DIANA PALMER

HEART of a STRANGER

HQN™

ISBN 0-373-77180-0

HEART OF A STRANGER

Copyright © 2006 by Harlequin Books S.A.

The publisher acknowledges the copyright holder of the individual works as follows:

SOLDIER OF FORTUNE

Copyright © 1985 by Diana Palmer

THE TENDER STRANGER

Copyright © 1985 by Diana Palmer

This edition published by arrangement with Harlequin Books S.A.

® and TM are trademarks of the publisher. Trademarks indicated with ® are registered in the United States Patent and Trademark Office, the Canadian Trade Marks Office and in other countries.

www.HQNBooks.com

Printed in U.S.A.

CONTENTS

SOLDIER OF FORTUNE

CHAPTER ONE

GABBY WAS WORRIED about J.D. It wasn't anything she could put her finger on exactly. He still roared around the office, slamming things down on his desk when he couldn't find notes or reminders he'd scribbled on envelopes or old business cards. He glared at Gabby when she didn't bring his coffee on the stroke of nine o'clock. And there were the usual missing files, for which she was to blame of course, and the incessant phone calls that interrupted his concentration. There was still the heavy scowl on his broad face, and the angry glitter in his brown eyes. But that morning he'd been pacing around his office, smoking like a furnace. And that was unusual. Because J.D. had given up smoking years before, even before she had come to work for the law firm of Brettman and Dice.

She still couldn't figure out what had set him off. She'd put a long-distance call through to him earlier, one that sounded like it came from overseas. The caller had sounded suspiciously like Roberto, his sister Martina's husband, from Sicily. Soon afterward, there had been a flurry of outgoing calls. Now it was silent, except for the soft sounds the computer made as Gabby finished the last letter J.D. had dictated.

She propped her chin on her hands and stared at the door with curious green eyes. Her long, dark hair was piled high on her head, to keep it out of her way when she worked, and loose strands of it curled softly around her face, giving her an even more elfin look than usual. She was wearing a green dress that flattered her graceful curves. But J.D. wouldn't notice her if she walked through the office naked. He'd said when he hired her that he'd robbed the cradle. And he hadn't smiled when he said it. Although she was twenty-three now, he still made the most frustrating remarks about her extreme youth. She wondered wickedly what J.D. would say if she applied for Medicare in his name. Nobody knew how old he was. Probably somewhere around forty; those hard lines in his face hadn't come from nowhere.

He was one of the most famous criminal lawyers in Chicago. He made waves. He ground up hostile witnesses like so much sausage meat. But before his entry into the profession five years earlier, nothing was known about him. He'd worked as a laborer by day and attended law school by night. He'd worked his way up the ladder quickly and efficiently with the help of a devastating intelligence that seemed to feed on challenge.

He had no family except for a married sister in Palermo, Sicily, and no close friends. He allowed no one to really know him. Not his associate Richard Dice, not Gabby. He lived alone and mostly worked alone, except for the few times when he needed some information that only a woman could get, or when he had to have Gabby along as a cover. She'd gone with him to meet accused killers in warehouses at midnight and down to the waterfront in the wee hours of the morning to meet a ship carrying a potential witness.

It was an exciting life, and thank God her mother back in Lytle, Texas, didn't know exactly how exciting it was. Gabby had come to Chicago when she was twenty; she'd had to fight for days to get her mother to agree to the wild idea, to let her work for a distant cousin. The distant cousin had died quite suddenly and, simultaneously, J.D. had advertised for an executive secretary. When she applied, it had taken J.D. only five minutes to hire her. That had been two years earlier, and she'd never regretted the impulse that had led her to his office.

Just working for him was something of a feather in Gabby's cap. The other secretaries in the building were forever pumping her for information about her attractive and famous boss. But Gabby was as secretive as he was. It was why she'd lasted so long as his secretary. He trusted her as he trusted no one else.

She was a paralegal now, having taken night courses at a local college to earn the title. She did far more than just type letters and run off copies on the copier. The office had added a computer system. She ran that, and did legwork for her boss, and frequently traveled with him when the job warranted it.

While she was brooding, the door opened suddenly. J.D. came through it like a locomotive, so vibrant and superbly masculine that she imagined most men would step aside for him out of pure instinct. His partner Richard Dice was on his heels, raging as he followed.

"Will you be reasonable, J.D.!" the younger man argued, his lean hands waving wildly, his red hair almost standing on end around his thin face. "It's a job for the police! What can you do?"

J.D. didn't even look at him. He paused at Gabby's desk, an expression on his face that she'd never seen before. Involuntarily, she studied the broad face with its olive complexion and deep-set eyes. He had the thickest, blackest eyelashes she'd ever seen. His hair was just as thick and had deep waves in it, threaded with pure silver. It was the faint scars on his face that aged him, but she'd never quite had the bravado to ask where and how he'd gotten them. It must have been some kind of man who put them there. J.D. was built like a tank.

"Pack a bag," he told Gabby, in a tone too black to invite questions. "Be back here in an hour. Is your passport in order?"

She blinked. Even for J.D., this was fast shuffling. "Uh, yes...."

"Bring lightweight things, it'll be hot where we're going. Lots of jeans and loose shirts, a sweater, some boots, and a lot of socks." He continued nonstop. "Bring that third-class radio license you hold. Aren't you kin to someone at the State Department? That might come in handy."

Her mind was whirling. "J.D., what's going...?" she began.

"You can't do this," Dick was continuing doggedly, and J.D. was just ignoring him.

"Dick, you'll have to handle my case load until I get back," he pressed on in a voice that sounded like thunder rumbling. "Get Charlie Bass to help you if you run into any snags. I don't know exactly when we'll be back."

"J.D., will you listen?"

"I've got to pack a few things," J.D. said curtly. "Call the agency, Gabby, and get Dick a temporary secretary. And be back here in exactly one hour."

The door slammed behind him. Dick cursed roundly and rammed his hands into his pockets.

"What," Gabby asked, "is going on? Will somebody please tell me where I'm going with my passport? Do I have a choice?"

"Slow down and I'll tell you what little I know." Dick sighed angrily. He perched himself on her desk. "You know that J.D.'s sister is married to that Italian businessman who made a fortune in shipping and lives in Palermo, Sicily?"

She nodded.

"And you know that kidnapping is becoming a fast method of funding for revolutionary groups?" he continued.

She felt herself going pale. "They got his brother-in-law?"

"No. They got his sister when she went alone on a shopping trip to Rome."

She caught her breath. "Martina? But she's the only family he has!"

"I know that. They're asking for five million dollars, and Roberto can't scrape it up. He's frantic. They told him they'd kill her if he involved the authorities."

"And J.D. is going to Italy to save her?"

"However did you guess?" Dick grumbled. "In his usual calm, sensible way, he is moving headfirst into the china shop."

"To Italy? With me?" She stared at him. "Why am I going?"

"Ask him. I only work here."

She sighed irritably as she rose to her feet. "Someday I'm going to get a sensible job, you wait and see if I don't," she said, her eyes glittering with frustration. "I was going to eat lunch at McDonald's and leave early so I could take in that new science-fiction movie at the Grand. And instead I'm being bustled off to Italy…to do what, exactly?" she added with a frown. "Surely to goodness, he isn't going to interfere with the Italian authorities?"

"Martina is his sister," Dick reminded her. "He never talks about it, but they had a rough upbringing from what I can gather, and they're especially close. J.D. would mow down an army to save her."

"But he's a lawyer," she protested. "What is he going to do?"

"Beats me, honey." Dick sighed.

"Here we go again," she muttered as she cleared her desk and got her purse out of the drawer. "Last time he did this, we were off to Miami to meet a suspected mob informer in an abandoned warehouse at two o'clock in the morning. We actually got shot at!" She shuddered. "I didn't dare tell my mama what was going on. Speaking of my mama, what am I supposed to tell her?"

"Tell her you're going on a holiday with the boss." He grinned. "She'll be thrilled."

She glared at him. "The boss doesn't take holidays. He takes chances."

"You could quit," he suggested.

"Quit!" she exclaimed. "Who said anything about quitting? Can you see me working for a normal attorney? Typing boring briefs and deeds and divorce petitions all day? Bite your tongue!"

"Then may I suggest that you call James Bond," he said, "and ask if he has any of those exploding matches or nuclear warhead toothpicks he can spare."

She gave him a hard glare. "Do you speak any Spanish?"

"Well, no," he said, puzzled.

She rattled off a few explicit phrases in the lilting tongue her father's foreman had used with the ranch hands back during her childhood. Then, with a curtsy, she walked out the door.

CHAPTER TWO

GABBY HAD SEEN J.D. in a lot of different moods, but none of them could hold a candle to the one he was in now. He sat beside her as stiff as a board on the jet, barely aware of the cup of black coffee he held precariously in one big hand.

Worst of all was the fact that she couldn't think of anything to say. J.D. wasn't the kind of man you offered sympathy to. But it was hard just to sit and watch him brood without talking at all. She'd rarely heard him speak of his sister Martina, but the tenderness with which he described her had said enough. If he loved any human being on earth, it was Martina.

"Boss..." she began uneasily.

He blinked, glancing toward her. "Well?"

She avoided that level gaze. "I just wanted to say I'm sorry." Her long, slender fingers fidgeted with the skirt of the white suit she was wearing. "I know how hard it must be for you. There's just not a lot that people can do in these kinds of situations."

A peculiar smile touched his hard features for a moment. He swallowed a sip of coffee. "Think not?" he asked dryly.

"You aren't serious about not contacting the author-

ities?" she persisted. "After all, they've got those special teams now, and they even rescued that one kidnap
victim…"

He glanced down at her. The look stopped her in
mid-sentence. "That was a political kidnapping. This
isn't. As for those special teams, Darwin, they're not in-
fallible. I can't take risks with Martina's life."

"No," she said. She stared at his hands. They were
so gracefully masculine, the fingers long and tapered
and as dark olive as his face, with flat nails and a sprin-
kling of hair, like that curling around the watch on his
wrist. He had powerful hands.

"You aren't afraid, are you?" he asked.

She glanced up. "Well, sort of," she confessed. "I
don't really know where we're going, do I?"

"You should be used to that by now," he reminded
her dryly.

She laughed. "I suppose so. We've had some adven-
tures in the past two years."

He pulled out a cheroot and lit it, staring at her nar-
rowly over the flame. "Why aren't you married?" he
asked suddenly.

The question startled her. She searched for the right
words. "I'm not sure," she said. "I suppose I just haven't
bothered to get involved with anyone. Until four years
ago, I was living in a small town in Texas. Then I came
up here to work for a cousin, he died, you needed a secretary…" She laughed softly. "With all due respect, Mr.
Brettman, you're kind of a never-ending job, if you
know what I mean. It just isn't a nine-to-five thing."

"About which," he observed, "you've never once
complained."

"Who could complain?" she burst out. "I've been around the country and halfway across the world, I get to meet gangsters, I've been shot at…!"

He chuckled softly. "That's some job description."

"The other secretaries in the building are green, simply green, with envy," she replied smugly.

"You aren't a secretary. You're a paralegal. In fact," he added, puffing on his cheroot thoughtfully, "I've thought about sending you to law school. You've got a lot of potential."

"Not me," she said. "I could never get up in front of a courtroom full of people and grill witnesses like you do. Or manage such oration in a summing up."

"You could still practice law," he reminded her. "Corporate law, if you like. Or deal in estates and partnerships. Divorces. Land transfers. There are many areas of law that don't require oratory."

"I'm not sure enough that it's what I want to do with the rest of my life," she said.

He lifted his chin. "How old are you?"

"Twenty-three."

He shook his head, studying the chignon, the glasses she used for close reading and now had perched on top of her head, the stylish white linen suit she was wearing, the length of her slender legs. "You don't look it."

"In about twenty years could you repeat that?" she asked. "By then I'll probably appreciate it."

"What do you want to be?" he asked, persisting as he leaned back in the seat. His vested gray silk suit emphasized the sheer size of him. He was so close she could even feel the warmth of his body, and she found it oddly disturbing.

"Oh, I don't know," she murmured, glancing out the window at the clouds. "A secret agent, maybe. A daring industrial spy. A flagpole sitter." She looked over her shoulder at him. "Of course, those jobs would seem very dull after working for you, Boss. And do I ever get to know where we're going?"

"To Italy, of course," he replied.

"Yes, sir, I know that. *Where* in Italy?"

"Aren't you curious, though?" he mused, lifting one shaggy eyebrow. "We're going to Rome. To rescue my sister."

"Yes, sir, of course we are," she said. It was better to agree with maniacs, she told herself. He'd finally snapped. It was even predictable, considering the way he'd been pushing himself.

"Humoring me, Miss Darwin?" he asked. He leaned deliberately past her to crush out his cheroot, and his face was so close that she could smell the spicy cologne he wore, feel the warm, smoky scent of his breath. As his fingers left the ashtray, he turned his head.

That look caused her the wildest shock she'd ever felt. It was like an earth tremor that worked its way from her eyes to the tips of her toes and made them want to curl up. She hadn't realized how vulnerable she was with him until her heart started racing and her breath strangled in her throat.

"I hesitated about taking you with me," he said quietly. "I'd rather have left you behind. But there was no one else I could trust, and this is a very delicate situation."

She tried to act normally. "You do realize that what you're thinking about could get her killed?"

"Yes," he said simply. "But not to act could get her

killed quicker. You know what usually happens in these cases, don't you?"

"Yes, I do," she admitted. Her gaze moved down to his broad mouth with its lips that seemed sculpted from stone and back up again to his dark eyes. He looked different so close up.

"I'm doing what I think is best," he said. His fingers nudged a wisp of hair back into place at her neck, and she felt trembly all over from the touch. "We're not sure that the kidnappers still have Martina in Italy. Roberto thinks he knows one of them—the son of an acquaintance, who also happens to own land in Central America. I don't have to tell you what a hell of a mess this could turn into if they take Martina there, do I?"

She felt weak all over. "But how are they dealing with Roberto?"

"One of the group, and there is a group, is still in Italy, to arrange the handling of the money," he answered. He let his eyes fall to the jacket of her suit, and he studied it absently with disturbing concentration. "We may do some traveling before this is all over."

"But first we're going to Italy," she murmured dazedly.

"Yes. To meet some old friends of mine," he said, his chiseled mouth smiling faintly. "They owe me a favor from years past. I'm calling in the debt."

"We're taking a team?" she asked, eyebrows shooting up. It was getting more exciting by the minute.

"My, how your eyes light up when you speak of working with a team, Miss Darwin," he mused.

"It's so gung ho," she replied self-consciously. "Kind of like that program I watch on TV every week, about the group that goes around the world fighting evil?"

"The Soldiers of Fortune?" he asked.

"The very one." She grinned. "I never miss a single episode."

"In real life, Miss Darwin," he reminded her, "it's a brutal, dangerous occupation. And most mercenaries don't make it to any ripe old age. They either get killed or wind up in some foreign prison. Their lives are overromanticized."

She glowered at him. "And what would you know about it, Mr. Criminal Attorney?" she challenged.

"Oh, I have a friend who used to sell his services abroad," he replied as he sat back in his seat. "He could tell you some hair-raising stories about life on the run."

"You know a real ex-merc?" she asked, eyes widening. She sat straight up in her seat. "Would he talk to me?"

He shook his head. "Darwin." He sighed. "What am I going to do with you?"

"It's your fault. You corrupted me. I used to lead a dull life and never even knew it. Would he?"

"I suppose he would." His dark eyes wandered slowly over her. "You might not like what you found out."

"I'll take my chances, thanks. He, uh, wouldn't be one of the old friends you're meeting in Rome?" she asked.

"That would be telling. Fasten your seat belt, Darwin, we're approaching the airport now."

Her eyes lingered on his dark, unfathomable face as she complied with the curt order. "Mr. Brettman, why did you bring me along?" she asked softly.

"You're my cover, honey," he said, and smiled sideways at her. "We're lovers off on a holiday."

"The way I look?" she chided.

He reached over and took the pins out of her coiffure,

loosening her hair. His fingers lifted the glasses from their perch atop her head, folded them, and stuffed them into his shirt pocket. He reached over again and flicked open the buttons of her blouse all the way down to the cleft between her high breasts.

"Mr. Brettman!" she burst out, pushing at his fingers.

"Stop blushing, call me Jacob, and don't start fighting me in public," he said gruffly. "If you can remember all that, we'll do fine."

"Jacob?" she asked, her fingers abandoning their futile efforts to rebutton her buttons.

"Jacob. Or Dane, my middle name. Whichever you prefer, Gabby."

He made her name sound like bowers of pink roses in bud, like the softness of a spring rain on grass. She stared up at him.

"Jacob, then," she murmured.

He nodded, his dark eyes searching hers. "I'll take care of you, Gabby," he said. "I won't let you get in the line of fire."

"You meant it, didn't you?" she asked. "You're going to try to rescue Martina."

"Of course," he replied calmly. "She and I, we had a tough time as kids. Our father drowned in a bathtub, dead drunk, when we were toddlers. Mama scrubbed floors to keep us in school. As soon as we were old enough, we went to work, to help. But I was barely fifteen when Mama died of a heart attack. I've taken care of Martina ever since, just the way I promised I would. I can't let strangers try to help her. I have to."

"Forgive me," she said gently, "but you're an attorney, not a policeman. What can you do?"

"Wait and see," he told her. His eyes surveyed her quietly, approving her elfin beauty. "I'm not in my dotage yet."

"Yes, sir, I know that," she murmured.

"Jacob," he repeated.

She sighed, searching his dark eyes. "Jacob," she agreed.

That seemed to satisfy him. He glanced past her as the plane started down, and he smiled. "The Eternal City, Gabby," he murmured. "Rome."

She followed his gaze and felt her heart lift as the ancient city came into view below. Already, she was leaping ahead to the time when she could actually see the Colosseum and the Forum and the Pantheon. But as she remembered the reason for their being in Rome, her enthusiasm faded. Of course there wouldn't be time for sightseeing, she reasoned. J.D. was going to be too busy trying to get himself killed.

The drive into Rome was fascinating. They went in on the Viale Trastevere, through the old part of the city, across the wide Tiber on an ancient bridge. The seven hills of Rome were hardly noticeable because of centuries of erosion and new construction, but Gabby was too busy gaping at the ruins they passed to notice or care.

They went right by the Colosseum, and her eyes lingered on it as they proceeded to their hotel.

"We'll find a few minutes to see it," J.D. said quietly, as if he knew how much it meant to her.

Her gaze brushed his hard face and impulsively she touched her fingers to the back of his hand. "It really isn't that kind of a trip," she said softly.

He searched her worried face. His big hand turned,

grasping hers warmly in its callused strength. "We'll have to pretend that it is, for a day or so at least," he said.

"What are we going to do?" she asked nervously.

He drew in a slow breath and leaned back against the seat, handsome and rugged-looking in his vested suit. It strained against massive muscles, and she tingled at the sight. J.D. had always affected her powerfully in a purely physical way. It pleased her eyes to look at him.

"I'm working on that. But one thing we'll be doing in the hotel," he added slowly, "is sharing a suite. Will that frighten you?"

She shook her head. "I'm not afraid of anything when I'm with you, Jacob," she replied, finding that his given name was more comfortable to her tongue than she'd expected.

He cocked a heavy eyebrow. "That wasn't the kind of fear I meant, actually," he murmured. "Will you be afraid of me?"

"Why would I be?" she asked, puzzled.

He blew out a harsh breath and looked out the window. "I can't think of a single damned reason," he growled. "I hope Dutch got my message. He's supposed to call me later at the hotel."

"Dutch?" she queried softly.

"A man I know. He's my go-between with Roberto," he replied.

"Roberto and Martina don't live in Rome, do they?" she asked.

He shook his head. "In Palermo. So, for all appearances, we'll be a couple on holiday, and there won't be anything to connect us with the kidnapping."

"Will this man Dutch know if Martina is still in the country?" she asked.

"He'll know," he said with certainty.

He was obviously irritated with her, so she didn't press him with any more questions, contenting herself with staring at every building they passed.

Their hotel was disappointingly modern, but the old-world courtesy of the Italian desk clerk made up for it. He was attentive and outgoing, and Gabby liked him at once. J.D., however, seemed to have misgivings about him. He didn't share them with her, but he stared aggressively at the poor little man.

He had booked them a suite, with two bedrooms. Gabby hadn't expected anything else, but J.D.'s behavior was downright odd. He glared at the elegant sitting room, he glared at her, and he especially glared at the telephone. He paced and smoked, and Gabby felt as if she were going to fly apart, he made her so nervous. She went into her bedroom and unpacked, just to have something to do. The sudden sound of the phone ringing startled her, but she didn't go back into the sitting room; she waited for J.D. to call her. Meanwhile, she changed into jeans and a silky green top, leaving her hair loose and her reading glasses in her purse. She did look like a tourist on holiday. That ought to perk up J.D.

He called to her about five minutes later, and she walked into the room to find him staring blankly out the window. He'd taken off his jacket and vest and opened the top buttons of his shirt. His thick, wavy hair was mussed, and one big, tanned hand was still buried in it. A smoking cigarette was in the other hand, which was leaning on the windowsill.

"Jacob?" she murmured.

He turned. His dark eyes focused on her slender figure, so intent that they missed the shocked pleasure in her own gaze as she took in this sudden and unexpected glimpse of his body. Where the shirt was loose, she could see the olive tan of his chest under curls of dark hair, and rippling muscles that made her hands itch. Her whole body reacted to his sensuality, going rigid with excitement.

"Dutch," he said, nodding toward the phone to indicate who his caller had been. "Martina's out of the country."

She caught her breath. "Where?"

"Guatemala. On a *finca*—a farm—owned by a revolutionary group."

Her eyes searched his hard face. "Why would they take her there?"

"Terrorism is international, didn't you know? They probably have holdings all over the world, but Guatemala is in such a state of unrest it's a good place to hide a kidnap victim." He laughed bitterly. His jaw tautened. "They'll kill her if they don't get the money. They may do it anyway."

"What are you going to do?"

"I've already done it," he replied. "I've given Dutch a sum of money to buy some things I'll need. I've also had him contact my old comrades. They'll meet us at the Guatemalan *finca* of a friend of mine."

She cocked her head at him, uncomprehending. "When do we leave?"

"Tomorrow," he said. "As much as I'd like to jump on the next plane, we can't do it that way. I need time to plan. And there's no sense in signaling our every move. Dutch was going to speak to Roberto for me to-night. I'll need to know the status of his fund-raising be-fore we leave."

"Will we fly into Guatemala?" she asked, feeling jittery.

"To Mexico," he said in answer. He smiled slowly. "As part of the holiday, of course," he added. "That will be broadcast to the right quarters."

"And now?" she asked. "What do I do?"

"We'll go see some of those ruins, if you like," he said. "It will help to pass the time."

Her eyes searched his. "I know you're worried, J.D. If you'd rather stay here…"

He moved closer to her, and the sudden proximity of his big body made her knees go weak. She lifted her face and found his dark eyes intent and unblinking.

"I don't think that's a good idea," he said quietly. He reached out and traced a slow path down her cheek to her throat, where her pulse went suddenly wild. "What would you like to see first?"

She found that her voice wobbled alarmingly. "How about the Forum?"

His dark eyes searched hers for a long moment. His fingers went to her mouth, touching it lightly, as if the feel of it fascinated him. His thumb dragged slowly, sensuously, over it, smearing her lipstick, arousing every nerve ending she had. She gasped, and her lips parted helplessly.

"The Forum?" he murmured.

She hardly heard him. Her eyes were held by his. Her body was reacting to the closeness of his in a new and frightening way. She could smell the musky cologne he wore and it made her head spin.

Her hands went to his chest in a small gesture of protest, but the feel of all that bare skin and matted hair made her jerk back.

He glanced down at her recoiling fingers with an odd expression. "It's only skin," he said quietly. "Are you afraid to touch me?"

"I've never touched anybody that way," she blurted out.

He tipped her face up to his and studied it with an odd smile. "Haven't you? Why?"

What an interesting question, she thought. What a pity she didn't have an answer.

"Don't tell me you haven't had the opportunity, Gabby," he said softly. "I wouldn't believe it."

"Mama said that it wasn't wise to do things like that to men," she told him doggedly, her chin thrust out. "She said they were hard enough to manage even when it didn't go beyond kissing."

"So there," he added for her with a faint smile. "She was right. Men get excited easily when they want a woman."

She felt the blush go up into her hairline, setting fire to her face. And he laughed, the horrible man!

She pulled away from him with a hard glare. "That was unkind," she grumbled.

"And you're delightfully repressed," he told her, but the look in his eyes was all tenderness. "You'd be pure sweet hell to initiate, Gabby."

"I don't want to be initiated," she said primly. "I want to see the Forum."

"All right, coward, hide your head in the sand," he taunted, holding the door open for her.

"It's safer that way, around you," she mumbled.

He caught her arm as she started past him, and she felt the warmth of his body like a drug. "I'll never hurt you," he said unexpectedly, drawing her stunned gaze to his face. It was hard and solemn. Almost grim. "You trust me in every other way. I want you to trust me physically as well."

"Why?" she asked.

"Because if I take you with me to Central America, I'll want you with me all the time. Especially at night," he added. "The men we'll be working with aren't particularly gentle. For all intents and purposes, you'll be my possession."

"To protect me from them?" she asked.

He nodded. "That means, in case you haven't worked it out, that you'll be sleeping in my bed."

She tingled from head to toe at the thought of lying in J.D.'s arms. It was something she'd contemplated in her own mind for a long time, and hearing it from his lips almost made her gasp. As it was, her flush told him everything anyway.

"In my bed," he repeated, searching her eyes. "In my arms. And I won't touch you in any way that I shouldn't. Even when we're back home and Martina is safe, and you're at your computer again, there won't be anything you'd be ashamed to tell your mother. All right?"

She couldn't find the words to express what she was feeling. J.D. felt protective of her. It was something she'd never expected. And uncharacteristically, she was disappointed. Did it mean that he didn't want her?

"All right, Jacob," she whispered softly.

His nostrils flared and his eyes flashed down at her. The hand holding her arm tightened until it hurt. "We'd better get out of here," he said gruffly. He let her go, turning away as if it took some effort.

Rome was the most exciting place Gabby had ever been. All of it seemed to be interspersed with history and crumbling ruins and romance. J.D. told her that the Colosseum, the Forum, the Ninfeo di Nerone—Nero's Sanctuary of the Nymphs—and the ruins of Nero's House of Gold residence were all near the Caelian, Capitolene, and Palatine hills. They decided to concentrate on that area of the city.

There was so much to see that Gabby's mind seemed to overload. They wandered around the ruins of the Forum first, and she just stared and stared like the eternal tourist.

"Just imagine," she whispered, as if afraid the ghosts might hear and take offense, "all those centuries ago Romans walked here just as we're walking today, with the same dreams and hopes and fears we feel. I wonder if they ever thought about how the world would be in the future?"

"I'm sure they did." J.D. stuck his hands in his pockets, and the wind ran like loving fingers through his crisp, dark hair. With his head thrown back like that, his profile in relief, he could have been one of the early Romans himself.

"Have you ever read *The Annals of Imperial Rome* by Tacitus?" she asked.

His head jerked around. "Yes. Have you?"

She grinned. "I was always a nut about Roman history. And Greek history. I loved Herodotus, even though he's been bad-mouthed a lot for some of his revelations."

"He was repeating what he'd heard or was told," he

said. "But it's fascinating reading, nevertheless." He smiled amusedly. "Well, well, a historian. And I never suspected. I thought your knowledge of other countries was limited to those sweet little romance novels you read."

She glared at him. "I learn a lot about the world from those books," she said, defending herself. "And about other things too."

He cocked a dark eyebrow. "What other things?"

She looked away. "Never mind."

"We can go and see the catacombs later, if you like. They're south of here."

"Where the early Christians were buried?" She shuddered. "Oh, no, I don't think so. It's kind of an invasion of privacy. I'm sure I wouldn't want someone walking through my grave."

"I suppose it depends on your point of view," he conceded. "Well, we'll drive up to the Colosseum then."

"What was the other thing you mentioned, the Ninfeo di Nerone?"

He looked down at her with dark, indulgent eyes. "The Sanctuary of the Nymphs. You'd have fit right in, with your long, dark hair and mysterious eyes."

"I wouldn't have liked the debauchery," she said with certainty, her green eyes flashing. "The morals in Rome in Nero's time were decadent. I read that he had his wife Octavia killed, in a horrible way, after some prodding by his mistress."

"That was in Tacitus," he recalled. "A lot of terrible things happened here in the early days. But if you think about it, honey, terrible things are still happening. Like Martina's kidnapping."

"The world hasn't really changed very much, has

it?" she asked sadly, watching the disturbance in his features at the thought of Martina and what she might be
going through. She reached out and touched his arm
gently. "They won't hurt her, Jacob," she said quietly.
"Not until they get the money. Will they?"

"I don't know." He caught her arms and jerked her
against his hard body, holding her there and staring intently
into her eyes. "Frightened?" he asked on a husky note.

"No," she lied.

His dark eyes held hers. "We're supposed to be lovers on a holiday," he reminded her. "Just in case anyone
is watching us…"

His head started to bend, and she caught her breath.
Her eyes dropped to his chiseled mouth and she suddenly became breathless.

"Haven't you ever wondered?" he asked tautly, hes-
itating when he saw the shock on her young face.

Her eyes fluttered up to his fierce ones and back
down again. "How it would be to…to kiss you?" she
whispered.

"Yes."

Her lips parted on a rush of breath. She felt her
breasts pressed softly against his shirtfront and was
aware of the hardness of warm muscles against their
hardening tips. She felt trembly all over just at the touch
of his body.

His hands slid up her arms, over her shoulders, and up
her throat to cup her face and look at it with searching eyes.

"For the record," he murmured quietly, "is it a distasteful thought?"

That did shock her. She couldn't imagine any woman
finding him distasteful.

"It's not that at all," she said. Her fingers flattened against his shirtfront, feeling the warm strength of his body. "I'm afraid that you'll be disappointed."

His eyebrows shot up. "Why?"

She moved restlessly. "I haven't kissed a lot of people. Well, you keep me too busy," she added defensively when his eyes twinkled.

"So your education has been neglected?" He laughed softly. "I'll teach you how to kiss, Gabby. It isn't hard at all. Just close your eyes and I'll do the rest."

She did, and the first contact with that hard, persuasive mouth made her breath catch. He lifted his head, studying her.

"What was that wild little gasp about?" he asked gently.

Her wide eyes searched his. "You're my boss...."

That seemed to anger him. "For today, I'm a man." His thumbs under her chin coaxed her face up still farther. His head bent, his mouth hovering just above hers. "Relax, will you?" he whispered. "I can hear your bones straining."

She laughed nervously. "I'm trying. You make me feel...stiff. I'm sorry, I'm kind of new at this."

"Stiff how?" He pounced on that, his expression giving nothing away, his eyes narrow and unblinking.

Her lips parted. Her fingers contracted on his shirtfront, her nails biting unconsciously into his chest, and he stiffened. "Now you're doing it too," she whispered.

His face relaxed, and there was a wild kind of relief in his dark eyes. He brushed his mouth over her forehead, her closed eyes. His hands slid behind her head and into the thick hair at her nape, cradling it.

"Gabby," he murmured as he tasted the softness of her cheeks, her forehead, "that stiffness…have you felt it before with anyone?"

It was a casual-sounding question, nothing to alarm her. "No," she murmured. She liked the soft, slow kisses he was pressing against her face. She felt like a child being loved.

"Would you like me to make it worse?"

She opened her dazed eyes to ask what he meant, and his open mouth crushed down on her lips. She gasped softly, letting her eyes close again. His mouth felt odd; it was warm and smoky tasting and very, very expert. Her fingers clung to the fabric of his shirt, twisting it into wrinkles. She stood quite still, her body tense with hunger, feeling the slow persuasion of his mouth grow rougher.

He lifted his mouth away from hers, his face so close that she couldn't see anything but his lips. "Who taught you that it was impolite to open your mouth when a man kissed it?" he whispered softly.

Her eyes went dazedly up to his dark ones. "Is it?" she whispered back, her voice sounding high-pitched and shaky.

"No," he breathed. His thumb gently tugged on her lower lip, coaxing her mouth open. "I want to taste you, Gabby. I want to touch you…inside…"

She started to tremble at the sensuality of the words and of his touch. His mouth eased hers open and slowly increased its hungry pressure. She felt the tiny bristle of a half day's growth of beard around his mouth and felt the hardness of his tongue slowly, delicately, penetrating her lips.

A tiny moan trembled in her throat.

"Don't be afraid," he whispered, his own voice oddly strained. "It won't hurt."

She did moan then, as the implied intimacy and the penetration all washed over her at once, and she drowned in the sensation of being possessed by him. He tasted of smoke and coffee, and her nails dug into his shoulders. She pressed her body into the hard curve of his and heard him groan.

"No," he said suddenly, pushing her away. He turned, walked off and lit a cigarette.

Gabby clutched her purse to her and stood staring helplessly after him, trembling all over. She'd never dreamed that it would feel like that!

Around them, a group of tourists was just entering the end of the Forum, which they'd had momentarily to themselves. Gabby got a glimpse of colorful clothing and heard murmuring voices as J.D. smoked his cigarette for several long moments before he turned and rejoined her.

"I shouldn't have done that," he said quietly. "I'm sorry."

She was struggling for composure, and it was hard won. "It's all right," she said. "I know you're worried about Martina…"

"Was I looking for comfort, Gabby?" He laughed mirthlessly. His dark eyes swept up and down her slender body.

"I'd rather it was that," she murmured, "than you needing a woman and having me get in the way."

"It wasn't that impersonal, I'm afraid," he said, falling into step beside her. He towered over her. "Gabby,

I'll tell you something. I've done it in every conceivable way, with a hell of a lot of women. But up until now, I've never wanted a virgin."

She stopped and looked up at him, puzzled.

He glanced down at her. "That's right," he said. "I want you."

Her face flushed.

"You'll have to remind me at odd intervals that you're a virgin," he continued, smiling faintly. "Because I'm not really out of the habit of taking what I want."

He was angry and frustrated and probably trying to warn her off, she thought. But she wasn't afraid of him. "If you seduce me," she told him, "I'll get pregnant and haunt you."

He stared at her as if he didn't believe his ears. And then he threw back his dark head and laughed like a boy, his white teeth flashing in his dark face.

"Then I'll have to be sure I don't seduce you, won't I?" he teased.

She smiled up at him, feeling oddly secure. "Please."

He drew in a long breath as they walked, sighed and took another drag from his cigarette. "I thought this was all going to be straightforward and simple," he murmured. "Maybe I'd better put you on a plane back to Chicago, little one."

"Cold feet?" she muttered.

"Not me, lady. But you might wish you'd stayed home. I don't know where my mind was when I dragged you over here."

"You said you trusted me."

"I do. Totally. That's why I wanted you with me. The way things are turning out, I'm going to need you more than ever. When we get to my friend's *finca*," he said quietly, "someone has to stay behind to handle communications. We'll have powerful walkie-talkies and we'll need updated information. The *finca* we'll be staying at is only miles from the one where Martina is being held."

She felt uneasy as she studied his hard face. "You're not going in there alone?"

"No—with those old friends I was telling you about."

"Couldn't you stay behind at your friend's finca?"

"Worried about me?" He laughed. "Gabby, I've dodged a lot of bullets in my time. I was in the Special Forces."

"Yes, you told me," she grumbled. "But that was a long time ago. You're a lawyer now, you sit behind a desk…"

"Not all the time," he said, correcting her. His eyes studied her quietly. "There are a lot of things you don't know about me. About my private life."

"You could get yourself killed."

"A car could hit me while I'm standing here," he countered.

She glared at him. "I'd be without work. One of the unemployed. Everything I'd do for the rest of my life would be horribly boring."

"I'd miss you too, I guess," he agreed, laughing. "Don't worry about me, Gabby. I can take it as it comes."

"Do I even get to meet this man you call Dutch?"

He shook his head. "You'll meet enough odd characters in Central America. And Dutch hates women."

"You aren't Mr. Playboy yourself," she muttered.

"Aren't you glad?" he asked, turning to look at her. "Would you like a man who had a different woman every night?"

The question shocked her. She struggled for an answer, but he'd already opened the door of the rental car and was helping her in.

The rest of the day went by in a haze. She went back to the hotel with him, her eyes full of ruins and Romans and maddening traffic. She had a bouquet of flowers that J.D. had bought from an old woman near the Fountain of Trevi. She couldn't wait to get into her room and press one of the flowers, to keep forever. She buried her nose in them lovingly.

Across the room, J.D. was speaking fluent Italian with someone on the phone. He hung up and turned back to her.

"I have to go out for a little while," he said. "Lock the door and let no one in, not even room service, until I get back. Okay?"

She studied him quietly. "You won't go getting into trouble while I'm not around to rescue you, will you?" she said, teasing him.

He shook his head. "Not a chance. Watch yourself."

"You too. Oh, Jacob!"

He turned with his hand on the doorknob. "What?"

"Thank you for the flowers."

"They suit you." He studied her face and smiled. "You look like one of them. *Ciao*, Gabby."

And he was gone. She stared at the door for a long time before she went to put her flowers in some water.

CHAPTER THREE

J.D. DIDN'T COME BACK UNTIL late that afternoon, and he was strangely taciturn. He shared a silent supper with Gabby and then went out again, telling her tersely to get some sleep. She knew he'd found out something, but whatever it was, he wasn't sharing it. Apparently his trust in her had limits. And that was disappointing. She climbed into bed and slept soundly and without interruption. Part of her had hoped for a nightmare or an earthquake that would bring him running into her room. All her wild fantasies ended with him running into her room and catching her up in his hard arms. She sighed. This was certainly not the trip she'd envisioned. It was turning into a wild tangle of new emotions. A week before, she couldn't have imagined that he would tell her he wanted her.

THEY FLEW TO MEXICO the following morning. Several hours into the flight Gabby shot a worried glance at J.D. He'd hardly moved in his seat since takeoff, and she'd busied herself looking at clouds and reading the emergency instructions and even the label on her jacket out of desperation.

He seemed to sense her searching gaze and turned his

head to look down at her. "What's wrong?" he asked softly.

She made an odd little gesture. "I don't know," she said inadequately.

His eyebrows lifted. "I'll take care of you."

"I know that." She let her eyes fall to the vest of his gray suit. "Will we stay in Mexico City?"

"Probably not. We're supposed to be met at the airport." He reached over and took her slender hand in his big one. The contact was warm and wildly disturbing, especially when she felt his thumb moving slowly, sensuously, against her moist palm. "Nervous?" he taunted.

"Oh, no. I always go running off into the dark unafraid," she replied with a grimace. She glanced up. "I come from a long line of idiots."

He smiled at her. It was a shock to realize that he'd smiled more at her in these two days than he had in two months back at the office. Her eyes searched the deep brown of his, and the airplane seemed to disappear. He returned the look, his smile fading. His nostrils flared and the hand holding hers began to move slowly, his fingers probing, easing between hers. It was so sensuous she felt herself tremble. His hand was pressed against hers, palm to palm, fingers tightly interlocked, and when it contracted it was almost an act of possession.

Her lips parted in a soft gasp, and his eyes narrowed.

"Bodies do that," he whispered under his breath, watching her reactions intently. "Just as slowly, just as easily."

"Don't," she protested brokenly, averting her face.

"Gabby," he chided gently, "don't be a child."

She ground her teeth together and struggled for composure. It wasn't easy, because he wouldn't let go of her hand despite her token protest.

"You're out of my league, Mr. Brettman," she said unsteadily, "as I'm sure you know. Don't…don't amuse yourself with me, please."

"I'm not." He sighed and turned sideways so that his head rested against the back of the seat. Then he coaxed her face around to his. "You've never known the kind of men you'll meet when we get where we're going. I thought," he continued, smiling at her stunned look, "that it might be easier for you if we got in a little practice along the way."

"What do you mean? What will we have to do…?" she began nervously.

"I mean, as I told you in Rome, that we'll have to be inseparable for the most part. We have to look as if we can't keep our hands off each other."

She stopped breathing, she knew she did. Her eyes wandered quietly over his face. "Is that why, at the Forum…?"

He hesitated for an instant. "Yes," he said deliberately. "You were far too jumpy with me to be taken for my lover. It has to look convincing to do us any good."

"I see," she said, fighting to keep her disappointment from showing.

He studied her eyes, her cheeks, and then her mouth. "You have the softest lips, Gabby," he murmured absently. "So full and tempting; and I like the taste of them all too much…" He caught himself and lifted his eyes. "You'd better remind me at intervals that you're off-limits."

She was so aware of him that she tingled, and the

thought that he might kiss her again made her go hot all over. She smiled strangely and looked away.

"What was that about, that tiny little smile?" he asked curiously.

"I never used to think of you that way," she confessed without thinking.

"How? As a lover?" he probed.

She lowered her eyes quickly. "Yes," she said shyly.

She felt his long fingers brush her cheek and then her neck, where the pulse was beating wildly.

"Oddly enough, I've hardly thought of you any other way," he said in a deep, gruff whisper.

Her lips opened as she drew a sharp breath, and she looked straight into his eyes. "J.D....?" she whispered uncertainly.

His thumb brushed across her mouth, a tiny whisper of sensation that made her ache in the oddest places. His own breath wasn't quite steady, and he frowned, as if what was happening wasn't something he'd counted on or expected.

His eyes dropped to her parted lips and she heard him catch his breath. In a burst of nervousness, her tongue probed moistly at her dry upper lip and he made a rough sound in his throat. "Gabby, don't do that," he ground out. His thumb pressed hard against her mouth, and his head bent. "Let me..."

In a starburst of sensation, she felt the first tentative brush of his hard lips against her own.

And just as it began, it was suddenly over. The loudspeaker blared out a warning for passengers to fasten their seat belts, and the delicate spell was broken.

J.D. lifted his head reluctantly, his eyes almost black

with frustration, his face pale. "The next time," he whispered gruffly, "I'll kiss the breath out of you, the way I wanted to at the Forum."

She couldn't answer him. She was swimming in deep waters, hungry for him in an unexpectedly desperate way. Her hands fumbled with her seat belt and she couldn't look at him. What was happening to them? she wondered, shaken. Just the morning before, they'd been employer and employee. And in a flash, they were something else, something frightening.

His hand caught hers, enfolding it. "Don't, please, be frightened of me," he said under his breath. "I won't hurt you. Not in any way, for any reason."

She glanced at him. "I'm all right," she said. "I'm just…just…"

"Stunned?" he asked wryly. "Join the crowd. It shocked me too."

Her eyes locked on their clasped hands. "But I thought you kissed me to—how did you put it—make it look better for the men?"

"I did. And to satisfy my own curiosity about you. And yours about me." He tilted her face up to his. "Now we know, don't we?"

"I think I'd be better off not knowing," she muttered.

"Really? At least now you've learned how to kiss."

"You have the diplomacy of a tank!" she shot at him.

He smiled, his teeth white against that olive tan. "You're spunky, Gabby. I'm glad. You're going to need spunk."

His words brought back the reason for their trip, and she frowned. The plane started to descend and she clung to J.D.'s strong fingers, wondering if in a few weeks this would all be nothing more than a memory. He'd said they'd have to seem involved; was this just a practice session? The frown deepened. She realized quite suddenly that she didn't want it to be. She wanted J.D. to kiss the breath out of her, as he'd threatened, and mean it.

They landed in Mexico City, and Gabby's eyes widened as they walked into the terminal. She smiled, dreams of Aztecs and ancient ruins going through her mind—until she remembered poor Martina, and the fact that they weren't here to look at tourist attractions.

She looked at J.D., standing tall and quiet at her side with a smoking cigarette in his hand. He stared slowly around the terminal while Gabby shifted restlessly beside him, their two small carry-on cases beside her.

After what seemed like a long time, J.D. began to smile as a tall, devastatingly attractive man strode toward them. He was wearing a beige suit and leather boots, and he looked debonair and a little dangerous—like J.D.

"Laremos." J.D. grinned as they shook hands.

"Did you think I'd forgotten you?" the other man asked in softly accented English. "You look well, Archer."

Gabby's eyebrows lifted curiously.

"Archer," the man explained, "is the name to which he answered many years ago, during our...acquaintance. You are Gabby Darwin, no?"

"Yes." She nodded. "And you are Señor Laremos?"

"Diego Laremos, *a sus ordenes,*" he said formally, bowing. He grinned. "A dish, Archer."

"Yes, I think so myself," J.D. said casually, smiling at her as he drew her unresisting body close to his side. "Did Dutch phone you?"

The smile faded and Laremos was at once something else, something out of Gabby's experience. "*Sí.* Drago and Semson and Apollo are here now."

"No sweat. How about my equipment?"

"Apollo got it from Dutch," Laremos said, his voice low and intent. "An Uzi and a new AK-47."

J.D. nodded while Gabby tried to decide what in the world they were talking about. "We'll need some RPGs."

"We have two," Laremos said. "And eight blocks of C-4, rockets for the RPGs, assorted paraphernalia, jungle gear, and plenty of ammo. The border is a massing point for the guerrillas these days—you can get anything if you have the money and the contacts."

J.D. smiled faintly. "Dutch said First Shirt has both. You made a smart move when you put him in charge of your ranch security."

"*Sí,*" Laremos agreed. "It is why I survive and many of my neighbors have not. The *finca* above mine was burned to the ground a month ago, and its owner..." He glanced at Gabby. "Forgive me, *señorita.* Such talk is not for the ears of women."

"I don't even understand it," she said, studying both men. "What is an RP...whatever it was? And what do you mean, rockets?"

"I'll tell you all about it later," J.D. promised. "Got the plane?" he asked Laremos.

The other man nodded. "We will have to go through customs. I assume you have nothing on you that it would be embarrassing to declare when we land; otherwise you would not have made it through Mexican customs."

J.D. chuckled. "Even with you along, I doubt they'd

look the other way if I boarded with the Uzi slung around my neck and clips of ammunition hanging out of my pockets."

Laremos laughed too. "Doubtless they would not. Come. We are gassed up and ready to go."

"Uzi?" Gabby queried as they followed him.

J.D. pulled her against him briefly. "An Uzi is an Israeli-made weapon. It's classified as a semiautomatic."

"Did you use one in the Special Forces?"

He laughed softly. "No."

"Then how do you…and why…and what…?"

He bent suddenly and pressed a hard, warm kiss on her startled mouth. "Shut up, Gabby, before you get us into trouble."

As if she could talk at all, after that. Her lips felt as though they'd been branded. If only they'd been alone, and it could have been longer…

Laremos had a twin-engine plane and a pilot to fly it. He settled into one of the comfortable seats in front of Gabby and J.D. and another man, small and young, brought them cups of coffee as the plane headed toward Guatemala City.

"I have told the appropriate people that you and your friend here are visiting me," Laremos said to J.D. and laughed. "It will put you under immediate suspicion I fear, because my past is no secret. But it will spare you the illegality of having to smuggle yourself across the border. I have friends high in government who will help. Oddly enough, the terrorists who have your sister attempted to kidnap me only weeks ago. First Shirt was nearby and armed."

"First Shirt doesn't miss," J.D. recalled.

"Neither did you, my friend, in the old days." Laremos studied the older man unsmilingly.

"How many men are there in the terrorist group?" J.D. asked. "Hard core, Laremos, not the hangers-on who'll cut and run at the first volley."

"About twelve," came the reply. "Maybe twenty more who will, as you say, cut and run. But the twelve are veteran fighters. Very tough, with political ties in a neighboring country. They are just part of an international network, with members in Italy who saw a chance to make some fast money to finance their cause. Your brother-in-law is an important man, and a wealthy one. And the decision to bring your sister here was most certainly devised by one of those twelve. They took over the *finca* only a month ago. I have little doubt that the kidnapping has been planned for some time." He shrugged. "Also, it is known that the Italian authorities have been successful in dealing with this sort of kidnapping. There is less risk here, so they smuggled her out of Italy."

"Roberto is trying to borrow enough to bargain with," J.D. said. "He's determined not to go to the authorities."

"He does not know about you, does he?" Laremos asked quietly.

J.D. shook his head. "I covered my tracks very well."

"You miss it, the old life?"

J.D. sighed. "At times. Not often anymore." He glanced at Gabby absently. "I have other interests now. I was getting too old for it. Too tired."

"For the same reasons, I became an honest man." Laremos laughed. "It is by far the better way." He stretched lazily. "But sometimes I think back and wonder how it would have been. We made good *amigos,* Archer."

"A good team," J.D. agreed. "I hope we still do."

"Have no fear, *amigo.* It is like swimming—one never forgets. And you, do you keep in condition?"

"Constantly. I can't get out of the habit," J.D. said. "Just as well that I have. Cutting through that jungle won't be any easy march. I've been keeping up with the situation down here, politically and militarily."

"What about this lovely one?" Laremos asked, frowning as he studied Gabby. "Is she a medic?"

"She'll handle communications," J.D. said shortly. "I want her at the ranch with you so that there's no chance she might get in the line of fire."

"I see." Laremos's dark eyes narrowed and he laughed. "Trust still comes hard to you, eh? You will never forget that one time that I let my mind wander..."

"No hard feelings," J.D. said quietly. "But Gabby runs the set."

Laremos nodded. "I understand. And I take no offense. My conscience still nags me about that lapse."

"Will somebody tell me, please, what's going on?" Gabby asked when she could stand it no longer.

"I've gotten together a group to get Martina out," J.D. said patiently. "That's all you need to know."

"The mercs! They're already here?"

"Yes," he murmured, watching her with a tiny smile on his face.

"Ah, I think the line of work of our *amigos* fascinates this one." Laremos grinned handsomely.

"Can I actually talk to them?" Gabby said, persisting, all eyes and curiosity. "Oh, J.D., imagine belonging to a group like that, going all over the world to fight for freedom."

"A lot of them do it for less noble reasons, Gabby," he said, searching her face with an odd intensity. "And you may be disappointed if you're expecting a band of Hollywood movie stars. There's nothing glamorous about killing people."

"Killing...people?"

"What in God's name did you think they did, turn water hoses on the enemy?" he asked incredulously. "Gabby, in war men kill each other. In ways you wouldn't like to know about."

"Well, yes, I realize that." She frowned. "But it's a very dangerous way to live, it's..." She stopped and searched for words. "Before I came to work for you I lived a quiet, kind of dull life, J.D.," she said, trying to explain. "Sometimes I thought that I'd probably never do anything more exciting than washing clothes at the Laundromat. Those men...they've faced death. They've learned the limits of their courage, they've tested themselves until the secrets are all gone." She looked up. "I don't suppose it makes sense, but I think I envy them in a way. They've taken all the veneer off civilization and come away with the reality of what they are. In a terrible way, they've seen the face of life without the mask. I never will. I don't think I really want to. But I'm curious about people who have."

He brushed the hair back from her face with a gentle hand. "When you see First Shirt, you won't have to ask questions. You'll be able to read the answers in his face. Won't she, Laremos?"

"But indeed." He chuckled.

"Is he a friend of yours?" she asked J.D.

He nodded. "One of the best I ever had."

"When you were in the Special Forces?" she asked.

He turned away. "Of course." He glanced at Laremos, and they exchanged a level gaze that Gabby didn't understand.

"You didn't want mines, did you?" Laremos asked suddenly.

"No. We could have carried in a few Claymores, but they're too much extra weight. The RPGs will be enough, and Drago can jury-rig a mine if he has to. I want to get in and get out fast."

"The rainy season hasn't started, at least," Laremos said. "That will be a bonus."

"Yes, it will. Have you still got my crossbow?"

"Above the mantel in my study." Laremos smiled. "It is a conversation piece."

"To hell with that, does it still work?"

"Yes."

"A crossbow?" Gabby laughed. "Is it an antique?"

J.D. shook his head. "Not quite."

"Is it easier to shoot than a bow and arrow?" she asked, pursuing the subject.

He looked uncomfortable. "It's just a memento," he said. "Gabby, did you pack some jeans and comfortable shoes?"

"Yes, as you saw in Italy." She sighed, beginning to feel uneasy. "How long will we be here?"

"Probably no more than three days, if things go well," he replied. "We need a little time to scout the area and make a plan."

"The hospitality of my *finca* is at your disposal,"

Laremos said. "Perhaps we might even make time to show Gabby some of the Mayan ruins."

Her eyes lit up. "Really?"

"Don't mention archaeological ruins around her, please," J.D. muttered. "She goes crazy."

"Well, I like old things," she retorted. "Why else would I work for you?"

J.D. looked shocked. "Me? Old?"

She studied his face. It wasn't heavily lined, but there was a lot of silver at his temples mingling with his black hair. She frowned. She'd always assumed he was pushing forty, but now she wondered.

"How old are you, J.D.?" she asked.

"Thirty-six."

She gasped.

"Not what you expected?" he asked softly.

"You...seem older."

He nodded. "I imagine so. I've got thirteen years on you."

"You needn't sound so smug," she told him. "When I'm fifty, you'll hate those extra thirteen years."

"Think so?" he murmured, smiling.

She glanced away from that predatory look. "Tell me about Guatemala, Señor Laremos."

"Diego, please," he said, correcting her. "What would you like to know?"

"Anything."

He shrugged. "We have hopes for a better future, *señorita,* now that we have new leadership. But the guerrillas are still fighting the regime, and the *compañitas* are caught in the middle, as always. The warfare is sometimes very cruel. We are primarily an agricultural country, with an economy based on bananas and coffee. There is a sad lack of the things your people take for granted. Indoor plumbing, automobiles, adequate medical facilities—these things even the poorest of your people can expect, but here... Did you know, *señorita,* that the life expectancy in my country is only 50 years?"

She looked shocked. "Will things get better? Will the fighting stop?"

"We hope so. But in the meantime, those who wish to hold their land must have security. Mine is excellent. But many do not have the financial wherewithal to hire guards. I have a neighbor who gets government troops to go with him every afternoon to check his cattle and his holdings. He is afraid to go alone."

"I'll never grumble about paying income taxes again," Gabby said. "I guess we tend to take it for granted that we don't have to defend our property with guns."

"Perhaps someday we will be able to say the same thing."

Gabby was quiet for the rest of the trip, while J.D. and Laremos discussed things she couldn't begin to understand. Military terms. Logistics. She studied her taciturn employer with new eyes. There was more than he was telling her. It had something to do with the past he never discussed, and he was obviously reluctant to share any of it with her. Trust, again. At least he trusted her enough to let her handle the communications for this insane rescue attempt. If only he'd let those men go into the jungle and stay behind himself. Maybe she could talk him into it. It was a job for a professional soldier, not a lawyer. She closed her eyes and began to think up things to say, knowing in her heart that J.D. wasn't going to be swayed by any of them.

CHAPTER FOUR

DESPITE GABBY'S UNVOICED FEARS, they went through customs with no hitches, and minutes later were met by a man J.D. obviously knew.

The man was short and sandy blond, with a face like a railroad track and a slight figure. He was much older than the other two men, probably nearing fifty. He was wearing jungle fatigues with laced up boots. At his side was a holstered pistol; over his shoulder, a mean-looking rifle.

"Archer!" The short man chuckled, and they embraced roughly. "Damn, but I'm glad to see you, even under the circumstances. No sweat, *amigo*—we'll get Martina out of there. Apollo came like a shot when I told him what was on."

"How are you, First Shirt?" J.D. replied. "You've lost weight, I see."

"Well, I'm not exactly in the right profession for getting lazy, am I, Boss?" he asked Laremos, who agreed readily enough.

"Laremos said Apollo and Drago were here, but how about Chen?" J.D. asked.

The short man sighed. "He bought it in Lebanon, *amigo*." He shrugged. "That's the way of it." His eyes were sad and had a faraway look. "It was how he'd have wanted it."

"Tough," J.D. said, agreeing. "Maps and radios, Shirt—we'll need those."

"All taken care of. Plus about twenty *vaqueros* for backup—the boss's men, and I trained 'em," he added with quiet pride.

"That's good enough for me."

"Shall we get under way?" Laremos asked, helping Gabby into a large car. He stood back to let J.D. slide in after her. They were joined by First Shirt, who drove, and another man with a rifle.

The topography was interesting. It reminded Gabby of photos of Caribbean islands, very lush and tropical and studded with palm trees. But after they drove for a while, it began to be mountainous. They passed a burned-out shell of what must have been a house, and Gabby shuddered.

"Diego," she said quietly, nodding toward the ruin, "the owners—did they escape?"

"No, *señorita*," he said.

She wrapped her arms around herself. J.D., noticing the gesture, pulled her closer. She let her head fall onto his shoulder quite naturally and closed her eyes while the men talked.

Laremos's *finca* was situated in a valley. The house seemed to be adobe or stucco, with large arches and an airy porch. It was only one story, and it spread out into a garden lush with tropical vegetation. She fell in love with it at first sight.

"You approve?" Laremos smiled, watching her with his dark, lazy eyes. "My father built it many years ago.

The servants in the house are the children and grand-children of those who came here with him, like most of my employees. The big landowners who hold the *fin-cas* provide employment for many people, and it is not so temporary as jobs in your country. Here the laborers serve the same household for generations."

They'd passed through a small village, and she re-membered glimpses of dark-eyed, dark-skinned, bare-footed children grouped around a big fountain, where women were drawing water in jugs. The apparent lack of modern conveniences made her grateful for her own life in Chicago.

She hadn't noticed anything unusual about the drive except that the small, dark man beside First Shirt had his rifle in his lap and kept watching the countryside. Now he stood beside the car, rifle ready, while the others went into the house.

It was dark for a moment until her eyes adjusted; then she began to see its interior. There were tiny statuettes, obviously Mayan, along with bowls of cacti, heavy wood furniture, and Indian blankets all around the big living room.

"Coffee?" Laremos asked. He clapped his hands and a small, dark woman about First Shirt's age came run-ning with a smile on her face. *"Café, por favor, Carisa,"* he told the woman in rapid-fire Spanish.

She nodded and rushed away.

"Brandy, Archer?" he asked J.D.

"I don't drink these days," J.D. replied, dropping onto the comfortable sofa beside Gabby. "First Shirt, have you been able to get any intelligence out of the other camp?"

"Enough." The short, sandy-haired man nodded, also refusing the offer of brandy. "She isn't being mistreated, not yet, at least," he said, watching the younger man relax just a little. "They're holding her in the remains of a bunkhouse on a *finca* about six clicks away. They aren't well armed—just some AK-47s and grenades, no heavy stuff. They don't have an RPG-7 between them."

"What is a click? And what's an RPG?" Gabby asked.

"A click is a kilometer. An RPG is a rocket launcher, Russian made," J.D. explained. "It makes big holes in things."

"Like tanks and aircraft and buildings," First Shirt added. "You must be Gabby. I've heard a lot about you."

She was taken aback. Everybody seemed to know about her, but she'd never heard of any of these people. She glanced at J.D.

"So I brag about you a little," he said defensively.

"To everybody but me," she returned. "You never even pat me on the head and tell me I've done a good job."

"Remind me later," he said with a slow smile.

"Could I freshen up?" Gabby asked.

"Of course! Carisa!" Laremos called.

The Latin woman entered with a tray of coffee, and he spoke to her again in Spanish.

"*Sí, señor,*" Carisa murmured.

"I've asked her to show you your room," Laremos explained. "Archer, you might like to take the bags and go with them. Then we can talk."

"Suits me." J.D. picked up the cases and followed Gabby and the serving woman down the hall.

The room had a huge double bed. It was the first thing Gabby noticed, and she felt herself go hot all over, especially when Carisa left and she was alone with J.D.

He closed the door deliberately and watched her fiddle with her cosmetic case as she set it down on the dresser.

"Gabby."

She put down a bottle of makeup and turned.

He moved just in front of her and framed her small face in his hands. "I don't want you out of my sight any more than you have to be. Laremos is charming, but there are things about him you don't know. About all these men."

"Including you, Mr. Brettman?" she asked gently, searching his eyes. "Especially you?"

He drew in a slow breath. "What do you want to know?"

"You were one of them, weren't you, J.D.?" she asked quietly. "They're more than old friends. They're old comrades-in-arms."

"I wondered when you'd guess," he murmured. His eyes darkened. "Does it matter?"

She frowned. "I don't understand. Why should the fact that you served in the Special Forces with them matter?"

He seemed torn between speech and silence. He drew in a breath and rammed his hands in his pockets. "You don't know about the years before you met me, Gabby."

"Nobody does. It has something to do with trust, doesn't it?"

He met her searching green eyes squarely. "Yes. A lot. I've lived by hard rules for a long time. I've trusted no one, because it could have meant my life. These men—First Shirt and Laremos and the rest—I know I can trust them, because under fire they never failed me. Laremos, maybe once—that's one reason I brought you along. Against my better judgment," he added dryly. "I'm still not sure I could live with myself if anything happened to you here."

"And that's why you want me in the same room with you?" she probed delicately.

"Not quite," he admitted, watching her. "I want you in the same room because I've dreamed of holding you in my arms all night. I won't make any blatant passes at you, Gabby, but the feel of you in the bed will light up my darkness in ways I can't explain to you."

She felt her heart hammering. He made it sound wildly erotic, to be held close to that massive body all night long, to go to sleep in his arms. Her breath caught in her throat; her eyes looked up into his and her blood surged in her veins.

His fingers moved down to her throat, stroking it with a deliberately sensuous lightness. "Is your blood running as hot as mine is right now?" he asked under his breath. "Does your body want the feel of mine against it?"

He bent and tilted her face up to his, so that he could watch her expression. His mouth opened as it brushed against hers.

"Stand very still," he whispered, opening her mouth with his. "Very, very still…"

She gasped as his hard, moist lips began to merge with her own. She tasted him, actually tasted the essence of him, as he built the intensity of the kiss. His hands moved down her back, bringing her torso against his and letting her soft breasts crush against the hardness of his chest. His teeth nipped roughly at her mouth as he drew slowly away. His eyes were blazing—fierce and passionate and hungry.

"I like it hard," he said under his breath. "Will I frighten you?"

She barely managed to shake her head before he bent again. This time it was a tempest, not the slight breeze of before. He lifted her in his hard arms and she felt the heat in him as his mouth opened wide. She felt his tongue go inside her mouth in a fencing motion that made her feel hot all over and dragged a smothered moan from her throat.

She was trembling, and her body couldn't seem to get close enough to his. She clung to him, trying to weld herself to him, but before she could move, he was putting her on her feet. His eyes blazed wildly in his pale face.

"No more of that," he said heavily. He freed her abruptly, and the blood rushed back into her upper arms, making her aware of the pressure of his unconscious hold on her. "My God, you were trembling all over."

She felt naked under his glittering gaze. She'd never been vulnerable like that with anyone, but to have it happen with J.D. was terrifying.

"I feel funny," she said with a shaky laugh.

"Do you?" He took a deep breath and drew her head to his shoulder. "I'm sorry. I'm sorry, Gabby. I'm not used to virgins."

"That never happened to me before." She hadn't meant to confess it, but the words came tumbling out involuntarily.

"Yes, I felt that," he murmured. His hands, tangled

in her hair, gently drew her closer to him so that her cheek rested against his chest. "Gabby, do you know what I'd like to do? I'd like to take off my shirt and feel your cheek against my skin, your lips on my body…" He groaned and suddenly pushed her away, turning on his heel. He seemed to go rigid, and his hands reached blindly for a cigarette while Gabby stood behind him and ached for what he'd just described.

"How long have we worked together…two years?" he asked in an odd tone. "And we spend two days posing as lovers and this happens. Maybe bringing you along wasn't such a good idea."

"You said you needed me," she reminded him.

He pulled out another cigarette and lit it, handing it to her with an oddly apologetic look. "It will steady you," he said gently. "Gabby, just don't tempt me, all right?"

"Do what?" she asked blankly, looking up at him with dazed eyes.

"Damn!" he growled and then sighed. "Gabby, what I'm trying to say is, let's not get emotional."

"You're the one who's cursing, counselor, not me," she reminded him coldly. "And I didn't start kissing you!"

"You helped," he reminded her, his eyes narrow. "You'd be a joy to initiate."

"I am not sleeping with you!"

His knuckles brushed her mouth, silencing her. "I was teasing. I won't do anything to you that you'll regret, Gabby, that's a promise. No sex."

She swallowed. "You scare me."

"Why?"

"Because of the way you make me feel," she confessed. "I didn't expect it."

"Neither did I. You're a heady wine, honey. One I don't dare drink much of." He lifted his hand to her hair. "You could be habit-forming to a man like me, who's been alone too long."

"Maybe I'd better resign when we get back…" she began, shaken as much by what she was feeling as by what he was telling her.

"No!" he said curtly. His fingers caught the nape of her neck and held on. "No. This is all just a moment out of time, Gabby. It's no reason to start getting panicky. Besides," he added heavily, "there's still Martina. And God only knows how this will turn out."

She went icy cold. "Jacob, please don't go with the others."

"I have to," he said simply.

"You could get killed," she said.

He nodded. "That could happen. But Martina is all I have in the world, the only person I've ever loved. I can't turn my back on her, not now. I could never call myself a man again."

What could she say to that? He touched her cheek lightly and left her alone in the room. She watched the door close with a sense of utter disaster. It didn't help that she was beginning to understand why she trembled so violently at his touch.

J.D. had always disturbed her, from the very first. But she'd assumed that it was because of the kind of man he was. Now, she didn't know. Just looking at him made her ache. And he'd kissed her…how he'd kissed her! As if he were hungry for her, for her alone.

She shook herself. Probably he just needed a woman and she was handy. He'd said not to get herself involved, and she wasn't going to. Just because she was all excited at the prospect of being part of a covert operation, that was no reason to go overboard for J.D.

She wondered at the way he'd reacted when she'd asked if he had been one of the group before. Didn't he remember that he'd told her he'd served in the Special Forces?

It was fifteen minutes before she rejoined the men, wearing jeans and a loose pullover top and boots. J.D. studied her long and hard, his eyes clearly approving the modest gear.

She stared back at him. He seemed like a different man, sitting there in jungle fatigues and holding some small weapon in his big hands.

"The Uzi," he told her when she approached and stared at the miniature machine gun curiously. "It holds a thirty-shot magazine."

"And what's that?" she asked, nodding toward a nasty-looking oversize rifle with a long torpedo-like thing on a stick near it.

"An RPG-7 rocket launcher."

"Is that Gabby?" a short black man asked, grinning at her.

"That's Gabby." J.D. chuckled. "Honey, this is Drago, one of the best explosives men this side of nuclear war. And over in the corner, being antisocial, is Apollo. He's the scrounger. What we need, he gets."

She nodded toward the corner, where a second black man stood. That one was tall and slender, whereas Drago was chunky.

"Hey, Gabby," Apollo said without looking up.

"Does everybody know my name?" she burst out, exasperated.

"Afraid so," First Shirt volunteered, laughing. "Didn't you know Archer was a blabbermouth?"

She stared at her boss. "Well, I sure do now," she exclaimed.

"Come here, Gabby, and let me show you how to work the radio," Laremos offered, starting to rise.

"My job," J.D. said in a tone of voice that made Laremos sit back down.

"But of course." Laremos grinned, not offended at all.

Gabby followed the big man out of the room to the communications room, where Laremos had a computer and several radios.

"J.D...." she began.

He closed the door and glared down at her. "He hurt a woman once. Badly. Can you read between the lines, or are you naïve enough that I have to spell it out in words of one syllable?"

She drew in a steadying breath. "I'm sorry, J.D. You'll just have to make allowances for my stupidity. I'm a small-town Texas girl. Where I come from, men are different."

"Yes, I know. You aren't used to this kind of group."

She looked up. "No. But they seem to be nice people. J.D., it just dawned on me that you must trust me a lot to bring me here," she murmured.

"There isn't anyone I trust more," he said in a deep, rough tone. "Didn't you know?"

He stared into her eyes until she felt the trembling come back, and something wild darkened his own before he turned away and got it under control.

"We'd better get to it," he said tautly. "And when we go back out there, for God's sake, don't say or do anything to encourage Laremos, you understand? He's a friend of mine, but I'd kill him in a second if he touched you."

The violence in him made her eyes widen with shock. He glanced at her, his face hard, and she knew she was seeing the man without the mask for the first time. He looked as ruthless as any one of those men in the other room and she realized with a start that he was.

"I'm territorial," he said gruffly. "What I have, I hold, and for the duration of this trip, you belong to me. Enough said?"

"Enough said, Jacob," she replied, her voice unconsciously soft.

His face tautened. "I'd like to hear you say my name in bed, Gabby," he breathed, moving close. "I'd like to hear you scream it..."

"Jacob!" she gasped as he bent and took her mouth.

She moaned helplessly as he folded her into his tall, powerful form, letting her feel for the first time the involuntary rigidity of his body in desire.

He lifted his lips from hers and looked into her wide eyes, and he nodded. "Yes, it happens to me just as it happens to other men," he said in a rough tone. "Are you shocked? Haven't you ever been this close to a hungry man?"

"No, Jacob, I haven't," she managed unsteadily.

That seemed to calm him a little, but his eyes were still stormy. He let her move away, just enough to satisfy her modesty.

"Are you frightened?" he asked.

"You're very strong," she said, searching his face. "I know you wouldn't force me, but what if...?"

"I've had a lot of practice at curbing my appetites,

Gabby," he murmured. He brushed the hair away from her cheeks. "I won't lose my head, even with you.

"Let me show you," he whispered, and she felt his mouth beside hers, touching, moving away, teasing, until she turned her head just a fraction of an inch and opened it to the slow, sweet possession of his lips.

She could barely breathe, and it was heaven as his arms came around her, as his mouth spoke to her in a wild, nonverbal way. The opening of the door was a shattering disappointment.

"Excuse me—" Laremos chuckled "—but you were so long, I thought you might be having trouble."

"I am," J.D. said in a voice husky with emotion, "but not the kind you thought."

"As I see. Here, let me go over the sequence with you and discuss the frequencies—they are different from the ones you are familiar with, no doubt," he said, sitting down in front of the equipment.

Gabby brushed back her hair and tried not to look at J.D. She tried not to think about the long night ahead, when she'd lie in his arms in that big bed and have to keep from begging him to do what they both wanted.

The radio wasn't difficult at all. It took only minutes to learn the routine. It was the code words that took longest. She made a list and walked around the house memorizing it while the men talked in the spacious living room. At the dinner table, she was still going over it.

Only Laremos, J.D., and Gabby ate together at the table. The others carried their plates away.

"They're still antisocial, I see," J.D. murmured over his food.

"Old habits." Laremos glanced at Gabby. "And I

think they do not want to disillusion this one, who looks at them with such soft eyes."

"I didn't embarrass them, did I?" she asked, contrite.

"No," J.D. said. "I think you flattered them. They aren't used to all that rapt attention." He chuckled.

"How did they come to be mercenaries?" she asked softly. "If you can tell me, I mean. I don't want to invade anyone's privacy."

"Well, Shirt was in the Special Forces, like I was," J.D. said, pausing over the sentence, as if he was choosing his words carefully. "After he got out of the service, he couldn't find anything he liked to do except police work, and he wasn't making enough to pay the bills. He had a contact in the mercenary network and he asked some questions. He was good with the standard underworld weapons and something of a small-arms expert. He found work."

"And Apollo?"

"Apollo started out as an M.P. He was accused of a crime he didn't commit, and there were some racial overtones." J.D. shrugged. "He wasn't getting any justice, so he ran for it and wound up in Central America. He's been down here ever since."

"He can't clear himself?" she asked.

"I expect I'll end up defending him one of these days," he told her with a quiet smile. "In fact, I can almost guarantee it. I'll win, too."

"I wouldn't doubt that," she murmured, tongue in cheek.

"How long have you worked with this bad-tempered one, Señorita Gabby?" Laremos asked.

"A little over two years," she told him, glancing at J.D.

"It's been an education. I've learned that if you shout loudly enough, you can get most anything you want."

"He shouts at you?"

"I wouldn't dare," J.D. murmured with a grin. "The first time I tried, she heaved a paperweight at my head."

"I did not," she protested. "I threw it at your door!"

"Which I opened at the wrong time," he continued. "Fortunately, I have good reflexes."

"You will need them tomorrow, I fear," Laremos told him. "The terrorists will not make things easy for us."

"True," J.D. said as he finished his coffee. "But we have the element of surprise on our side."

"That is so."

"And now, we'd better go over the maps again. I want to be sure I know the terrain before we set out in the morning."

Gabby went on to bed, feeling definitely in the way. She took a quick bath and settled in on one side of the big double bed, wearing the long, very modest nightgown she'd brought along. Unfortunately, the material was thin, but perhaps J.D. would be too busy with his thoughts to notice.

She lay there trying to stumble through a Guatemalan newspaper, but she couldn't concentrate. She tingled all over, thinking of the long night ahead, of spending it lying in J.D.'s arms. Had he really meant that? Or had it just been something to tease her with? And what if he did hold her in his arms all night—would she be able to resist tempting him beyond his control?

She tossed the newspaper onto the floor and wrapped her arms around her knees, staring apprehensively at the door. Her long hair hung softly around her shoulders, and she brushed strands of it away from her face. She wanted him. There was no use denying that she did. But if she gave in, if she tempted him too far, what would she have? One single night to remember, and it would be the end of her job. J.D. didn't want any kind of permanent relationship with a woman, and she'd do well to keep her head. He was worried about his sister, justifiably nervous about tomorrow's foray into the jungle, and he might do something insane if she pushed him.

But for just a moment she thought how it would be, to feel his hair-roughened skin against every inch of her, to let him touch her as he'd no doubt touched other women. She sighed huskily. He'd be gentle, she knew that, and patient. He'd make of it such a tender initiation that it would surpass her wildest dreams of belonging to a man. But it would cheapen what she was beginning to feel for him, and it would do no good for his opinion of her. She attracted him because she was a virgin, untouched. And if she gave herself to him, she wouldn't be that anymore. It was even possible that he'd hold her in contempt for joining the ranks of his lovers.

With a weary moan, she turned out the light and burrowed under the covers. It was a lovely dream, anyway, she told herself, and closed her eyes.

She hadn't meant to go to sleep so soon, but the first thing she knew the dawn light was streaming in through the windows, bringing her wide awake.

Sleepily she stretched, and became suddenly aware of where she was. She sat up, eyes wide, and looked around for J.D. It took only a second to find him. He was standing at the window, his profile to her, looking out. And he didn't have a stitch of clothing on his body.

Her eyes were riveted on him. She'd seen men without clothes. These days, with all the explicit films, it was impossible to avoid nudity. But she'd never seen a nude man close up, like this. And she imagined that J.D. would please even the eyes of an experienced woman.

He was all powerful muscle, with dark shadows of hair feathering every inch of him. His legs were long and muscular, his hips narrow, his stomach flat. His chest was broad and bronzed and a wedge of thick black hair curled over it. She stared at him helplessly, unashamedly—until she happened to look up and saw him watching her.

Her lips trembled as she tried to speak, but she couldn't get anything out.

"It's all right," he said quietly. "If I'd found you in the same condition, I'd be staring just as hard. There's nothing to be embarrassed about.

"I don't wear pajamas," he murmured with an amused look. "I expected to be awake before you were. It was a hot night."

"Yes," she managed, choking.

He moved back toward the bed, and she sat there frozen, unable to make even the pretense of looking the other way. It didn't seem to bother him at all. He bent down, catching her by the arms, and dragged her out of the bed and against his body.

He laughed deep in his throat, the sound of it predatory, primitive. "Touch me," he dared her. His hands caught hers and ran them over his sleek hips, up his spine, and around to the matted tangle of hair over his warm chest.

Her breath was trapped somewhere beneath her ribs, and her fingers burrowed into the crisp hair over his heart.

"Yes, you like it, don't you?" he asked in a voice like rough velvet, his eyes narrow and black and hot on her face. "But not half as much as I do. I've dreamed about this, night after endless night, about how your hands would feel touching me. What do I look like to those innocent eyes, Gabby? Do I frighten you...please you? Which?"

She was drunk with the feel of him, the smell of him. Her hands roamed over his chest, his rib cage. With a long sigh she leaned her forehead on his collarbone. "You please me," she whispered. "Can't you tell? Oh, Jacob...!" Her hands pressed harder, more urgently. "Jacob, I want to do such shameless things."

"Such as?" he asked in a whisper. "Such as, Gabby?" He covered her hands with his own and she felt their faint tremor. "I won't hurt you. Do whatever you want to do."

It wasn't fair that he should have such power over her, she thought dazedly. She was too intoxicated, too hungry, to listen to the cool voice of reason. Her hands smoothed over his chest, around his back, and with an instinct she didn't even know she had, her mouth opened and pressed against the center of his chest.

He groaned harshly, shocking her. She lifted wide, curious eyes to his.

"I like it," he whispered huskily. "Do it again."

She moved closer, and his hands caught her head, guiding her mouth to the places he wanted it, while the silence lengthened and grew around them and J.D.'s breath came raggedly and in gasps. She learned so much about him all at once. That she drove him wild when she rubbed her cheek across his taut nipples, that he liked the curl of her tongue around the tangled hair. That she could nip him gently with her teeth and make him go rigid. That he wanted her badly enough to tremble.

"This isn't fair, Jacob," she whispered shakily, "I'm making you miserable, I'm…"

His thumb pressed across her mouth. His face looked strained, but his eyes were blazing. "I want it," he whispered roughly.

"But I'm hurting you," she said achingly.

"Such a sweet hurt," he whispered, bending. "So sweet, so beautiful…let me make you ache like this, Gabby. I won't seduce you, I promise I won't, but let me touch you…"

His hand moved between them and lightly touched her breast. The gown was thin, and his fingers were warm, and the sudden intimacy was shocking and pleasurable, all at once.

She gasped and instinctively caught his fingers. He lifted his head and looked down, and he smiled.

"Habit?" he whispered.

Her fingers lingered on his hairy wrist. "I…I haven't ever let…" she began.

"You'll let me." His face nuzzled hers, his cheek rubbed gently against hers and he found her mouth, cherishing it with a whispery soft pressure that was wildly exciting.

And all the while, his fingers were shaping, probing, lightly brushing until they caused a helpless reaction in her body. He drew the gown tightly around her breasts and lifted his head.

"Look," he said softly, directing her eyes down to the rigid peaks outlined under the gown. "Do you know what it means, what your body tells me when that happens?"

Her lips opened as she tried to breathe. "It means...that I want you," she whispered back.

"Yes." He brushed her lips apart with his, tracing the line of them with his tongue. His teeth caught her upper one and nibbled gently, tugging it, smiling as she reached up to do the same thing to his.

"Jacob," she whispered. Her hands crept around his neck. "Jacob..." She arched and pressed herself to him, and froze, shocked at what his taut body was telling hers.

"Body language," he whispered, coaxing her mouth open again. "Now listen. I'm going to strip you out of that gown and hold you to me, just for a second, and then I'm going to get the hell out of here before I go crazy. I don't know what we'll be walking into today. I want one perfect memory to take with me, you understand?"

She did. Because it was just dawning on her that she was in love with him. Why else would she be doing this?

She felt his hands unbuttoning the garment and she looked up because she wanted to see his face, she wanted to remember always the expression on it. In case anything happened...

He eased the gown off her shoulders and she felt it suddenly drop to the floor. She felt the whisper of the breeze against her bare skin. J.D.'s eyes blazed as he looked down at her body. And then he drew her to him, and she felt herself go rigid all over.

"I won't live long enough to forget how this feels," he whispered. "Now kiss me, one last time."

And she did, with all her heart and soul, without a single inhibition. And her arms held him and they fused together in a silence gone mad with tangible hunger.

He groaned as if he were being tortured and his arms

hurt her, his lips hurt, his tongue thrust into her mouth in a deliciously fierce invasion. Finally he drew back, shaking, and put her from him.

He bent, picked up the nightgown, and gently drew it back on her without a single word.

"Worth dying for," he whispered, studying her luminous eyes, her swollen mouth, her flushed cheeks. "God, you're sweet."

"Jacob, don't go out there," she pleaded.

"I have to." He bent and retrieved his clothes from a chair where he must have flung them the night before and began to dress.

"But you're a lawyer," she persisted. She wiped away a tear and sat down heavily on the side of the bed, her green eyes wide and frightened. "You aren't a soldier."

"But I was, honey," he said as he tugged on his jungle fatigues. He turned, buttoning the shirt, his eyes dark and mysterious as they searched hers. "You still haven't worked it out, have you, Gabby?"

"Worked what out?"

He tucked in the shirt. "I served only three years in the Special Forces. I joined when I was eighteen."

She was trying to do mathematics with a mind still drugged by pleasure. "You were twenty-one when you got out."

"Yes. But I didn't start studying for my degree until I was twenty-five."

She stared at him, uncomprehending. "That means...you did something else with those four years."

"Yes." He met her searching gaze levelly. "I was a

mercenary. I led First Shirt and the others for the better part of four years, in some of the nastiest little uprisings in the civilized world."

CHAPTER FIVE

GABBY STARED AT HIM as if she'd never seen him before. J.D., a mercenary? One of those men who hired out to fight wars, who risked their lives daily?

"Are you shocked, honey?" he asked, his eyes searching, his stance challenging.

Her lips parted. "I never realized...you said you served with them, but I never realized...I thought you meant in the Special Forces."

"I was going to let you go on thinking that, too," he said. "But maybe it's better to get it out into the open."

Her eyes went over him, looking for scars, for changes. She'd noticed the tiny white lines on his stomach and chest, partially hidden by the hair, but until now it hadn't dawned on her what they were.

"You have scars," she began hesitantly.

"A hell of a lot of them," he said. "Do you want to hear it all, Gabby?"

"Yes."

He rammed his hands into his pockets and went to stare out of the window, as if it was easier to talk when he didn't look at her. "I stayed in the service because it meant I made enough to keep Martina in a boarding school. We had no relatives, you see. Mama was gone."

He shrugged. "But when I got out of the service, I couldn't get a job that paid enough to get Martina through school. I wasn't trained for much except combat." He fumbled in his pocket for a cigarette and lit it. "I thought I'd given this up until the kidnapping," he said absently, holding the cigarette to his lips. He drew in and blew out a cloud of smoke. "Well, Shirt was recruiting, and he knew I was in trouble. He offered me a job. I took it. I spent the next four years globe-trotting with my crossbow and my Uzi. I made money, and I put it in foreign banks. But I got too confident and too careless, and I got shot to pieces."

She held her breath, waiting for him to continue.

"I spent weeks in a hospital. My lungs collapsed from shrapnel and they thought I was going to die. But I lived through it. When I got out, I realized that there was only one way I could go from there, and it was straight downhill. So I told Shirt I was quitting." He laughed mirthlessly. "But first I went on one last mission, just to prove to myself that I still had the guts. And I came out of that one without a scratch. I came back to the States afterward. I figured that someday the guys I'd served with might need a lawyer, and I needed a profession. So I got a job and went to school at night."

"You aren't a fugitive?" she asked.

"No. In one or two countries, perhaps, if I were recognized. But not in the States." He turned, studying her through narrowed eyes. "That's why I guard my past so meticulously, Gabby. And it's why I don't like reporters. I'm not ashamed of the old life. But I don't like being reminded of it too often."

"Do you miss it?" she asked, probing gently.

He sighed. "Yes. Part of me does. Life is so precious when you've touched death, Gabby. You become alive in a way I can't explain to you. Life is pretty damned tame afterward."

"This is why you came after Martina, isn't it, Jacob?" she asked, fitting the puzzle pieces together. "Because you knew that you and the group could succeed where a larger group might fail."

"We're the only chance she has, honey," he said quietly. "In Italy I might have stayed out of it. But down here…the government has its hands full just trying to keep the economy from failing, and there are other factions fighting for control as well. Besides all that, damn it, she's my sister. She's all I've got."

That hurt. He might want Gabby, but he didn't care about her. He'd made that perfectly clear. She lowered her eyes to the skirt of her nightgown.

"Yes, I can understand that," she said in a subdued tone.

"I had a long talk with Laremos last night," he said. "I told him that if he touched you, I'd kill him. You'll be safe here."

Her head jerked up. "I'm not afraid for myself," she said. "Only for you and the others."

"We're a good team," he said. "The way you and I have been for the past two years. Do you want to quit now, Gabby? Are you disillusioned?"

He sounded coldly sarcastic. He lifted the cigarette to his lips with a short laugh.

"Are you firing me?" she threw back, angered by the unexpected and unwarranted attack.

"No. If you leave, it's up to you."

"I'll think about it," she said.

He crushed out his cigarette in an ashtray. "You'd better get dressed. I want to go over those codes with you one last time before we get under way."

"Yes, of course," she murmured. She got up and went to find her clothes. Before she could turn around, the door opened and he'd gone out.

She got dressed and sat down on the bed and cried. To go from dream to nightmare in such a short space of time was anguish. And the worst thing was that she didn't even know what had happened.

It didn't matter to her that he'd been a soldier of fortune, she thought miserably. How could it, when she loved him?

Loved him. Her eyes pictured him, dark and solemn and strong, and a surge of warmth swept over her like fire. She would have followed him through that jungle on her knees without a single complaint. But despite his obvious hunger for her, he didn't want anything emotional between them. He'd pretty well spelled that out for her. Martina was the only person on earth he loved or would love, and he'd said so. What he felt for Gabby was purely physical, something he couldn't help. She was a virgin and she excited him. He wanted her, but that was all. And he could have had her that morning, without a protest on her part. He must have known it too. But he hadn't taken her, because he was strong. He didn't want her getting involved with him, so he'd told her all about his past.

That was the final blow, that he'd shared his past with her, only to put a wall between them. She hid her face in her hands and tried to hold back the tears. How was she going to manage to work with him day after day now, when he couldn't help but see how she felt?

But that wasn't the worst of it. He was going out into the jungle after kidnappers who could kill him. Her heart froze in her chest. She couldn't stop him. All she could do was sit there and pray for him.

All the pleas in the world wouldn't hold him back, not when Martina's life hung in the balance. If there was a chance of any kind, he would take it. But if he died…oh, God, if he died, there would be nothing of worth left in Gabby's life. Tears welled up in her soft green eyes as she tried to imagine a world without him. She wanted to go with him, to risk her life at his side, to die with him if that was what lay in store. But even as she thought it, she knew that nothing would convince him to take her along. He might not love her, but he was fiercely protective of her. He wouldn't allow her to risk her life. And she couldn't fight him.

With a resigned sigh, she got up, combed her hair, and went into the living room where the men were assembled. It took the last ounce of courage she possessed to smile at them. She couldn't meet J.D.'s searching gaze at all. It would cut her to the quick to see indifference in his eyes.

There was a new face in the room. It belonged to a dark, lithe man with pale blue eyes.

"Semson," J.D. told her, indicating the newcomer. "He's been out scouting for the past day or so."

"Gabby?" the new man murmured and grinned at her. "How do you stand working for this dude?"

She smiled wanly. "Oh, it has its moments," she confessed, but she didn't look at J.D. as she said it.

J.D. had picked up an automatic weapon something like a machine gun and slung it over his shoulder, but he was carrying the crossbow. Gabby stared pointedly at it and suddenly realized what it was for.

She looked up, and he seemed to read the thought in her mind.

He nodded. "Sentries," he said, confirming her suspicions. "If there are any."

She felt her throat go dry. She'd never been in a situation like this, and she could have kicked herself for coming along. It was one thing to watch an operation like this in a fictional TV show. But to realize that any one of these men, especially J.D., might never come back from the rescue attempt…that was altogether different.

"Hey, Gabby, don't look so grim," Apollo chided. "I won't let this big turkey get himself hurt."

Gabby laughed despite herself. "Thanks, Apollo," she said. "I've gotten kind of used to him."

"That works both ways. Laremos, take care of her," J.D. told the other man.

Laremos nodded. "Be assured that I will. Now, shall we double-check our coordinates and codes?"

They did, and Gabby felt her palms sweating as she rattled off the codes from memory. She knew how important they were, and that made her more nervous than ever.

"Calm down," J.D. said quietly. "You're okay."

She smiled for him. "Sure. You guys take it easy out there, okay?"

"We're sort of used to this kind of thing," First Shirt said with a wink. "Okay, guys. Hit it."

And just that quickly, they left. Gabby stood at the front door with her wide, unblinking gaze riveted on J.D.'s broad back. He didn't turn or say anything to her. It hurt terribly.

"How long will it take them to get there, Diego?" she asked the man at her side.

"At least an hour or two, Gabby," he replied. "The terrain is rugged, and they require much stealth."

She glanced up to see that his eyes were concerned. "Are you worried?"

"Of course not," he said, but he was lying and she knew it. His smile didn't reach his eyes.

"I'll get a cup of coffee, if I may, and sit beside the receiver."

He studied her closely. "Archer—you care very much for him."

"Yes," she said simply.

"Will you believe me if I tell you that of all the men I have known, he is the most capable under fire?" he said gently. "I have seen him come back from the grave. And their opponents have traveled far, *señorita,* and are already decimated in numbers. They will not expect such an attack here. We have seen to it that their intelligence is distorted."

"But what if something goes wrong?" she burst out.

He sighed. "Then it is in the hands of God, is it not?"

She thought about that for the next three hours, pacing and sweating and worried out of her mind.

"Shouldn't we have heard something?" she asked finally, her face contorted with fear.

Laremos frowned. "It is rugged terrain," he reiterated.

"Yes, but…listen!"

The radio broke its silence, and Gabby made a dive for it. She gave the correct identification and waited.

"Panther to Red Rover," J.D.'s voice said curtly. "Bravo. Tango in ten. Out."

She keyed the mike. "Red Rover here. Alpha. Omega. Out."

The code words meant that the group had arrived undetected and would make their play in ten minutes. She'd radioed back that the message was understood and that there was no new intelligence to convey.

She looked up at Laremos, feeling her heart go wild as she realized how close the danger was. "Ten minutes," she said.

"The waiting is the hardest, is it not?" he asked quietly. "I will have Carisa fix us another pot of coffee."

He strode away, and Gabby prayed and chewed her nails and stared at the microphone as if it held the key to salvation.

Long, agonizing minutes later, the static came again. "Panther to Red Rover," J.D. said tightly, as gunfire and an explosion of some sort sounded in the background. "Charlie Tango! Heat up the coffee. Out!"

Her fingers trembled as she returned, "Red Rover to Panther. Bravo. Omega. Out!"

She'd just signed off when Laremos came tearing into the room, eyes flashing.

"Raise them quickly! One of my men just reported that he's sighted a large guerrilla force moving toward Archer's position!"

She grabbed the mike. "Red Rover to Panther. Red Rover to Panther. Come in, Panther!"

But there was no answer. Frantically she tried again and again, and still there was no answer. Her frightened eyes went to Laremos.

"They must be under fire," he said heavily, "or they

would answer. We can only pray that they spot the new-comers in time."

She stared at the mike, hating it. Her cold fingers keyed it again, and again she gave the message. There was no answer.

Her mind went wild. J.D., answer me, she pleaded silently. I can't lose you now, I can't!

As if he heard her, somewhere miles away, the radio blared. "Red Rover, we're cut off by guerrillas, lots of them," J.D. said sharply. "Going into the jungle coordinates two clicks from position Delta. Gabby, get the hell out of there, they're heading in your direction...!"

The radio went dead. Gabby stared at it helplessly and then at Laremos.

"*Madre de Dios,*" he breathed. "I should have realized...Carisa!" he yelled. A stream of Spanish followed, and Laremos grabbed one of the weapons J.D. had called an AK-47. He thrust it into Gabby's numbed fingers.

"Carry it. I will teach you to use it when I must," he said curtly. "Come, there is no time. Aquilas!" he yelled, and the short man who'd driven in from the airport with them came running in. There was another stream of Spanish.

"My men will cover us," Laremos said curtly. "We must hurry. The guerrillas will not care who are terrorists and who are not, they will cut us down regardless. Aquilas says the government troops are not too far behind. But we cannot involve them." His wary eyes sought hers. "You understand?"

"Because of the rescue," she said, smiling wanly. "It's all right, *señor.* Just, please, get me to J.D."

He looked at her searchingly. "I understand. But do

not underestimate the group, *señorita*. We were once…quite something."

He led her out of the house, and together they headed quickly into the jungle. She carried the heavy weapon with no real sense of its weight and no earthly idea of how to use it. As she followed Laremos through dense undergrowth at a breakneck pace, she wondered what her mother back home in Lytle, Texas, would think if she knew where her only daughter was.

"Quick, get down," Laremos hissed, pushing her under the dense foliage and cautioning her to be quiet.

She froze, her heart pounding painfully in her chest. She felt weak all over. What would happen if they were seen? She couldn't fire the weapon, she didn't know how! Her eyes felt as if they were going to pop out of her head, and she wished she were with J.D. Laremos would do his best, but if she had to die, she wanted to be with Jacob when it happened. Her eyes closed and she prayed silently while sweat poured down her cheeks.

There was a wild thrashing nearby, and she had a glimpse of ragged-looking men with rifles, wearing some sort of soldiers' garb. She knew without being told that they were the guerrillas Laremos had spoken about. They were muttering among themselves, but they didn't seem to be looking for anyone. They were joking and laughing, their weapons hung over their shoulders as they trailed through the jungle.

Gabby bit almost through her lower lip as she studied the weapons they were carrying. She could feel terror in her throat, strangling her. What if they were spotted? There were worse things than being killed, especially for a woman, and she remembered what she'd read about this part of the world. Her eyes closed. The bravery she'd thought she had was nowhere to be found.

It seemed to take forever for the men to march out of sight and finally out of earshot.

"Courage," Laremos whispered. "We will wait just another minute and then proceed."

"We can't go back to your *finca?*" she whispered back, hating her own cowardice.

He shook his head. "This is only a small part of the main force. Unless I am badly mistaken, the rest are camped at my *finca.*" He shrugged. "The government troops will come and drive them out. But for the meantime, we have little choice. We either try to join our comrades or risk being killed."

"I'm much too young to die," she told him with a quiet smile. "How do I shoot this thing if I have to?"

He showed her, quickly and efficiently, and she felt a little more secure as they started out again. But her eyes darted every which way, and she was so afraid that she could taste the fear in her mouth. Death seemed to lurk behind every tree.

She was learning something about courage. It wasn't being unafraid. It was being stubborn.

It was slow going. Laremos had a pedometer, a compass, and a map, and he was using all three. They had been walking for over an hour when suddenly gunfire erupted all around them.

"Oh, my God," Gabby squealed, dropping down with her hands over her head, the AK-47 falling to the ground.

"Don't panic," Laremos said tautly as he came down beside her. "Listen."

She heard bullets whizzing, but Laremos was grinning!

"What...?" she tried to ask, gathering enough courage to grab her weapon and hold onto it with cold fingers.

"The Uzi," he whispered. "I know the sound, oh, so well, *señorita,*" he said with a grin. He moved behind a tree and peered out into the jungle. All at once, he stood up. "Archer!" he yelled. "Here!"

Then there was a flurry of wild movement, crashing sounds, gunfire, and explosions, and in the middle of it came J.D., with a small, dark-haired woman under one arm and the Uzi under the other. Around him, Shirt and Apollo and Semson and Drago were covering each other and firing on the run as they joined Laremos and Gabby.

"Martina, Gabby," J.D. said as he piled in with them and let go of his sister. "Okay, honey?" he asked Gabby with a quick glance.

"Fine, now," she whispered shakily, clutching the weapon.

"They're right on our tails," J.D. said. "Apollo, got any of that C-4 left?" he yelled.

"Working on it right now, big man," came the reply. "Just enough to make a big splash. We'll have to draw them in."

"Tell me when," J.D. called back.

"The guerrillas have taken my *finca,*" Laremos said. "We barely escaped in time."

"I'm sorry about that," J.D. said as he reloaded the small automatic weapon.

"Are you both all right?" Gabby asked J.D. in a quavering voice as she crawled over to Martina and clutched the frightened woman's hand.

"A few scratches, but we'll make it," he returned, but his eyes were fierce and tormented as they searched Gabby's face. "How about you?"

"I'm learning to be a crack shot," she replied with a nervous laugh. "Laremos even told me how to cock this thing."

"If you have to fire it," J.D. said intently, "be sure you brace it hard against your shoulder so that the recoil doesn't break a bone. Take a breath, let half of it out, and squeeze the trigger, don't jerk it."

"I'll be a natural," Gabby told him, but she was trembling.

"I wish I could help," Martina whispered shakily. "But I'm so tired…!"

"God knows you've reason to be," J.D. said. He ruffled her hair. "But you're a trooper, sis."

She managed a smile for him. "Like my big brother. I knew you'd come, I knew you would. Thank God for your Special Forces training." Martina added with a laugh, "But however did you find these other men?"

J.D. and Gabby exchanged a quiet look. "I hired them," he said blandly. "Roberto can reimburse me."

"My poor darling." Martina sighed. "He'll be so frantic."

"How are we going to get out of here?" Gabby asked J.D.

"Wait and see." He glanced toward Apollo. "Ready?" he called.

"Ready!"

"I'm going to draw them out for you. Don't let me down!"

"J.D., no!" Gabby burst out as he leaped out of the

brush and started firing toward rustling noises in the undergrowth ahead.

She lost her mind. Afterward it was the only explanation she could come up with. The guerrillas came forward in a rush, and suddenly Gabby was on her feet. She saw a sniper taking dead aim at J.D.; she turned and lifted the heavy weapon and sighted it and pulled the trigger.

It was a miracle that she even hit the guerrilla's shoulder, her aim was so wide. But she did, and with terror she realized that the man had taken aim at her and was about to fire.

"Gabby!" J.D. yelled wildly.

Simultaneously she pulled the trigger again, forgetting to brace the gun in her terror. She was knocked to the ground when she fired. There was a burst of gunfire and, suddenly, a huge, horrible explosion that rocked the ground.

"All right, let's hit it!" First Shirt yelled out.

J.D. dragged Gabby to her feet, and his face showed such terrible fury that she closed her eyes. He didn't even speak. He jerked the gun out of her hands and pushed her ahead of him as he bent to lift Martina to her feet.

"Are you all right, *señorita?*" Laremos asked gently as he joined Gabby.

"My shoulder hurts a little, but I'm…I'm fine," she whispered. She started to turn around, to look behind them, but J.D. was suddenly there.

"Don't look," he said in a tone that dared her to argue. "Get moving."

He was a stranger now, a man she'd never known. His face was like stone, and there was something wild and dangerous in his eyes and in the set of his big body. She didn't say another word. She kept quiet all the long way through the jungle.

"Where are we going?" she finally asked Laremos as they kept moving through the endless jungle.

"In a circle, around my *finca*," he told her. "We have hopes that by now the government troops have rounded up the guerrillas. Apollo has gone in to check."

"So quickly?" she asked, brushing back a strand of matted hair from her sweaty face.

"So quickly," he confirmed. "Your shoulder, it is better?"

"A little bruised, that's all," she said. She felt sick to her stomach. All she wanted was to lie down and forget the past two days altogether.

"I'm so tired," Martina murmured. "Can't we rest?"

"Soon," J.D. said, gently now. "Just a little longer, honey."

"Okay, big brother. I'll trudge along. Gabby, are you holding up okay?"

"Yes, thanks, Martina."

There was a sudden crackling sound and J.D. and the others whirled with their guns leveled as Apollo came leaping through the growth, grinning.

"We're clear!" he shouted. "The government troops just marched the guerrillas away."

"What about the men in the terrorist camp?" Gabby asked.

"They scattered," First Shirt replied. "The guerrillas would have shot them if they'd found them before the government troops showed up. The terrorists have no friends here in Guatemala."

"How sad for them," Martina said, but her eyes flashed. "I do not pity them, not after the ordeal they put me through. Oh, I want my Roberto!"

"We'll send for him the minute we get to my *finca*," Laremos promised her. "The very minute."

Gabby dropped back to put a comforting arm around the smaller, older woman and smiled reassuringly. "It won't be long," she said.

"Absolutely," Laremos agreed. "There. We are home."

The *finca* looked so good that Gabby wanted to kiss it. The outside bore no marks of violence, but inside it was a different story. The furniture was wrecked, the floors scarred. Laremos's dark eyes glittered as he saw the evidence of the brief guerrilla occupation.

"I'm sorry about your house, *señor*," Martina said gently.

"*Señora*, that you are safe is the most important thing," Laremos said with pride, turning to bow in her direction. "My poor house can be repaired. But your life, once lost, would not have been restored."

"I owe you a great debt," Martina said. Her clothes were torn and her hair hung in wild strands. But she looked spunky for all that. She reached up and kissed Laremos on his tan cheek. "*Muchas gracias.*"

Laremos looked embarrassed. "My pleasure, *señora*. I regret that I could not have done more."

"Is everybody all right?" Gabby asked, looking around at the battle-scarred little group with concerned eyes.

"Gabby, you'll spoil us if you worry about us," Apollo said, chuckling.

"Not me." First Shirt glowered at Apollo. "Worry all

you want, Gabby. I'll just sit here like a sponge and soak it up."

The others joined in, all except J.D. He kept to himself, looking dangerous and unapproachable until Martina and Gabby left to go up to the room Gabby had shared with him.

"A bath." Martina sighed, taking advantage of the facilities. "I feel so dirty!"

"It must have been horrible," Gabby said, digging out fresh clothes.

"Not as horrible as it could have been. I wasn't abused, at least. That surprised me." She came out of the shower minutes later, toweling her long hair dry. "Your turn. I imagine you feel as mucky as I did."

"Yes, I do." Gabby laughed. "My shoulder hurts and I feel shaky all over."

"You saved J.D.'s life," was Martina's quiet comment. "I can never thank you enough for that. But don't expect him to," she added dryly. "I think his pride's dented. He's very quiet."

"He's been through a lot. They all have. What a great bunch of guys," she said fervently.

"Tell me!" Martina laughed, and despite the weariness in her drawn face, there was joy. "I'd like to kiss every one of them twice. I can't tell you how I felt when I saw J.D. come breaking in that door! Wasn't it lucky that he had that military training?"

Obviously Martina didn't know everything about J.D.'s past, and Gabby wasn't about to betray him. "It sure was," she agreed and disappeared into the bathroom.

Her shoulder was turning blue, but she was grateful to be alive. She still couldn't believe what she'd done.

It had been pure instinct when she saw the weapon pointing at J.D. Let him be angry at her—she couldn't be sorry about what she'd done. Even if the man had shot her, it would have been worth it to deflect his aim. If anything had happened to J.D., she might as well have died. She loved him—so much!

The next day, Roberto drove in from the airport and there was a wildly emotional reunion. Gabby, watching, couldn't help the twinge of jealousy she felt. Roberto was crying as he embraced his wife, and unashamedly at that. Gabby's eyes darted to J.D., who hadn't said a single word to her since they'd come out of the jungle. They'd all had a good night's sleep, Martina and Gabby sharing the big double bed this time, but his dark mood hadn't lifted. He wouldn't even look at Gabby, and that hurt most of all. She'd only wanted to save him, but it seemed that she'd committed some unforgivable sin.

CHAPTER SIX

ROBERTO WAS VERY ITALIAN, if someone who lived in Sicily could be called Italian, Gabby mused. He was of medium height and thin, with a charm that was immediately apparent when he bent over Gabby's hand.

"It is a pleasure to meet you," he said. He grinned, glancing at J.D., who was talking quietly with Apollo in the living room. "Martina's brother mentions you often."

"Does he?" Gabby asked conversationally, privately wondering whether she even had a job to go back to, now that it was all over. J.D. still hadn't looked in her direction.

"It was bad, Gabby," Martina said from her husband's side, her dark eyes meeting the other girl's green ones warmly. "Jacob and the others...well, it was a miracle that any of us got out. He'll get over it. It has been a long time since he was in the service, you know. It had to affect him."

"Yes, of course," Gabby said, smiling faintly. She couldn't let Martina know the truth. "You look awfully good for somebody who went through what you did."

Martina clung to her husband's arm and smiled. "I have my whole world back again. I feel good. Just a little shaken and homesick." She glanced up at Roberto. "Can we go back today?"

He inclined his head. "As soon as our pilot finishes the meal Laremos was kind enough to provide."

"It will be good to have familiar things around me." Martina sighed. "But I do not think I ever want to go shopping alone again." She shuddered. "From now on, my husband, I will listen when you warn me against such things."

"I had feared that it would happen," Roberto confessed, with a glance at the men scattered around the living room. "Thank God your brother and his friends knew so well what to do. I am sure that the kidnappers would never have let you live." He pulled her into his arms and held her convulsively, his eyes closed, his face contorted. "*Dio,* I could not have lived myself!" he whispered hoarsely.

"Shh," Martina said, comforting him and smiling. She clung to him, and Gabby could only imagine how it felt to be loved so possessively. She experienced a twinge of envy, because nobody had ever cared for her that way. J.D. surely hadn't. He looked as if he were frankly sick of the whole thing, especially Gabby.

"You had better spend a little time with Jacob while you can," Roberto said, releasing Martina. "It may be another year before we see him again." He smiled. "Hopefully, the next time will be under happier circumstances."

"Oh, yes," Martina said wholeheartedly. "Gabby, you must come to Palermo with him next time and visit. Our villa overlooks the sea, and it is so beautiful."

"I'd like that," Gabby said noncommittally. She was thinking that J.D. would probably never take her as far as the corner again, but she didn't say it.

Martina approached her brother, and as J.D. stood up Gabby got a glimpse of his face. It softened magically for his sister. When he smiled at her it was like the sun coming out. Gabby couldn't bear the contrast between the way he'd looked at her in the jungle and the way he looked at his sister. She turned and went toward the bedroom to finish packing.

Later, as she was folding clothes, Martina tapped at the door and entered the room quietly, smiling sheepishly.

"I hate to ask, but do you have some makeup I could borrow?" J.D.'s sister asked. "I feel like a hag."

"Yes, of course, I do," Gabby said quickly, taking her cosmetic case from the dresser. "I didn't bring much, though," she said apologetically as she handed it over, along with a brush. "I kind of figured that we weren't going to be going places that I'd need to dress for."

"Thank you," Martina said and seated herself in front of the mirror. "There!" she exclaimed, smiling ruefully at her face. "Such pleasure, from such a mundane thing," she murmured. "Gabby, there were times when I thought I'd never live long enough to do this again."

"It must have been awful," the taller girl said quietly. "I'm so sorry, Martina."

"My own stupidity," came the reply. "Roberto warned me, but I take after Jacob, I'm afraid. I'm bull-headed and I like my own way." She sat down on the bed and studied Gabby for a long moment. "He will not speak to you, and that hurts, doesn't it?"

Gabby shrugged, taking a long time to fold a T-shirt. "A little."

"If you could only have seen his face in that split second before the recoil threw you to the ground," Martina said solemnly. "It would have been a revelation to you. In all the years of my life, I can only recall once or twice when I've seen that expression in his eyes. Once," she added quietly, "was just after our mother died."

Gabby stared at the pale garment in her hand. "I was so afraid for him," she confided. "I saw that man level his rifle at Jacob, and…" She shivered. "It all happened so quickly."

"Yes, I know." Martina stood up. "Gabby, he isn't an easy man. And he's been very restless the past few years. But I think perhaps in you he has found his future. Did you know," she added with a wicked grin, "that you're all I hear about when he calls me these days?"

Gabby laughed nervously, desperate even for crumbs. Her green eyes glowed softly as she looked at Martina. "I'd give anything to be his future," she said quietly. "But he's already said he doesn't want ties or commitment. And I'm dreadfully old-fashioned. Everybody else sleeps around and thinks nothing of it, but I'm just not built for loose affairs."

Martina pursed her lips and then grinned. "Well, well. Poor Jacob."

"Anyway," Gabby said, sighing, "it's probably just a flash in the pan. I've worked for him over two years and he's never looked twice at me until this came up." She glanced at Martina and smiled. "I'm just so glad that you came out of it all right. We were all worried about you, not just J.D."

"Roberto and I must go home today," Martina said. "But you will come and visit us one day. I believe that, even if you don't." Impulsively, she hugged Gabby. "Take care of Jacob for me. He doesn't know that he needs taking care of, so we mustn't let on. But he's so alone, Gabby."

Gabby felt as if she were choking. "Yes," she said. "I know." And it hurt to think just how alone he was, and how much it affected her.

Later, as she wandered around the house restlessly, she met First Shirt coming down the hall, and he stopped to talk to her. "Why the long face, little lady?" he asked with an affectionate smile.

"Work is going to seem like peeling onions from now on," she lied, smiling impishly at him.

He laughed heartily. "Now you know why the guys and I don't retire. Hell, I'd rather die on my feet than deteriorate behind a desk." He shrugged. "But it seems to suit Archer."

Her eyes fell. "Yes, I suppose so."

"Hey."

She looked up, and he smiled at her.

"He doesn't like being helped out," he said knowingly. "I ought to know. He threw a punch at me one time when I spotted a guy with a grenade and got to him first. He doesn't like making mistakes. He'll get over what happened out there."

"Will he?" she asked, her eyes wide and sad. "He won't even talk to me."

"Reaction. You have to remember, Gabby, he's been out of action for a while. This sort of thing—" he waved his hand "—you don't forget, but sometimes it brings back bad memories. He got shot up pretty bad once."

"He told me," she said absently.

His eyes narrowed. "Now, that's interesting."

"Just to satisfy my curiosity," she added.

"I used to wonder if he was ever going to settle down," he said enigmatically. "But there was never a special woman."

"I suppose he liked leaving his doors open," she murmured, "in case he couldn't adjust to a desk job."

"Yes, that's what I thought," First Shirt said. His chest rose and fell on a deep breath. "None of us have ties. They're too much of a luxury in this kind of work." He searched her wide eyes. "I'm glad our paths crossed. Take care of Archer. He's gone too far to come back to us, but maybe he doesn't realize it yet."

"I wish you were right, First Shirt," she said with a sad smile.

"My name—my given name—is Matthew."

She smiled. "Matthew."

"Keep in touch once in a while, will you?" he asked as he turned. "Archer's a damned bad correspondent."

"I'll do that," she promised, flattered.

Her eyes followed his lean figure down the hall. She was already thinking about Christmas. Socks, she decided. Lots of socks and gloves. She started back toward the bedroom.

It was deathly quiet after Martina and Roberto left, and one by one the men seemed to vanish. Later she learned that everybody except First Shirt had already left the country for other places, just as secretively as they'd come. She'd grown attached to them in that short space of time. Of course, the circumstances were unusual, to say the least.

Laremos was his charming self at the evening meal, but J.D. was still brooding and he wouldn't look at Gabby.

"When are we going back?" she asked J.D. finally, in desperation.

"Tonight." He bit the words off.

"I'll double-check to make sure I've packed everything." She stood up. "Señor Laremos, thank you for your hospitality. Under different circumstances, it would have been lovely. I'm sorry we didn't get to see the Mayan ruins."

"So am I, Gabby," he said sincerely. "Perhaps you may return someday, and it will be my pleasure to show them to you." He made her a handsome bow and she smiled at him as she left the room.

Minutes later, J.D. joined her, presumably to get his own things packed. He had slept downstairs with the men the night before, but his case was still in the bedroom. Gabby had considered packing for him, but she was nervous about antagonizing him any more.

She looked up from her suitcase when he closed the door. His face was still hard as granite, and his eyes glanced off hers coldly. He didn't say a word as he began to fill the small bag on the chair across from the bed.

"Are you all right?' she asked finally, when the silence became uncomfortable.

"Yes, I'm all right," he said gruffly. "Are you?"

She shrugged and smiled wanly. "It was the experience of a lifetime."

"Wasn't it, though?" he asked curtly. His eyes blazed as he studied her flushed face.

"Why are you so angry?" she asked.

He dropped his eyes to the bag and shoved his combat fatigues into it. "What makes you think I am?"

"You've barely spoken to me since we came back."

She moved around the bed to stand beside him, her emotions in turmoil, her mind confused. She looked at his big body and remembered with staggering clarity how it looked without clothing, how it felt to be held by those hard arms and kissed by that mouth.

"Jacob, what have I done?" she asked softly, and touched his arm.

His hard muscles tensed beneath her touch, and when he looked down at her she had to fight the urge to back away.

"What the hell did you think you were playing at out there?" he asked coldly. "Didn't you realize that the bullets weren't blanks, that we weren't acting out some scenario from a television show? You're a dull little secretary, not a professional soldier, and if the force of the recoil hadn't knocked you down, you'd have been killed, you stupid child!"

So that was it. Shirt had been right, his pride was hurt because Gabby had seen a threat and he hadn't. "J.D., if I hadn't shot him, he'd have killed you," she said, trying to reason with him.

He slammed the bag back down. "Am I supposed to thank you?"

Her temper was blazing now too. "Don't strain yourself," she told him icily. "And I am not a dull little secretary!"

"Don't kid yourself," he said, staring at her. "You aren't Calamity Jane and you're never likely to be. You'll get married to some desk jockey and have a dozen kids."

Her face paled and his eyes narrowed when he saw it. "What's wrong, honey?" he taunted. "Were you expecting a proposal from me?"

She turned away. "I expect nothing from you."

"Liar." He caught her arm roughly and swung her around. Seconds later, she was flat on her back on the bed and he was looming over her, holding her down with hands that hurt.

"Jacob, you're bruising me!" she burst out, struggling.

He threw a long, powerful leg across hers and spread-eagled her, his hands on her wrists. "Now fight," he said coldly, "and see how far you get."

She gave up finally and lay breathing heavily, glaring up at him. "What's this supposed to prove, that you're stronger than I am? Okay, I'm not arguing."

His dark eyes wandered slowly over her body, lingering on the curves outlined by her tight jeans and the expanse of bare skin where her sweatshirt had ridden up during the struggle. Her breath caught, because she wasn't wearing a bra, and the hem of the garment was just below the curve of her breasts.

"I wanted you yesterday morning," he said bluntly. "And if you hadn't been a virgin, I'd have taken you. But any woman would have done. You were just a body to me, so if you've been weaving me into your future, forget it."

Her heart leapt in her chest. It was true, she had, but she couldn't let him see just how involved she was emotionally. Very obviously, that wasn't what he wanted from her.

"I haven't asked you for any promises, have I?" she asked quietly, searching his dark eyes. "You're safe, Jacob. I'm not trying to tie you down."

His fingers contracted. "Let's make sure of that, shall we?" he asked in a menacing tone. "Let's make damned sure that you don't ever want to try."

Her lips parted to ask the question, but he moved suddenly. One hand imprisoned both of hers above her head. The other pulled up the sweatshirt, baring her taut breasts to his eyes.

"Now, Gabby, let me show you how a real mercenary treats women."

He did, and she couldn't fight, because he was so much stronger than she was. She lay still, feeling half-afraid of him as he treated her body like a piece of used merchandise. He shamed her, humiliated her, covering her with his own taut body, while his hands touched and gripped and his body moved suggestively, making a travesty of everything she felt for him.

"Do you like it?" he growled against her bruised mouth as his hands moved lower on her pinned body and contracted, grinding her hips against his. "Because this is how it would be if I took you. Quick and rough and purely for my own pleasure. And if you're remembering yesterday morning, don't," he added. "Because that was a flash in the pan. This is the reality. This, and this...!"

He hurt her, and the crush of his mouth was as suggestive as the motion of his hard body. She tried to struggle away from him, but that only made it worse. He forced her arms down into the mattress and his body overwhelmed hers in an intimacy that made her gasp.

He laughed coldly. "Are you shocked? You wanted it yesterday. Come on, honey. I won't let you get pregnant. How about it?" And he kissed her again, cruelly, oblivious to the tears of shame and humiliation running hotly down her cheeks as he whispered graphic, crude remarks before his mouth forced hers open and penetrated it.

When he finally tired of the game and rolled away, she couldn't even move. She lay there, bruised and emotionally devastated, her face pale, her eyes closed. Tears ran in a flood down her cheeks and her body shook with sobs.

"Damn you, J.D.," she wept, flushed with fury. "Damn you!"

"That's how I am with a woman," he said coldly, ignoring the trembling of her body, the terrible hurt in her eyes. "That's how it would have been yesterday if I'd had the time and I could have coaxed you into it. Your body arouses me and I want it. But anything would have done. I just needed to forget what was ahead, the same way I've forgotten it a hundred times before with a hundred other women." His voice was bitter and he turned away. "So set your sights on some other man, and don't weave romantic daydreams around me. I've just shown you the reality. Remember it."

She didn't move. She couldn't. She was trembling too much, and she felt sick and empty. Her eyes looked up into his, bright with furious anger. Something of her pain and shame must have shown in them, because he turned away and, grabbing up his suitcase, went to the door without another glance.

"Bring your bag and let's go," he said in a harsh tone.

She watched him close the door and then she managed to get to her feet. His taunting voice would haunt her as long as she lived. She would resign, of course, but she didn't know how she was going to manage to look at him while she worked out a two-week notice. Maybe he'd let her go immediately. The only problem was that she didn't have another job to go to. Her rent and car payments wouldn't wait while she went without work.

Minutes later, wearing a fresh green pullover blouse with a matching sweater and the same jeans, and with her hair carefully pulled back in a bun, she left the bedroom, her suitcase in hand. She was still pale, but makeup had camouflaged the rest of what J.D. had done to her.

He didn't even glance in her direction as she came back into the living room. Apparently, he'd shut her out of his mind already, and she wished she had the ability to do the same with him. The scars his brutality had left on her emotions would be a long time healing. She'd loved him. How could he hurt her that way? How could he?

She tried to disguise her anguish and hoped that she succeeded. She said goodbye to Laremos and got into the station wagon with First Shirt while J.D. said his own farewells.

Shirt gave her a brief but thorough scrutiny and laid one lean, wiry hand over the steering wheel. "What did he do to you?" he asked.

She lifted a startled face. "Why...nothing."

"Don't lie," he said gently. "I've known him a long time. Are you okay?"

She shifted restlessly in the seat, refusing to let her eyes go past Shirt to J.D., who was standing apart with Laremos. "Yes, I'm okay," she said. "Of course, I'll be a lot better once I get out of his life."

"Whew." He whistled ruefully. "That bad?"

"That bad." She gripped her purse tightly in her lap.

"Gabby," he said gently, with a tiny smile, "have you ever known a fighting fish to lie down when he hit the bait? Don't expect to draw him in without a little effort."

She glared at him. "I'd like to put a hook in him, but not to land him."

"Give it a little time," he said. "He's been alone most of his life. It's new to him, needing someone."

"He doesn't need me," she said shortly.

"I'm not convinced of that," he replied. He studied her affectionately. "I think he's met his match. You're a pretty damned good shot for a lady who's never used an automatic weapon before. Laremos said you learned fast."

She pursed her lips, studying her purse. "It wasn't a hard weapon to learn," she told him. "There were only three positions to remember with the change lever—top for safety, middle for bursts and bottom for single shots. And actually, I have shot a .22-caliber rifle before. Mama and I used to hunt rabbits. But it didn't have a kick like that AK-47."

He smiled as she rubbed her shoulder. "I don't imagine so. Is your mother still alive?"

She nodded, smiling back. "She lives in Lytle, Texas. There's a small ranch, and she has a few head of cattle. It's not nearly as big as the one she and Daddy had, but when he died, she decided to retire. Sort of."

"And she hunts?" he asked.

"Hunts, rides, ropes, and can outcuss most veteran cowboys," she told him. "She's quite a character."

"You're a character yourself," he said. "When J.D. told me he took you along on secret meetings, I began to realize that he had an unusual relationship with you. J.D. doesn't trust anybody except his sister and me."

That wasn't bragging, either, she realized. Just a statement of fact. "He doesn't trust Laremos."

"Neither do I," he whispered, smiling.

She burst out laughing, but the amusement faded immediately as J.D. started toward the car, and she felt herself freezing up. But she needn't have worried. J.D. climbed into the back seat and slammed the door, waving to Laremos.

"Be back in a few hours, Boss," Shirt called to him. Laremos grinned and waved, and they were under way.

It was a long trip to the airport, not because of distance but because of the tension between Gabby and J.D. Despite First Shirt's efforts to keep things casual, Gabby drew into herself and didn't say a word all the way.

It was like that during the flight back as well. Gabby was relieved to find that their seats were not together. She was sandwiched between a businessman and a young girl. J.D.'s seat was farther back. Not one word had passed between them when they landed at O'Hare airport in the wee hours of the morning.

It took her a long time to find a place in the swollen ranks of departing passengers. She didn't look back to see where J.D. was either. Her only thought was to get back to her apartment. After that she'd face the thought of leaving J.D. forever, of finding another job and getting on with her life.

At last she reached the front of the terminal and stepped out into the breezy night air that carried the sound of distant car horns and city smells that had become so familiar. There was no cab in sight, but Gabby wasn't daunted. She'd just call one.

"Come on," J.D. said tersely, appearing just behind her. "I'll drive you."

She glared at him. "I'd rather be mugged."

"You might be, at this hour, alone," he said matter-of-factly. "What's the matter, afraid of me?" he taunted.

She was; he'd made her afraid. But she was too proud to let him see how much.

After a minute, she turned and followed him toward the parking lot. A little later, they were winding their way back into Chicago.

"Have you decided what you're going to do?" he asked.

She knew instinctively what he meant. "Yes. I'm going to try to find a job in the computer field. I like working with them."

He glanced toward her. "I thought you enjoyed legal work. It's too bad, to let that paralegal training go to waste."

"I'm tired of legal work," she said noncommittally. What she meant was that she couldn't take the risk of running into J.D. accidentally after she'd quit. It would be too painful.

He shrugged and calmly lit a cigarette as he drove. "It's your life. You'd better call that agency Monday morning and have them send over some applicants. I'll let Dick do the interviewing this time," he added with a cold laugh.

Her fingers clenched on her purse. She stared out of the window at the river.

"No comment?" he prodded.

"About what?" she asked indifferently.

He sighed heavily and took another draw from the cigarette. One more turn and he pulled the car into a parking spot in front of her apartment building.

She got out and waited for him to get her carry-on bag. "Don't bother walking me up," she said.

He glared down at her. "I wasn't aware that I'd offered."

Her anger exploded. "I hate you," she said in a venomous whisper.

"Yes, I know you do," he said with a cold smile.

She whirled on her heel and started toward the door of the building.

"Gabby," he called curtly.

She stopped with her hand on the door, but didn't turn. "What?"

"You'll work a two-week notice. Every day of it. Or I'll make sure you don't work again. Clear?"

She'd been thinking about not showing up at all on Monday. But when she turned and saw his eyes, she realized, not for the first time, what a formidable adversary he made. She hated to give in, but the necessity of finding a new job made her do so gracefully.

"Why, Mr. Brettman, I wouldn't miss a minute of it," she said with sweet mockery. "See you Monday."

CHAPTER SEVEN

THE LAST THING SHE FELT like doing Monday morning was going into the office. To make things worse, her shoulder was aching like mad. But that didn't stop Gabby. She put on a beige suit with a jazzy, multicolored blouse, pinned up her hair, and went to work. Might as well get it over with, she told herself. She'd go back to the office, work out her notice, and get another job. Sure. Simple.

Explaining that to her mother back home in Lytle, Texas, had not been quite so simple.

"But I thought you loved your job!" her mother had gasped. "Why are you quitting? Listen, Gabby, what's happened?"

"Nothing, Mama," she'd said quickly. "It's just that Mr. Brettman may not be in Chicago much longer." She lied on impulse. "You see, he has prospects in another area, and I don't really want to relocate."

"Where would he go?"

"Now, Mama," she said, "you know I don't like to pry into Mr. Brettman's business."

"That Mr. Dice, his partner, why couldn't you still work for him?" her mother demanded gruffly. "Better yet, why don't you come home and get married?"

Gabby chewed on her lip so that she wouldn't say anything hasty. She had visions of her mother providing a groom, a minister, and a loaded gun for motivation. It made her want to giggle, which would have infuriated her mother.

"Gabby, you aren't in trouble?" her mother had added in a strange tone.

"No, Mama, I'm not in trouble. Now don't get upset. It may all fall through anyway."

"I like Mr. Brettman," her mother said roughly. "That one time I met him when I visited you, he seemed like a nice man to me. Why does he want to move anyway? He isn't getting married?"

"J.D.? Get married?" Gabby laughed mirthlessly. "That would make the world record books."

"He'll have to get married someday," came the curt reply.

"Think so?" Already Gabby could picture him in fatigues rushing some stronghold with Shirt and Apollo. But she couldn't tell her mother that!

"Of course. It happens to everybody. He'll get tired of living alone someday. Your father did. That's when I nabbed him." Gabby could almost see her grin.

"Are you tired of living alone?" Gabby asked suddenly. It had been ten years since her father's death. Yet her mother didn't even date.

"I don't live alone, baby. I live with my memories. I had the best man God ever made. I don't want second best."

"You're just fussy," Gabby said accusingly.

"Yes, I am. You be fussy too. Honey, think about coming home. That Chicago place is pretty big, and if Mr. Brettman isn't going to be around, I'd worry about you."

"I'll think about it," Gabby promised.

She hated thinking about it. It made her face the fact that she wouldn't be seeing J.D. again. Whether or not he went back to the old life, he'd made it impossible for her to work for him anymore. He'd forced her into resigning, whether consciously or unconsciously. And now here she was losing her boss, her job, and her heart all in the space of three days. So little time to change so much of her future. It might have been better if she'd stayed behind and never known the truth about J.D.

When she got to the office, it was clear that J.D. had not yet come in. Richard Dice was sitting on her desk with his arms folded across his chest, looking murderous.

"Morning, Dick," she said with a forced smile.

"Thank God you're back." He sighed. "That temporary girl didn't work out, and the agency hasn't called me about a replacement. Where's J.D.?"

"Don't ask me," she replied, calmly shedding her jacket and putting her purse in the desk drawer. She tucked her glasses on top of her head while she searched through the calendar for appointments that had been made by both the temporary girl and herself.

"Didn't he come back?" Dick persisted.

"Yes." She stared at him. "You mean he hasn't been in touch with you?"

"Not yet. Well?" he burst out. "What happened? How's Martina? Did they pay the ransom?"

"You're chock-full of questions." She sighed in turn. "Yes, Martina's safe. No, they didn't have to pay the ransom. And anything else you want to know, ask J.D., because I don't want to talk about it."

Dick looked at the ceiling. "You disappear for days, and all I get is one long-winded sentence?"

"You should have come with us," she said conversationally. "Then you wouldn't have to take up my time asking questions. Did you take care of Mrs. Turnbull's divorce yesterday?"

"Yes," he murmured absently. "Judge Amherst called. He wants to discuss the Landers case with J.D. before he makes a decision about the trial date."

Gabby made a note of it.

Dick was studying her closely. "You look bad."

She smiled. "Thank you. What a lovely thing to be told."

He flushed. "I mean, you look worn out."

"You try crawling through a jungle on your belly with an AK-47 and see how you look," she replied.

"Jungle? On your belly? What's an AK-47?"

She got up from her desk and started filing some folders that Dick had left there. "Ask J.D."

"But he isn't here!"

She glowered at the file folders. "Maybe he's out buying a new crossbow," she muttered.

"A what?" But she didn't hear him. He grumbled something and walked into his office, slamming the door behind him. She glanced over her shoulder. "Well, somebody's in a snit," she said to the filing cabinet.

It was a good two hours before J.D. came in, looking as neat as a pin in his vested gray suit.

"Any messages?" he asked Gabby, just as he used to.

"No, sir," she replied, and she sounded the same too, except that she wouldn't meet his eyes. "Dick took care of the Turnbull case for you, and Judge Amherst wants you to call him."

He nodded. "What have I got on the calendar for this afternoon?"

"Mr. Parker is coming by at one to get you to draw up that incorporation for him, and you have three other appointments after him."

He turned toward his office. "Get your pen and pad and let's get the correspondence out of the way."

"Yes, sir."

"Oh, there you are, J.D.," Richard called from the doorway of his own office. "Welcome back. Would you tell me what happened? Gabby's got a case of the clams."

"So have I," J.D. informed him. "Everything's okay. Martina and Roberto are back in Palermo by now, and the kidnappers were taken care of. How about lunch?"

"Sorry," Richard said, smiling. "I've got a luncheon appointment with a client. Rain check?"

"Sure."

Gabby followed J.D. into the office and left the door open. If he noticed, or cared, he didn't let on. He eased his formidable frame into the big swivel chair behind the desk and picked up a handful of letters.

He started dictating and she kept her eyes on her pad until he finished. Her fingers ached and so did her back from sitting so straight, but she didn't move an inch until he dismissed her.

"Gabby," he called as she started toward the door.

"Yes, sir?"

He fingered a pencil on his desk, and his dark eyes stared at it. "How's your shoulder?" he asked.

She shrugged. "It's still a little sore, but I can't complain." She clasped the pad tightly against her breasts. She studied his impassive face quietly. "By the way, do you need written notice, or is a verbal one satisfactory?"

His eyes came up. "Wait," he said quietly.

"I have to get another job. I can't do that if I'm obligated to you for more than two weeks," she said with remarkable calm.

His jaw clenched. "You don't have to quit."

"Like hell I don't!" she returned.

"Things will get back to normal!" he roared. "Is it too much to ask you to give it a chance? We got along well enough before!"

"Yes, we did, before you treated me like a streetwalker!" she burst out.

He saw the hatred in her eyes, in her rigid posture. His gaze fell to the pencil again. "You won't be easy to replace," he said in an odd tone.

"Sure I will," she said venomously. "All you have to do is call the agency and ask for somebody stupid and naïve who won't get too close and loves being shot at!"

His face paled. "Gabby…"

"What's going on?" Richard asked from the open door. He looked aghast. He'd never heard Gabby raise her voice in the two years he'd known her, and here she stood yelling at J.D. at the top of her lungs.

"None of your business," they chimed in together, glaring at him.

He hunched his thin shoulders and grinned sheepishly. "Excuse me, I feel a sudden urge to eat lunch. Goodbye!"

They didn't even notice his leaving. J.D. glared at Gabby, and she glared back.

"I'm too set in my ways to break in somebody new," he said finally. "And you'd be bored to death working for anybody else and you know it."

"It's my life," she reminded him.

He got up from the desk and she backed away, her eyes wide and angry and afraid. The fear was what stopped him in his tracks.

"I wasn't going to make a grab for you, Miss Darwin."

"Shall I drop to my knees and give thanks?" she asked, glaring back. "You'll never make the list of the ten top lovers, that's for sure."

"No, I don't imagine so," he said quietly. "But I didn't realize how much I'd frightened you." He studied her closely. "Gabby, I never meant to go that far."

"I wasn't going to try to drag you in front of a minister," she said, lowering her voice. "I was curious about you, just as you were curious about me. It's over now. I don't want ties either."

"Don't leave," he said quietly. "I'll never touch you again."

"That isn't the point," she told him, shifting restlessly from one foot to the other. "I...I don't want to work for you anymore."

His dark eyes searched hers slowly, quietly. "Why?"

That was rich. Was she going to tell him that her heart would break if she had to work with him day in and day out, loving him hopelessly, eating her heart out for him? That was what would happen too. She'd go on mooning over him and never be able to date anybody else. Worse, she'd sit cringing as the days went by, wondering when he would throw it all in and rush back to First Shirt and Apollo. Now that he'd gotten a taste of the old, free life again, she had to expect that it would happen.

"There's no job security here," she said finally, putting her nameless fears into mundane words that couldn't possibly express her real feelings.

He drew a cigarette from his pocket and lit it, staring at her through the smoke. "You're guessing that I'll go back to the old life?" he asked coldly.

She shook her head. "No, J.D.—anticipating. Shirt said that you had the bug again," she confided. "I want a dull, routine employer who won't go rushing off to save the world at a minute's notice."

His jaw tightened. "It's my life. How I live it is my business."

"But of course," she said with a sickeningly sweet smile. "That's exactly what I meant. Out of sight, out of mind."

That made him angry. His dark eyes glittered as he scowled at her. "After what we shared in that room at Laremos's house?" he asked bluntly.

Her eyes narrowed. "Perhaps we're thinking of different things," she retorted. "I have a very vivid memory of being treated like the worst kind of Saturday-night pickup!"

He turned away and went to the window, his back rigid. "There were reasons."

"Of course there were!" she shot back. "You wanted to make sure that I didn't get any ideas about you just because you made a pass at me. Okay! I got the message and I'm going, just as fast as I can!" she said. "Do you really think I could forget what happened in Guatemala and go on working for you?"

He studied the cigarette in his fingers. "Maybe I'll settle down," he said after a minute.

"Maybe you will, but what concern is that of mine?" she asked. "You're my employer, not my lover."

He turned just as the phone on her desk rang. She rushed to answer it, grateful for the diversion. Fortunately, it was an angry, long-winded client. She smiled wickedly as she transferred the call to J.D.'s phone. While he was talking, she escaped to lunch, leaving him listening helplessly to the venomous divorcée on the other end of the line.

But once she was out of the office and eating a hamburger at a local fast-food restaurant, the smile vanished and gloom set in. She'd read about men who couldn't marry, who were too freedom-loving for marriage. But until J.D. came along, she hadn't known what anguish there could be in loving someone like that. Now she did, and her nights would be plagued with nightmares about hearing someday he'd died in combat. Or worse, that he was serving time in some filthy foreign jail for interfering in the internal politics of another nation.

If Martina had known the truth, maybe she could have helped talk some sense into him. But Gabby hadn't dared to tell her. J.D. would never forgive Gabby if she did.

An hour later, she dragged herself back into the office, only to find J.D. gone. There was a terse note on her desk, informing her that he'd gone to meet a client and that she was to cancel his appointments; he wouldn't be in until the next day.

She picked up the phone and started dialing. Was he really seeing a client? The thought tormented her, even after she left the office. Perhaps he'd already packed his bag and gone off in search of the sun. She cried herself to sleep, hating herself for worrying. If this was any indication of the future, she'd do well to hurry about finding another job.

The next day she forced herself to search the want ads for positions in between answering the phone, using the copier, and running the computer. J.D. still hadn't come in, and she was grateful for Dick's dictation and the hectic rush of the office. It kept her from thinking about J.D.

When he walked in the door just before lunch, it was all she could do not to jump up and throw herself into his arms. But she remembered that he didn't want ties so she forced herself to greet him calmly and hand him his messages.

"Worried about me?" he asked with apparent carelessness, but his eyes were watchful.

She looked up with hard-won composure, her eyebrows arched behind her reading glasses. "Worried? Why?"

He drew in a slow breath and turned on his heel to walk into his office. He slammed the door behind him.

She stuck out her tongue at it and picked up her purse. "Going to lunch," she said into the intercom and started out the door.

"Gabby."

She turned. He was standing in his office doorway, looking lonely and hesitant.

"Have lunch with me," he said.

She held up the newspaper. "Sorry. I'm going interviewing."

His face hardened, his eyes narrowed. "Don't."

Her soft heart almost melted under that half pleading stare. But she couldn't give in, not now. In the long run, it would be easier to eat her heart out from a safe distance. She'd die working with him, knowing that all he was capable of giving her was lust or a business relationship.

"I have to," she said quietly. "It's for the best."

"For whom?" he demanded.

"For both of us!" she burst out. "I can't bear to be in the same office with you!"

Something indescribable happened to his face. And because it hurt to see him that way, she turned and all but ran out the door. It didn't occur to her until much later how he might have taken her remark. She'd meant she couldn't bear to be with him because she loved him so, but he probably thought it was because of his brutal treatment of her at the *finca*. Well, he had been brutal. But he'd apologized, and some part of her understood why he'd acted that way. He was just trying to open her eyes to the futility of loving him. To spare her more hurt. Anyway, she told herself, her remark wouldn't faze him. He didn't care about her, so how in the world could she hurt him?

She applied for two jobs in offices a few blocks away. In one job she would be operating a computer. She knew how to do that, so it would be easy. The other was to work as a secretary for an international firm.

When she went back to the office, J.D. was gone again. Just as well, she thought. She had to get used to not seeing him. The thought was excruciatingly painful, but she was realistic enough to know that the pain would pass one day. After all, as J.D. himself had said, there was no future for her with him. He'd gone to elaborate lengths to make sure she knew that. And since she couldn't spend the day crying, she forced herself to keep her mind strictly on the job.

CHAPTER EIGHT

J.D. WAS SO RESERVED after that day that he barely spoke to Gabby at all, except when absolutely necessary for business. And all the time he scowled and snapped, like a wounded animal.

"Have you heard anything about your job interviews yet?" he asked Friday morning, glaring at her over a piece of correspondence to which he had just dictated an answer.

"I hope to hear Monday about the computer job," she said quietly. "The other one didn't work out."

He pursed his lips thoughtfully. "So it may not be all that easy to find something else," he commented.

She met his level stare. "If nothing works out in Chicago, I'm going home."

He didn't move. He studied her intently. "To Texas."

She lowered her gaze to her steno pad. "That's right."

"What would you do in Texas?"

"I'd help Mama."

He put down the letter. "'Help Mama,'" he scoffed, glaring at her. "Your mother would drive you to drink in less than a week, and you know it."

"How dare you…!" she began hotly.

"Gabby, your mother is a sweet lady," he said, "but her

lifestyle and yours are worlds apart. You'd fight all the time, or you'd find yourself being led around like a lamb."

Her breasts rose and fell softly. "Yes, I know," she said after a minute. "But it's better than the unemployment line, isn't it?"

"Stay with me," he said. "I think, if you'll just give it time, it will work out. Can't you forget how I treated you that one time?"

"Don't make it harder for me," she said.

"Is it hard, to walk out that door and never see me again?" he asked bluntly.

Her chin trembled just a little. "You've got nothing to give—you told me so. You've left me no choice but to leave."

"Yes, that was what I said," he agreed. "I went to impossible lengths to show you just how uncommitted I was, to make sure that you didn't try to cling too closely." He sighed heavily and his hands moved restlessly on the desk. "And now I can't look myself in the mirror, thinking about the way you cringe every time I come near you." He got up from the desk and stared out of the window, stretching as if he were stiff all over. "I've never needed anyone," he said after a minute, without turning. "Not even when I was a boy. I was always looking out for Martina and Mama. There was never anyone who gave a damn about me except them. I've been alone all my life. I've wanted it that way."

"I've told you until I'm blue in the face, I'm not trying to trap you!"

He lifted his head and looked at her. "Yes, I realize that now. I want you to try to understand something," he said after a minute. "I spent a lot of my life in the military. I got used to a certain way of doing things, a certain way of life. I thought it had stopped being important to me. And then Martina was kidnapped."

"And you got a taste of it again," she said quietly, searching his face. "And now you're not sure you can be just a lawyer for the rest of your life."

"You read me very well."

"We've worked together for a long time." She stared down at the steno pad and pen in her hands, glad that he couldn't see her heart breaking. "I'll miss you from time to time, J.D. Whatever else this job was, it was never dull."

"If you stay," he said quietly, "I might be able to stay too."

"What do I have to do with it?" she asked with a nervous laugh. "My goodness, the world is full of competent paralegals. You might like your next one a lot better than you like me. I have a nasty temper and I talk back, remember?"

"I remember so much about you," he said surprisingly. "When I started trying to tear you out of my life, I discovered just how deep the taproot went. You've become a habit with me, Gabby, like early morning coffee and my newspaper. I can't get up in the morning without thinking about coming to work and finding you here."

"You'll find new habits," she said. Was that all she was, a habit?

"I'm trying to make you understand that I don't want to acquire any new habits," he growled. "I like things the way they are, I like the routine of them."

"No, you don't," she told him, glaring. "You just said so. You want to go back to all the uncertainties of being a mercenary, and risking your life day after day. You want to go adventuring."

"You make it sound like a disease," he said shortly.

"Isn't it? You're afraid to feel anything. Shirt, Apollo, Semson, all of them are men who've lost something they can't live without. So they're looking for an end, not a beginning. They don't have anything to lose, and nothing to go back to. I learned so much in those three days, J.D. I learned most of all that I have everything to live for. I don't want that kind of freedom."

"You've never had it," he reminded her.

"That's true," she agreed. "But you've spent five years working to build a life for yourself, and you've made a huge success of it. Several people owe their lives, and their freedom, to you. Are you really crazy enough to throw all that away on a pipe dream?"

"Freedom isn't always won in a court of law," he growled.

"How then—with an Uzi and a few blocks of C-4?" she asked. "There are other ways to promote change than with bombs and bullets!"

He drew in a short breath. "You don't understand."

"That's right, I don't. And for your information, I've lost all my illusions about the exciting life of a soldier of fortune." She stood up with her pad in hand. "I'll go and transcribe this."

He watched her walk to the door. "Wait a minute," he said.

She paused with her hand on the doorknob and watched him come around the desk. She felt a twinge of fear as he came close to her. He towered over her, his blue pin-striped suit emphasizing the strength of his muscular body.

She opened the door and moved through it, trying not to show fear, but he saw right through her.

"No," he said softly, shaking his head. "No, don't run. I won't hurt you."

"You used to say that a lot, and I listened one time too many," she said with a nervous laugh. She backed up until she got the width of her desk between them. "I have to get these typed," she added, lifting the steno pad.

His dark eyes had an oddly bleak look in them. "It's real, isn't it, that fear?" he asked.

She sat down in her chair, avoiding his piercing gaze. "I have work to do, J.D."

He propped himself on the corner of the desk with a graceful, fluid movement.

"Don't panic," he said quietly. "I'm not coming any closer than this."

She stiffened. She couldn't help it.

"I should never have hurt you that way," he said, staring down at her clenched fingers. "I overreacted. Someday I'll try to explain it to you."

"There won't be any 'someday,'" she said tersely. "You'll be off blowing things up and I'll be programming computers."

"Will you stop that?" he growled. He fumbled for a cigarette.

"Would you mind waiting until I cover my diskettes?" she asked coldly, reaching to pull them out of the double-disk-drive computer. "Smoke and dust can cause them to crash."

He waited impatiently until she'd replaced the diskettes in their envelopes and stored them in their box before he lit the cigarette.

She glared at him. "I can't transcribe your letters until I can use the computer," she said matter-of-factly.

"So the letters can wait," he said. "Gabby, I swear to God I didn't mean to frighten you that much. I was shaken by what we'd been through, I was half-crazy…" He ran a hand through his hair. "I forgot how innocent you were too. I want you to know that under ordinary circumstances it wouldn't be like that for you with a man."

"With another man, perhaps not." She bit off the words.

"Gabby, what happened the morning before the mission didn't frighten you."

She felt herself go hot all over at the reminder, at the memories that flooded her mind. She remembered the touch of his hard mouth, the feel of his body, the tenderness of the fingers that searched over her soft, aching flesh….

"You were a different man then," she shot back. "You wouldn't even speak to me when we got back to the *finca*, you wouldn't look at me. You acted like a stranger, and then you attacked me!"

He stared down at the cigarette in his hand. "Yes, I know. I've hardly slept since."

His chest rose and fell slowly. He leaned over to crush out his cigarette in the spotless ashtray on her desk. He was so close, she could see the harsh shadows under his eyes.

"Would you consider having supper with me?" he asked.

Her heart jumped, but she didn't take time to decide whether it was from anticipation or fear. "No," she said bluntly, before she had time to change her mind.

He sighed. "No." His broad, hard mouth twisted into a rueful smile. He let his eyes wander slowly over her face. "Somehow, storming that terrorist camp seems like kid stuff compared to getting past your defenses, Gabby."

"Why bother?" she asked quietly. "I'll be here only another week."

The light went out of his eyes. He got to his feet and turned back toward his office. He paused at the doorway with his broad back to her. He seemed about to say something, about to turn. Then he straightened, went on into his office, and closed the door quietly behind him. Gabby hesitated just for a minute; then she booted up the computer again and concentrated on typing the business letters he'd dictated.

Saturday morning arrived sunny and with the promise of budding flowers. Gabby hated the city on such delightfully springlike days. She was brooding in her apartment, in the midst of doing her laundry, when a knock sounded at the door.

She couldn't imagine who might be visiting, unless her mother had gotten worried and had come all the way from Lytle to see her. That thought bothered her, and she went rushing to open the door.

J.D. lifted a heavy eyebrow. "Were you expecting me?" he asked with a faint grin.

She faltered, trying to think of a graceful way to ask him to leave. While she was debating, he walked into the apartment and sat down on her sofa.

"I thought you might like to have lunch with me," he said out of the blue, studying her slender figure in faded jeans and a striped pullover knit shirt.

She realized as she stared down at him that he looked different, and then she noticed what he was wearing. She'd never seen J.D. in anything but neat suits or jungle fatigues. But now he was wearing blue jeans as worn and faded as her own, with a western-style blue chambray shirt and boots. She stood there staring at him because she couldn't help it. He was so devastatingly handsome and masculine that he made her feel weak-kneed—from a distance, at least. She was still a little uneasy being alone with him.

"I won't pounce," he said softly. "I won't make a single move that you don't want. I won't even touch you, if that's what it takes. Spend the day with me, though, Gabby."

"Why should I?" she asked curtly.

He smiled wistfully. "Because I'm lonely."

Something in the region of her heart gave way. It must have been her soft brain, she told herself, because there was no logic in giving in to him. It would only make it harder to leave. And she had to leave. She couldn't bear staying around him, feeling the way she felt.

"You've got friends," she said evasively.

"Sure," he said, standing. He stuck his hands in his pockets, stretching the jeans flat across his muscular stomach and powerful thighs. "Sure, I've got friends. There's Shirt, and Apollo…"

"I mean…friends here in the city," she said hesitantly.

He was silent for a moment. "I've got you. No one else."

She gave in. Without another argument. How did you fight a flat statement like that, especially when you knew it was true? He'd said himself that he trusted no one except her. Friendship naturally involved trust.

"Okay," she said after a minute. "But just lunch."

"Just lunch," he agreed. And he didn't come close to her, or pressure her, or do anything to make her wary of him. He waited patiently while she closed the apartment door and locked it, and he walked beside her like a graceful giant as they left the building and got into his car.

CHAPTER NINE

IT WAS AN ODD KIND of day for Gabby. She thought she knew every one of J.D.'s moods, but that day he was different, in a way that she couldn't quite define.

He strolled beside her through the trees in the nearby park, then along the beach that edged the lake, watching birds rise and soar, watching boats sail and putter by. The wind tossed his dark hair and the sun made it glint blue-black. And Gabby thought she'd never felt like this in her life, free and yet protected and wildly excited, all at the same time. It was hard to remember that this was more of an end than a beginning. J.D. had a guilty conscience about the way he'd treated her and was trying to make amends before she left. That was all. She had to stop trying to make more out of it.

His fingers brushed hers as they walked, and he glanced down, watching her carefully.

"Looking for warts?" she asked, attempting to lessen the tension between them.

"Not really," he murmured. "I'm trying to decide what you'd do if I made a grab for your hand."

That irrepressible honesty again. She smiled and gave him her slender fingers, feeling trembly as he slowly locked them into his own. She was remembering that flight to Mexico and how he'd caressed her fingers with his own, and the remark he'd made about bodies fitting together that way. Her face burned.

He chuckled softly. "I wonder if you could possibly be thinking about the same thing I am, Gabby?" he murmured.

"I wish you'd mind your own business," she told him.

"I'm trying, but you're pretty transparent, honey. You still blush delightfully."

She tugged her fingers away and, to her disappointment, he let them go.

"No pressure," he said when she gave him a puzzled glance. "None at all. I'll take only what you give me."

She stopped, facing him. Nearby, the lake lapped softly at the shore and some children made wild sounds down the beach as they chased each other.

"What are you trying to do?" she asked.

He sighed. "Show you that I'm not a monster," he said.

"I never thought you were," she replied.

"Then why does this happen every time I come close to you?" he asked. His big hands shot out and caught her by the waist, dragging her against him.

She panicked. Her body twisted violently, her hands fought him. It was all over in seconds, but his face had gone white, and her own was flushed with exertion and anger.

She drew her lower lip between her teeth and bit it. J.D. looked...odd.

He gave a hard laugh and turned away. With unsteady fingers, he managed to light a cigarette despite the breeze. He took a long, steadying draw from it.

"Oh, God." He laughed bitterly. "I did a job on you, didn't I?"

Her legs were none too steady, but she managed to calm her voice enough to trust it with speech. "I'd never been handled roughly by a man before, J.D.," she told him. "And you said some pretty harsh things."

He turned, staring down at her. "Some pretty explicit ones." His dark eyes wandered slowly down her body, lingering on the soft curves as he lifted the cigarette to his mouth. "By the time I got around to that, I'd long forgotten my motives."

She blinked. "I don't understand."

His eyes found the horizon across the lake, and he smoked his cigarette quietly. "It doesn't matter," he said vaguely. He finished the cigarette and ground it out under his boot.

"You've gone back to smoking all the time," she said.

His shoulders rose and fell. "There doesn't seem much point in quitting now."

She wrapped her arms tightly across her breasts as she watched him walk down the beach. She followed him, searching for words.

"If you hadn't grabbed me like that, I wouldn't have fought you," she said curtly. She hadn't wanted to tell him that, but he looked as if her reaction to him had devastated him. Her marshmallow heart was going to do her in, she told herself when he stopped in his tracks and gaped at her.

"What?" he burst out.

She turned away, letting the wind blow her long, dark hair around. She couldn't manage another word.

He moved closer, but slowly this time. His hands came up to her face, hesitantly cupping it. Her heart pounded, but she didn't pull away.

His chiseled mouth parted as he looked deeply into her eyes. His face was rigid with control. She could feel the warm threat of his body against her, smell the musky scent of his cologne.

"Half of what I told you in that room was true," he said in a husky whisper. "In my younger days, I never gave a damn about the woman I took. But now, it matters. What I did to you, the things I said…I can't sleep, I can't eat. It haunts me."

"Why?" She, too, whispered.

His thumbs edged toward her mouth. "I…cared."

Her pupils dilated, darkening the green of her eyes. "Cared?"

He bent, and his hands were unsteady as they cupped her face. "I kept thinking about how close I came to losing you out there in the jungle," he whispered against her lips. "I wanted to purge myself of the memory and the emotion. So I hurt you." His face hardened, his heavy brows drew together. "But what I did to you…hurt me more." His hard lips brushed hers, nibbled at them. "You've seen me at my worst. Trust me now, Gabby. Let me show you…how tender I can be."

She wanted it almost frantically. She wanted a memory to take down the long, lonely years with her. So she let him have her mouth, as he wanted it. And his lips taught hers new sensations, new ways of touching and exploring.

He moaned softly, and his hands contracted, but his mouth was still tender even though she could feel his big body going rigid against her.

Her eyes opened and found his watching her, passion blazing out of them, a hunger like nothing she'd ever seen in him.

He lifted his head, his breath unsteady on her moist, parted lips. "Don't go cold on me," he whispered. "Not yet."

She swallowed, and her breasts lifted and fell with her breath. "Jacob…"

His eyes closed as though he were in pain. "I thought I'd never hear you say my name like that again," he said harshly.

Her hands were against the front of his shirt, and she didn't even know how they'd landed there. She was all too aware of what was under it, of how it felt to bury her fingers in that thick, cool mat of curling hair.

"Don't make it difficult for me," she whispered helplessly.

His hands slid around to the back of her head, tilting her face upward. "Do you think it's easy for me, letting you go?"

"Yes," she said with a trembling smile. "You said yourself that you didn't want any ties."

"Then why in God's name do I die a little every time I walk away from you?" he asked curtly. "Why do I wake up with your name on my lips?"

"I can't be your lover!" she whispered. "I can't!"

His nose brushed against hers, his lips hovered above her mouth, teasing it, coaxing it to follow his. "It would be so easy," he said softly, in a voice like dark velvet. "So easy. All it would take is ten minutes alone together with my mouth on yours and my hands under your blouse, and you'd give yourself with glorious abandon, the way you wanted to before I went to rescue Martina. Remember?" he breathed against her lips. "Remember, Gabby? You stood in my arms and let me touch you, and we rocked together and moaned..."

"Jacob." She hid her hot face against him. "Jacob, don't, please!"

His hands slid slowly down her back until they reached her hips and brought them into the curve of his, holding her there, pressing her there, so that she knew all too well what he wanted of her.

"This is a public place," she managed to say weakly, clinging to him.

"Where you're safe," he replied thickly. "Because if I did this anywhere else, I couldn't help what would happen. I want you so much."

"This is only making it worse," she told him. She leaned her forehead against his chest. She could smell the tangy soap he used, the clean scent of the shirt he wore. Her hands spread over his hard muscles.

His breath quickened at the almost imperceptible movement. "Unbutton it." He breathed roughly. "Touch me there."

"There are people...!"

"Yes." His lips touched her closed eyelids, her forehead. "Touch me."

She could hardly breathe at all. He was drowning her in sensation, and she loved him so much it was torture. It was just going to be harder to leave him, but how could she fight this? Part of her was frightened of his strength, but a larger part remembered how it had felt when he was tender, when he'd been so careful not to hurt her.

"I won't ever hurt you again," he whispered, lifting her fingers to the top button. "Not ever. I won't overpower you, or make crude remarks to you. I'll teach you to trust me, if it takes the rest of my life. Gabby…"

She closed her eyes. Tentatively her fingers fumbled the first button free. He tensed as she found the second, and the third. She stopped there, resting against him, and eased her fingers just inside. They tingled as they came in contact with firm muscle and curling hair.

He caught his breath, shifting his chest so that her fingers slid farther under the fabric.

"You did that," he reminded her in a sensuous undertone, "when I started to touch you under your nightgown, at the *finca*. Remember? You shifted and moved so that I could touch you more easily."

What she remembered most was the way it had felt when he'd touched her. Her eyes slowly opened, and he turned her face so that he could look into them.

His own eyes were black with desire; his face was hard and drawn, his lips were parted. "Yes, I like that," he whispered as she curled her nails against him and dragged them softly over his skin. "I like that." His chest rose and fell heavily and still his eyes held hers. "If we made love, you could do that to every inch of me. And I could do it to you, with my mouth."

She trembled. He felt it and drew her slowly into his arms. He stood like that, just holding her, in a strangely passionless embrace while the world became calm.

"Words," he said over her head, his tone light and solemn at the same time. "So potent… Until you came along, I'd never made love to a woman with my mind."

She stared out at the sailboats on the lake and involuntarily one hand pressed closer against him. "We're at an impasse," she said after a minute.

His cheek nudged her dark hair. "How?"

She laughed bitterly. "J.D., I'm leaving next Friday."

"Maybe," he said, and his arms tightened.

"Definitely." She pulled away from him, and he let her go immediately. She looked up. "Nothing has changed."

He let his eyes roam over her soft body. "At least you've stopped cringing."

"Thank you," she replied. "For removing the scars. Now I can go on to a lasting relationship."

"Why not have it with me?" he asked. "I'm well-off. I'm sexy—"

"You're unreliable," she said, interrupting him. "I want someone who doesn't know an Uzi from a blender!"

He sighed heavily, and his dark eyes were thoughtful. "I need a little time."

"Time won't help," she said. "You're hooked again. It's like the cigarettes, only worse. I can't live my life standing at windows and waiting for telephones to ring."

"You'll do that regardless."

She stopped dead and turned around, gaping at him. "What?"

"You'll do that anyway," he said matter-of-factly, watching her. He pulled a cigarette from his pocket with a what-the-hell smile and lit it. "You'll miss me. You'll want me. You're leaving the office, but the memories are portable and indestructible. You won't forget me any more than I'll forget you. We started something we haven't finished, and it's going to be between us all our lives."

"It's just sex!" she yelled at him.

Two young men walked past, grinned at J.D., and winked at Gabby, who was wishing she could sink into the sand. She hadn't even heard them approach.

She turned and fled back down the beach at a trot. J.D. was right beside her, effortlessly matching her steps and still smoking his cigarette. He finished it just as they reached the car, and he crushed it out before he joined her in the luxurious interior.

"It isn't just sex," he said, turning to face her, one arm across the back of the seat and an odd expression on his face. He smiled slowly. "But sex is going to be one big part of our relationship in the not-too-distant future."

She glared at him. "You'd be lucky!"

"No, you would," he said, cocking an eyebrow. "When I mind my manners, I'm a force to be reckoned with. What I did to you in that bed was all bad temper and irritation. What I did to you the morning before was what it's really like."

She couldn't control her heated response to that intimate remark. Her breasts tingled at the memory. His eyes dropped slowly to her breasts, and he smiled wickedly. Following his gaze, she saw why and crossed her arms over her chest.

"Too late," he murmured. "Your body will give you away every time. You haven't forgotten what we did together."

Her nostrils flared. "There are other men in the world."

"Sure," he agreed pleasantly. "But you don't want other men. You want me."

"Conceited ass," she enunciated clearly.

His fingers touched her mouth and parted her lips, as

if their texture fascinated him. "You risked your life for me," he said absently. "Why?"

She laughed nervously. "Maybe I just wanted to try out the gun."

He tilted her face up and leaned over to brush his mouth tenderly across her trembling lips. "Maybe there was a reason you don't want me to know," he murmured. He drew back and looked at her. "Hungry?"

The change of topic threw her. He had switched from lover to friendly companion in seconds. She managed a smile. "Yes. What did you have in mind?"

"Cheeseburgers, of course." He chuckled and started the car.

"I like those myself."

He glanced at her. "Let's talk," he said unexpectedly. "Really talk. I want to know everything about you. What you like to read, how it was to grow up in Texas, why you've never gotten involved with a man...everything."

That sounded intriguing. It suddenly occurred to her that she knew very little about him. What he liked and disliked, what he felt. She tried to read his face.

"Curious about me too?" he asked, glancing sideways. "I'll tell you anything you want to know."

She laughed uneasily. "'Anything' covers a lot of territory."

"And requires a hell of a lot of trust on my part," he added with a smile. "Anything, Gabby."

Total honesty. She stared down at her hands and wondered why they were trembling. She wasn't sure of his motives, of where this was leading. She looked up and all her uncertainty was on her face.

He reached over and caught one of her hands, lifting it to his thigh. Her palm tingled at the contact.

"Make me stay here," he said unexpectedly.

"What?" she asked.

"Make me stay," he repeated. His eyes caught hers briefly. "You can give me something that all the unholy little wars on earth couldn't. If you want me, show me. Give me a reason, half a reason, to settle down. And I might surprise you."

She stared out through the windshield and felt as if she were floating. It was a beginning that she wasn't sure she wanted. She might hold his interest briefly, until he tired of her body. But what then? He was offering nothing more than a liaison. He wasn't talking about permanent things like a house and children. Her eyes darkened with pain. Perhaps it would have been better if he hadn't gotten rid of her fear of him.

Her troubled eyes sought his profile, but it was as unreadable as ever. The only thing that gave her hope was the visible throbbing of his pulse and the searing desire in his eyes. He wanted her so desperately that she couldn't help wondering whether he didn't feel something for her, too. But it would take time to find out, and she wasn't going to withdraw her resignation. As much as it might hurt, in the long run it would be saner to leave him than to try to hold him. Gabby wasn't built for an affair. And she wasn't going to let him drag her into one, just to occupy himself while he decided between practicing law and soldiering.

CHAPTER TEN

THEY SAT IN A BOOTH at a nearby fast-food restaurant, where J.D. put away three cheeseburgers, a large order of french fries, and two cups of coffee before Gabby's fascinated eyes.

"I'm a big man," he reminded her as he was finishing the third one.

"Yes, you are," she agreed with a smile, running her eyes over the spread of muscle under his chambray shirt.

His eyes narrowed with amusement. "Remembering what's under it?" he said softly, teasing her.

She flushed and grabbed her coffee cup, holding it like a weapon. "I thought this was a truce," she muttered.

"It is. But I fight dirty, remember?"

She looked, studying his hard face. "What was it like, those four years when you were a mercenary?" she asked.

He finished the cheeseburger and sipped his coffee, leaning back with a heavy sigh. "It was hard," he said. "Exciting. Rewarding, in more ways than just financial." He shrugged. "I suppose I was caught up in the romance of it at first, until I saw what I was getting into. One of the men I joined with was captured and thrown into jail the minute we landed in one emerging African country. He hadn't fired a shot, but he was executed just like the men who had."

She caught her breath. "But why?" she asked. "He was just…"

"We were interfering with the regime," he told her. "Despite all our noble reasons, we were breaking whatever law existed at that time. Shirt and I managed to get away. I owe him my life for his quick thinking. I was pretty new to the profession back then. I learned."

"He told me his name was Matthew," she remarked with a smile.

He cocked an eyebrow. "Be flattered. It was three years before I found that out."

She toyed with her crumpled napkin. "I liked him. I liked all of them."

"Shirt's quite a guy. He was the one who pushed me into law," he said with a laugh. "He thought I needed a better future than rushing around the world with a weapon."

"You think a lot of him," she observed.

He shrugged. "I never knew my father," he said after a minute. "Shirt looked out for me when we served in Vietnam together. I don't know—maybe he needed somebody too. His wife had died of cancer, and he didn't have anybody else except a brother in Milwaukee who still doesn't speak to him. I had Martina. I suppose Shirt became my father, in a sense."

She cupped her hands around her coffee mug and wondered what he'd say if she told him that Shirt had said the door to the past was closed for J.D. Probably he'd laugh it off, but she decided she didn't want to find out.

He looked up. "How about your family? Any sisters, brothers?"

She laughed softly. "No. I was an only child. My father owned a ranch, and my mother and grandfather and grandmother had gone to San Antonio on vacation. Mother met Dad then and ran away to marry him over the weekend." She grinned. "My grandparents were furious."

"I can imagine." He searched her face. "You look like your mother. How about him? Was he big?"

She shook her head. "My father was small and wiry and tough. He had to be, you see, to put up with Mama. She'd have killed a lesser man, but Dad didn't take orders. There were some great fights during my childhood."

He cocked an eyebrow. "Did they make up eventually?"

She sighed. "He'd send her roses, or bring her pretty things from town. And she'd kiss him and they'd go off alone and I'd go see Miss Patty who lived in a line cabin on the ranch." She grinned. "I visited Miss Patty a lot."

He chuckled. "They say the making up can be pretty sweet."

She studied his hard face. "Yes, so I hear."

He lifted his eyes to hers. "We've had a royal falling out. Want to make up?"

She hesitated, and he concentrated on finishing his coffee and reaching for a cigarette.

"Sorry," he said quietly. "I'm rushing things."

Hesitantly, she reached across the table and touched the back of the big hand resting there. It jerked. Then it turned and captured hers in its rough warmth.

"J.D., what do you want from me?" she asked.

"What do you think I want, Gabby?' he asked in turn.

She gathered all her courage and put her worst fears into words. "I think you want to make amends for what happened in Guatemala, before you fly off into the sun. I think you want to have an affair with me."

"That's honest, at least," he said. His eyes fell to their clasped hands, and he watched his thumb rub softly against her slender fingers. "You want something more permanent, I gather."

She couldn't answer that without giving herself away. She drew her hand away from his with a light laugh. "Aren't we getting serious though?" she asked. "I need to go home, J.D. I left the laundry in the washing machine, and I've got a week's cleaning to do."

His face hardened. "Can't it wait until tomorrow?"

"Tomorrow's Sunday."

"So?"

She lifted her eyes to his. "I go to church on Sunday."

He frowned slightly. "I haven't been to church since I was a boy," he said after a minute. He studied the smoking cigarette in his hand. "I don't know what I believe in these days."

It was a reminder of the big differences between them. She frowned too, and got to her feet slowly.

"It would bother you," he murmured, watching her. "Yes, I suppose it would."

She half turned. "What would?"

"Never mind." He sighed as he put the remains of their meal into the trash can and replaced the tray in the rack on their way out. "Just a few adjustments that have to be made, that's all."

That didn't make sense, but she didn't pressure him. He didn't pressure her either, leaving her outside her apartment building with a rueful smile.

"I hate being stood up for the damned laundry," he muttered, hands in his pockets.

"New experiences teach new things," she murmured dryly. "Besides, I can't finish out the week in dirty clothes."

That put a damper on things. Her smile faded at the memory of how little time they had left together. His face grew harder.

"Well...thanks for lunch," she said awkwardly.

"We could do it again tomorrow," he said before she went inside.

Her eyes lifted. She wanted to. She wanted to, desperately. She tried to convince herself that it would be a mistake, but her body tingled and her heart surged at the idea.

"Yes," she said under her breath.

His chest rose and fell, as if in relief. "Suppose I pick you up about ten-thirty?"

She hesitated. "Church is at eleven."

"Yes, I figured it would be," he said with a rueful smile. "I hope the angels won't faint at having me in their midst."

All the color drained out of her face as she stared up at him, and she couldn't have said a word to save herself.

"Well, I won't embarrass you," he muttered curtly. "I do know not to stand up and yell 'Hallelujah' every five minutes or to snore in the front pew."

"I didn't say anything," she said.

"I still have a soul too, even if it has taken a few hard knocks over the years." He lifted his shoulders and let them fall. "I...need to go back. All the way back." His eyes held hers. "Gabby?"

"I'm Methodist," she said.

He smiled. "I used to be Episcopalian. The denomination doesn't matter so much, does it?"

She shook her head. "We can walk from my apartment."

He nodded. "See you tomorrow."

He turned to get back into the car, but she moved forward and touched his arm. The light contact of her fingers froze him. He looked down at her.

"Would you...bend down a minute?" she whispered.

Like a sleepwalker, he bent his tall frame and she stood on tiptoe to put her mouth warmly, hungrily to his.

He moaned, starting to reach for her, but she drew back with a wicked, warm smile.

"Try that again when we aren't in a public place," he said, challenging her.

Her heart jumped. "Dream on."

He lifted an eyebrow. "I've done very little else this past week," he said, letting his eyes roam over her slender body. "Gabby, have you ever thought about having children?"

She could hardly believe what she was hearing. Her face burned with pleasure, her heart sang with it. "Oh, yes," she whispered huskily.

"So have I." He started to speak, caught himself, and smiled hesitantly. "See you in the morning."

"'Bye." She stood there and watched him drive off.

It was probably all some wild daydream and she'd wake up back in the office, typing. But when she pinched herself, it hurt. She went upstairs and put the clothes in the dryer and tried to convince herself that J.D. had actually said he was going to church with her.

But the next morning, she was sure she'd misunderstood him. She dressed in a pretty Gibson Girl-style white outfit with matching accessories and at precisely ten-thirty, she started out the door. Of course, J.D. wasn't going to church, she told herself firmly. What a stupid thing to…

The doorbell rang as she was opening the door. And there he was. He was wearing the same vested gray suit she'd seen him in earlier that week, but he looked different now. More relaxed, more at ease, much less rigid.

"Shocked?" he asked wickedly. "Did you expect I'd changed my mind and gone fishing instead?"

She burst out laughing and her green eyes sparkled. With her long hair piled in an old-fashioned coiffure, she seemed part of another era.

"Little Miss Victorian," he murmured, studying her. "How exciting you look. So demure and proper."

He looked as if he'd give a lot to change that straight-laced image, and she dropped her eyes before he could see how willing she felt.

"We'd better get started," she murmured, easing past him.

"I like that gauzy thing," he remarked minutes later as they walked up the front steps of the gray fieldstone church.

"You can wear it sometimes, if you like," she said teasingly.

His eyes promised retribution. She eased her hand into his, and all the fight went out of him. He smiled at her, and his eyes were warm and possessive.

J.D. paid a lot of attention to the sermon, which was about priorities and forgiveness and grace. He sang the hymns in a rich baritone, and he seemed thoughtful as the benediction was given.

"Mind waiting for me?" he asked as they rose to file out at the end of the service.

She searched his hard face and shook her head. "Not at all."

He left her and went to speak to the minister who was waiting until the rest of the congregation had left. The two men stood talking behind the rows of pews, both solemn, their voices low. Then they shook hands and smiled at each other. J.D. came back and grasped Gabby's hand warmly in his for a minute.

"I'm taking your minister to lunch instead of you," he said with a mischievous smile. "How about getting into something casual and I'll pick you up in a couple of hours?"

She looked hard at him. "Are you all right?" she asked. She was trying to see beyond the fixed smile to something deep and wounded inside him.

He drew in a slow breath and the smile faded. "You frighten me sometimes, Gabby," he said softly. "You see too much."

She couldn't think of any response to that. She touched his hand briefly and watched him walk away.

Something was in the wind, a change. She frowned as she turned toward her apartment, her steps slow and deliberate. She wondered why he was taking her minister to lunch, if he had something on his conscience.

She changed into jeans and a button-up blue cotton blouse and then paced the floor for the next two hours. Wild thoughts raced through her mind, the wildest one being that J.D. might decide to chuck it all and go in search of First Shirt and Apollo.

It was three hours before he showed up. By then Gabby had consumed half a pot of coffee and chewed two fingernails to the quick. Her nerves were raw, and she actually jumped when the knock came at the door.

She let him in, too shaken to disguise the frightened uncertainty in her wide eyes.

"I thought you'd stood me up." She laughed nervously. "I was just about to give up and start watching a movie on TV. Do you want some coffee, or some cake…?"

He put a finger across her mouth to stop the wild words. His dark eyes looked into hers. "We have to learn to trust each other a little more," he said softly. "And the first thing you need to know about me is that if I ever give my word, it's good for life. I'm not going back to Shirt and the others, Gabby. That's a promise."

Tears burst from her eyes like rain from a storm cloud. She put her face in her hands and walked away.

"I'm sorry," she choked out, hating the fact that she'd given her feelings away.

He didn't say a word. He followed her, and when he

caught up to her, he lifted her gently in his big arms and headed straight for the bedroom.

She had just enough sanity left to realize where they were going. She opened her mouth to protest, and his came down on it, open and moist and tenderly possessive.

"Jacob…" she whispered into his mouth.

He smiled against her trembling lips. "What?"

Her nails bit softly into his shoulders as he laid her down on the crisp white chenille bedspread. "I can't," she whispered.

"Can't what?" He sat down beside her and calmly removed his jacket, vest, and tie and then unbuttoned his shirt while she watched him, spellbound as the hard, heavy muscles came into view under that mat of crisp hair.

"I can't have an affair with you," she said.

He leaned over and began to unfasten the buttons on her blouse. "That's nice."

"Jacob, did you hear me? Will you stop that…!"

He ignored her protests and her frantic efforts to stop his fingers. "Stop what?"

"Undressing me!" she burst out with an hysterical laugh. "Jacob, I'm wearing nothing underneath, for heaven's sake…!"

"So I see," he murmured with a wicked smile, as he opened the blouse and revealed the pink and mauve rise of her breasts.

"Will you listen…" she began breathlessly.

"Shut up, darling." He bent over her and put his open mouth against one breast, letting her feel the texture of his warm lips and his tongue before he moved closer and increased the ardent pressure.

She gasped and arched and then moaned sharply, a high-pitched sound that made him lift his head.

"Did I hurt you?" he asked. "I'm sorry, I thought I was being gentle."

Her fists were clenched beside her head, and her eyes were wide with mingled fear and desire. "You know very well it didn't hurt," she whispered fiercely.

His eyes moved back down to her bareness and he smiled slowly, watching her breasts lift and fall with her quickened breathing. "Lovely, lovely creature," he said under his breath. His fingers traced her rib cage and he held her eyes, watching the recklessness come into them, the deep passion.

Her breath was coming still quicker now, and the tracing of his fingers was driving her mad. She arched her head back into the pillow, lifting her body toward him in a slow, helpless movement.

"Want me to put my mouth there again and make it stop aching?" he whispered.

"Yes," she moaned softly. "Please."

She felt the whisper of his warm breath against her skin, felt his hands go under her to slide abrasively against her bare back. He lifted her, and his mouth moved with delicate precision from one taut breast to the other. His face nuzzled her, savored her softness.

Her fingers tangled in his thick, cool hair and worked at it like a cat kneading a blanket. Pleasure washed over her in waves, waves that lifted and twisted her body.

"Jacob," she whispered as his mouth slid over hers and down to her ear, while his hands made magic on her upthrust breasts. "Jacob, teach me how to make you feel this way."

"I already do," he murmured at her ear. "Touching you like this, kissing you, makes me wild, didn't you know?"

"Really?"

He lifted his head. "Really." He rolled onto his back and eased her down over him, smiling lazily as he studied her rapt face, as his eyes wandered to where her breasts were crushed softly against his hard, hair-matted chest. His hands unfastened her hair and arranged it over her shoulders, his eyes heavy-lidded and steady as they wandered over her body.

She watched his face and moved. Just a little. Just enough to let him feel the texture of her body.

"Is that an invitation?" he asked quietly, watching her.

Her breath caught in her throat. Was it, indeed? She searched his hard face with awe and love in every line of her own. Her fingers twined in his thick hair, and she could feel his heartbeat under her.

His hands smoothed over her back. He shifted her body this time, softly rubbing her breasts against the mat of hair on his chest. He heard her catch her breath as she bent her forehead to rest it on his.

His hands shifted, so that his thumbs could tease the hard peaks of her breasts. "I ache with wanting you," he said quietly. "Shall I let you feel how much?"

"You started it," she reminded him, nuzzling her forehead against his. She moved suddenly, so that the whole soft length of her body pressed down over him, and she knew then that she wasn't going to stop him.

"Hold me like this," she whispered as she bent to put her mouth over his. "Hold me hard, Jacob."

His big hands spread at the base of her spine, moving her in a sweet, tender rotation against his hips, and he moaned deeply.

"I won't stop you this time," she whispered over his mouth. "I won't stop you, Jacob, I won't…" Her hands slid between them, into the thick cloud of hair over his chest. "Jacob…!"

"Tell me…why," he managed to say in a tortured voice.

"You know," she breathed, crushing her mouth against his in a frenzy of hunger. Her body moved against him, she trembled with unleashed desire. And suddenly he rolled her over, covering her with his crushing weight, lifting her up to him while his mouth possessed hers absolutely. She felt the wild, demanding thrust of his tongue and met it with a wildness of her own, giving him everything he demanded of her.

"Tell me," he insisted, lifting his head to let his wild eyes glitter down into her own. He shifted, grinding his hips into hers. "Tell me, Gabby!"

"I love you," she said fiercely. Her voice was trembling, but she met his eyes unafraid. "I love you, I love you!"

He seemed to stop breathing. His body was rigid above her, but his eyes were alive, burning, blazing with emotion. His hands moved slowly up her body, over her breasts, to touch her face. His big body shuddered with the effort to control his passion.

"I'm going to die from this," he told her with a faint, harsh smile. And all at once, he rolled away from her and lay on his stomach. He groaned once, as if he were hurting in unbearable ways. His body stiffened and he clenched the pillow so hard his fingers went white.

"Jacob?" she whispered, sitting up, frightened.

"Don't touch me, baby," he whispered back, his voice tormented.

She sat there watching him, a little nervous and uncertain. He'd forced that reckless admission from her, and then he'd stopped. Why? What did he want?

Slowly his body relaxed and he sighed wearily. "Oh, God, I never thought I'd be able to stop," he murmured. "That was as close as I've ever come to losing control, except for that time at the *finca*."

Her wide eyes studied the pale face he turned toward her. "That morning?" she murmured.

He laughed dryly. "That night," he said. "Gabby, it wasn't punishment, there at the last. It was loss of control. I very nearly took you."

Her eyebrows went up. "But you let me think…!"

"I had to," he said. "I was going out of my mind trying to decide how to handle it. In the beginning, I wanted an affair with you. But I couldn't seem to get close enough, or make you see me as a man. Then, when we were in Rome, I'd had all I could stand and I forced the issue." He laughed softly. "My God, it was the end of the rainbow, and I was floating. Until I realized you were a virgin, and I had to rethink it all. I'd decided that I'd have to fire you, and then we went into the jungle and I died a thousand deaths when that terrorist pointed his rifle at you." He rolled over onto his back and caught her fingers in his, holding them to his mouth feverishly. "That was when I realized what had happened to me. I was like a boy, all raging desire and frustration and fear. I wanted to frighten you off before I was trapped by what I felt for you. Only it backfired. I started to hurt you and went crazy wanting you instead. I can't wait anymore," he added with an apologetic smile, "and after a week from Saturday I won't have to."

"A week from Saturday?" She frowned.

"There were two reasons I took your Reverend Boone to lunch," he said. "The first was to discuss some things I had on my conscience. The second was to arrange a wedding."

She froze; her face was flushed, and her eyes were disbelieving. It was like having every dream she had ever dreamed come true at once.

He sat up, taking both her hands in his. "Gabby, the one thing I can't do is go on living without you," he said matter-of-factly.

"But...but you said you didn't know whether you could settle down."

He rubbed his thumbs over the backs of her hands and sighed. "Yes, I know. And all the while I was wondering how I'd survive if you refused me. I was trying to get a reaction out of you, to see if I'd frightened you so badly that I'd chased you away." His face hardened as he stared at her hands. "I told you once that I was used to taking what I wanted. That ended with you. I couldn't take you. It had to be a mutual wanting."

"It was," she breathed softly. "It is. I love you with all my heart."

He smiled quietly, lifting hungry eyes to hers. "Do you know what I feel for you?"

She lifted her shoulders restlessly. "You want me," she said with a shaky smile. "Maybe you like me a little."

His chest rose and fell heavily and his eyes never left hers. "I've never said the words and meant them before. It's harder than I thought."

She moved close to him and slid her arms under his, pressing her cheek against his broad chest.

His hands hesitated on her back and then slid around her, cherishing, comforting, protective. He sighed, and she felt his breath on her ear.

"I…" He nuzzled his face against her cheek and then her throat. He laid her back on the bed so that he could find her soft breasts and brush them with his lips. His teeth nipped her tenderly, his hands lifted her. With a sound like a rough, low growl, he slid his body alongside hers and kissed her until she moaned and clutched at him.

"I love you," he breathed fiercely, looming over her. His face was so taut with passion that it would have frightened her once. "Worship you, adore you. I'll go down into the dark crying your name, wanting your mouth, your voice. Is that enough?"

Tears welled in her eyes. "Oh, yes, it's enough," she said unsteadily. "But will I be enough for you?"

"Yes," he said simply. "You and the children." He bent to her mouth again. "Reverend Boone said you hadn't joined the church. I thought we'd do it together. The kids are going to need a good foundation to build on, aren't they?"

She hid her face against his throat. "I'll like having your babies," she whispered.

He trembled convulsively. "Say things like that to me, and you'll find yourself wearing scarlet at the wedding. Hush!"

She managed to laugh. "You taught me how."

"That isn't all I'll teach you. But not now." He rolled away from her and got to his feet reluctantly, stretching as if his muscles were in torment.

She propped herself on an elbow and smiled at him wistfully. "You've got to be the sexiest man alive," she murmured. "I used to stare at you in the office and wonder what you looked like without your shirt..."

"Gabby," he said in a mock threatening tone.

She arched her body softly, wanting him, loving him, loving the way his eyes followed her movement with such obvious hunger.

"Jacob," she whispered, lying back so that the blouse slid away from her body and he could see every soft curve.

His chest rose and fell sharply. He seemed a little unsteady on his feet.

She loved that vulnerability. She'd never realized before just how much power she had over him, and it was a heady knowledge. With a small, triumphant smile, she held out her arms to him.

"I can't, honey," he whispered. "If I come back down there, I'll take you."

Her body tingled with the very thought of how it would be. She could already picture them, his hair-darkened body crushing her bare pink one down into the mattress, his voice whispering those wildly exciting things while she moaned and wept...

He reached down, and she arched toward him. And

all at once, before she realized what was going on, she was out of the bed, being buttoned back into her blouse.

"And don't try that again," he murmured with a wicked smile. "Hussy."

"But…"

"When we're married," he said firmly, kissing her mouth. "Now let's go look at houses. I drove by two yesterday that looked promising. How do you feel about living on the lake?"

She slid her hand into his as they walked into the living room. "I'll like living anywhere with you," she said with feeling. "I imagine just watching television is going to be an adventure from now on."

He chuckled softly as he opened the door, his eyes narrowing. "You can't imagine the plans I have for the symphony concerts on the educational channel," he remarked with a wicked smile.

She went ahead of him out the door. "Oh, I think I might have some vague idea," she said musingly, glancing over her shoulder. "By the way, what did you do with the crossbow?"

"What crossbow?" he asked grinning.

She sighed and leaned her head against his shoulder for an instant. "Do you reckon First Shirt would give me away if we asked him?"

"I imagine he'd be pretty flattered," he said. "Want to invite the rest of the gang too?"

"Could we?"

"Sure," he told her. He smiled as they got into the elevator. "Don't look so worried. I won't try to leave with them, I promise."

"No regrets?" she asked softly.

His eyes were wistful for a moment before he sighed and drew her into his arms. "Only," he whispered, bending, "that I waited so long to tell you how I felt."

"So long?"

"Gabby," he said against her mouth, "I fell in love with you two years ago."

She started to speak, but he was kissing her, and the wildness of it made her question go right out of her head.

"You never said anything," she murmured eventually.

"I couldn't," he returned. "You were so young. I felt guilty for wanting you the way I did. But you dated, you seemed so sophisticated sometimes." He touched her hair gently. "I had too many doubts about being able to settle down to make a heavy pass at you. Too, I was afraid you might quit, and I wasn't sure I could stand that." He shrugged his broad shoulders. "It wasn't until that day in the jungle that I knew how much I cared. I spent a miserable weekend trying to convince myself that I could go back to what I was and not miss you. I failed. After that, it was a matter of trying to convince you that I wouldn't be brutal again. You can't imagine how it hurt, when you cringed away from me…"

But she could. The anguish was in his face. She reached up and kissed his closed eyes gently, tenderly. "It wasn't so much a physical fear," she confessed, "as an emotional one. I was afraid you only wanted an affair. And that you'd walk away." She laughed bitterly. "I knew I couldn't survive that. I loved you too much."

"We won't be apart again," he said quietly. "Not ever.

Even when you have the children, I'll be with you every step of the way."

Tears misted her eyes. "I'll like that."

SIX DAYS LATER, there was a quiet ceremony in the Methodist church. Gabby, in a street-length white silk dress, walked slowly down the aisle on the arm of a wiry little man in a new gray suit, who looked even more out of place than the other people in the church. A tall black man standing beside J.D. was tugging uncomfortably at his tight collar and tie, and several other awkward-looking men were sitting in the front pew. Gabby noticed Richard Dice and two secretaries who worked in her building casting strange glances at the assembly. Her mother seemed equally perplexed.

Gabby just grinned and walked on, feeling proud and happy as J.D. grinned at her from where he stood near the altar.

It was a brief but solemn ceremony, and at its end, after Gabby had enthusiastically kissed her new husband, she threw her arms around Matthew and hugged him.

"Thank you," she told him with a beaming smile.

First Shirt looked faintly embarrassed. "I enjoyed it. Uh, Gabby, your mother's giving us a strange look."

"Mother's always been strange, Matthew," she informed him. "I'll show you. Mother, come meet Matthew," she called while J.D.'s partner Richard congratulated him and bent to kiss Gabby's cheek.

"All the best, Gabby, J.D.," Richard said with a grin. "What a shock, to be invited to your wedding. Especially after all that's happened the past week."

"The road to love is rocky," Gabby grinned at him. "As you'll discover someday."

"Not me," Richard retorted. "I run too fast!"

"That's what I thought," J.D. murmured with a wicked glance toward Gabby. She stuck out her tongue at him, and went to drag her mother away from the secretaries.

Mrs. Darwin, resplendent in a white linen suit and a hat that looked three sizes too big, followed her daughter slowly. She looked as out of place as Matthew and Apollo and the rest.

"I hate dressing up," she muttered, casting a curious eye at Matthew. "Give me my jeans anytime."

"I hear you shoot and cuss and ride," Matthew told her, pursing his lips.

Mrs. Darwin actually blushed. She lowered her eyes and grinned. "Well, a little, Mr...?"

"Matthew," came the reply. "Matthew Carver. Archer's...I mean, J.D.'s like a son to me." He held out his hand, took hers, and lifted it to his lips. "What a lovely mother-in-law he's getting," he murmured.

Gabby left her blushing mother and went to greet Apollo, Semson, Laremos, and Drago.

"Hi, guys," she said, grinning at them.

"Hey, Gabby," Apollo greeted her. "Good thing you know the ropes—we won't have to run you through the training course or anything."

"Now, just hold on," she informed him. "I am going on a honeymoon. My adventuring days are over. I can just see me, pregnant and crawling through underbrush with an AK-47..."

"Oh, we'd carry it for you, Gabby," he said, all seriousness.

"How gentlemanly!" She laughed.

"Unspeakable ruffian," Laremos said with a mock frown as he stepped forward to kiss Gabby's hand. "Congratulations. And of course you will not be crawling through the jungle." He grinned. "We will carry you."

Semson and Drago added their comments, and Gabby clutched J.D.'s arm, all but collapsing with laughter.

A strange man stood up farther down the pew and walked closer as the other guests paused on their way out to congratulate Gabby and J.D. He was the last. Tall, blond, and heavily muscled, he had a face as rugged as Jacob's and a tan that emphasized his sun-bleached hair.

He had brown eyes, and they studied Gabby for a long moment before he spoke. He was wearing a tan suit that looked as new as those J.D.'s men friends had on, and there was something familiar about the way he shook hands with J.D.

"I thought you hated weddings," J.D. remarked with a cool smile.

"I do. I just wanted to see who caught you." He pursed his lips and narrowed one eye, looking Gabby over in a way that made her nervous. Finally, one corner of his mouth tugged up a little and he gave a short laugh. "Well, if she can shoot and doesn't start screaming at gunfire, I guess she's okay."

"Okay?" she returned with a cold stare. "I'll have you know I'm terrific. I can even hit what I aim at."

The laugh mellowed a little and his dark eyes twinkled. "Can you?" He held out his hand. "I'm Dutch."

Her eyes widened. She remembered that he'd met J.D. in Rome and was the intelligence-gathering logistics man for the team.

"Well, miracles never cease," she murmured. "I thought you'd be bowlegged and chew tobacco."

Dutch burst out laughing. Impulsively, he drew her into a friendly embrace and hugged her. "Oh, J.D., you lucky son of a..."

"Dutch!" First Shirt burst out, interrupting him. "Where did you come from?"

"Lebanon," came the reply. "I need a few grunts. Interested?"

"Maybe," Matthew said. He glanced at the others. "Let's go talk. J.D., take care of her. And yourself." He clasped hands with the younger man. "I'll be in touch."

Gabby hugged him. "Thanks for giving me away. Let me know where you'll be at Christmas. I'll send you a box of thick socks."

Matthew kissed her forehead. "I'll do that." He leaned toward her ear. "Write down your mama's address for me too," he added in a whisper. "I like a lady who can shoot and cuss."

She laughed. "I'll do that."

The others filed out after brief goodbyes, and Gabby glanced at J.D.'s impassive face as they thanked Reverend Boone and started on their way to take Gabby's mother back to the airport.

"Call me once in a while, baby," her mother said to Gabby at the entrance to the waiting area.

"I will." She hugged the older woman. "Matthew took to you."

Her mother grinned. "I took to him too."

"There's just one thing…" Gabby began, wondering how much to tell her mother.

"He'll settle one day, just like J.D. did," came the quiet reply, and her mother gave her a knowing smile. "Some men take longer. Meanwhile, I write a sweet letter." She winked. "Come and visit."

"We will," J.D. promised, coming up to join them. He hugged his new mother-in-law and watched as she walked away with a wave.

Gabby slid her hand into the crook of his arm, and they walked back toward the parking lot.

"You've been very quiet since we left the church," he said softly. "Were you afraid I'd want to go with them?"

She was startled by his perception. "Yes, I think so. A little," she admitted.

He stopped beside the car and turned her to him, looking down into her troubled face. "I'll be honest with you, because anything less would cheat us both. I did feel a sense of loss when the others left without me, because in Guatemala I had a taste of the old, wild life and it brought back memories of days when I had more freedom than I have now. But I'm a realist, Gabby. Matthew said he told you, before we left Guatemala, that I'd gone too far to come back to them, to their way of life." She nodded and he touched her mouth softly with his fingers. "He was right. I've built a future for myself, for you. I've invested too much of my life in building it to throw it away for a little excitement. Besides," he murmured, lifting her slender hand to his chest and pressing it hard, "there are different levels of excitement."

His eyes studied hers with an intensity that made her knees go weak. He slid her fingers inside his vest, against his white shirt, letting her feel the warmth of his skin and the thunder of his pulse.

"You have the same effect on me that being caught under fire does," he whispered huskily, moving her fingers across one hard male nipple. "Except that you're a little less dangerous than a bullet."

"Only a little?" she whispered back, moving close, so that she could feel the length of his body touching hers.

His dark head bent and his mouth hovered just above hers. His hand moved between them to stroke one soft, high breast. It immediately went taut; his nostrils flared and his eyes burned with undisguised hunger.

"Are you afraid to have sex with me?" he whispered.

Her face flushed, but she didn't drop her eyes. "No. I love you," she whispered. "And it won't be sex. It will be…loving."

His mouth parted hers softly, sensuously. "In broad daylight, Gabby," he breathed.

"Yes, I know," she murmured, meeting his lips hungrily. "We can watch each other."

He looked into her eyes and saw the wildest kind of jungle there. He bent and caught her against him, kissing her hungrily and hard, feeling her response. He could hardly catch his breath when he finally lifted his head. "I don't need to go looking for adventure anymore. Not while I have you," he said gruffly. "A woman with an adventurous heart is excitement enough for me."

"Take me home, Jacob," she whispered. "Teach me."

He looked into her misty eyes and reluctantly let her go. "What an utterly delicious thought." He laughed unsteadily, and the lessons were already in his eyes. She looked at him and saw them as they would be, mouth to mouth, his body over hers, hard and warm and ardent, her eyes looking into his as they came together on crisp, cool sheets with his dark body overwhelming her soft, pink one with the same pleasure she felt when he stroked her bare flesh, only much more intimate, more intense…

She trembled softly in anticipation, wanting to be alone with him, wanting his hands, his mouth, his absolute possession. "I can hardly wait," she said, her voice trembling.

He put her into the car and paused for an instant, glancing toward the sky where a military plane was passing over. His face hardened for an instant as he stood quietly watching it until it was out of sight. But when he climbed in beside Gabby and looked at her glowing face, her bright, loving eyes, the hardness drained away. His dark eyes narrowed with the first stirrings of possession. And he smiled.

THE TENDER STRANGER

CHAPTER ONE

THE SEAT WAS MUCH TOO LOW for his tall frame; he had barely enough room without the paraphernalia his companion was shifting in her own seat. He gave her a short glare through deep brown eyes. She flushed, her gaze dropping to her lap as she tucked her huge purse on the other side of her and struggled with her seat belt.

He sighed, watching her. A spinster, he thought unkindly. From her flyaway brown hair to the eyes under those wire-rimmed glasses, from her bulky white sweater down to her long gray skirt and sensible gray shoes, she was definitely someone's unclaimed treasure. He turned his eyes back to the too-narrow aisle. Damn budget airlines, he thought furiously. If he hadn't missed the flight he'd booked, he wouldn't be trying to fit into this sardine can of a seat. Next to Miss Frump here.

He didn't like women. Never less than now, when he was forced to endure this particular woman's company for several hundred miles from San Antonio down to Veracruz, Mexico. He glanced sideways again irritably. She was shifting books now. Books, for God's sake! Didn't she know what the baggage hold was for?

"You should have reserved a seat for them," he muttered, glaring at a stack of what was obviously romance novels.

She swallowed, a little intimidated as her eyes swept over a muscular physique, blond hair and a face that looked positively hostile. He had nice hands, though. Very lean and tanned and strong-looking. Scars on the back of one of them...

"I'm sorry," she murmured, avoiding his eyes. "I've just come from a romance writer's autographing in San Antonio. These—these are autographed copies I'm taking back for friends after my Mexican holiday, and I was afraid to trust them to the luggage compartment."

"Priceless gems?" he asked humorlessly, giving them a speaking glare as she tucked the sackful under her seat.

"To some people, yes," she acknowledged. Her face tautened and she didn't look at him again. She cast nervous glances out the window while the airplane began to hum and the flight crew began once more the tedious demonstration of the safety equipment. He sighed impatiently and folded his arms across his broad chest, over the rumpled khaki shirt he wore. He leaned his head back, staring blankly at the stewardess. She was a beauty, but he wasn't interested. He hadn't been interested in women for quite a few years, except to satisfy an infrequent need. He laughed shortly, glancing at the prim little woman next to him. He wondered if she knew anything about those infrequent needs, and decided that she didn't. She looked as chaste as a nun, with her nervous eyes and hands. She had nice hands, though, he thought, pursing his lips as he studied them. Long fingers, very graceful, and no polish. They were the hands of a lady.

It irritated him that he'd noticed that. He glared harder at her.

That caught her attention. It was one thing to be impatiently tolerated, but she didn't like that superior glare. She turned and glared back at him. Something danced briefly in his dark eyes before he turned them back to the stewardess.

So she had fire, he thought. That was unexpected in a prim little nun. He wondered if she was a librarian. Yes, that would explain her fascination with books. And love stories…probably she was starving for a little love of her own. His eyes darkened. Stupid men, he thought, to overlook a feisty little thing like that just because of the glitter and paint that drew them to her more liberated counterparts.

There was murmuring coming from beside him. His sensitive ears caught a few feverish words: "Hail Mary, full of grace…,"

It couldn't be! He turned, his eyes wide and stunned. Was she a nun?

She caught him looking at her and bit her lip self-consciously. "Habit," she breathed. "My best friend was Catholic. She taught me the rosary and we always recited it together when we flew. Personally," she whispered, wide-eyed, "I don't think there's anyone up there in the cockpit flying this thing!"

His eyebrows levered up. "You don't?"

She leaned toward him. "Do you ever see anybody

in there?" She nodded toward the cockpit. "The door's always closed. If there isn't anything to hide, why do they close the door?"

He began to smile reluctantly. "Perhaps they're concealing a robot pilot?"

"More likely, they've got the pilot roped into his seat and they don't want us knowing it." She laughed softly, and it changed her face. With the right cosmetics and a haircut that didn't leave her soft hair unruly and half wild, she might not be bad-looking.

"You've been reading too many of those," he observed, gesturing toward the sack of books.

"Guilty." She sighed. "I suppose we need dreams sometimes. They keep reality at bay."

"Reality is better," he replied. "It has no illusions to spoil."

"I'd rather have my illusions."

He studied her openly. Wide, bow-shaped mouth, straight nose, wide-spaced pale gray eyes, heart-shaped face. She had a stubborn chin, too, and he smiled slowly. "You're a strange little creature," he said.

"I'm not little," she returned. "I'm five feet six."

He shrugged. "I'm over six feet. To me, you're little."

"I won't argue that," she said with a shy smile.

He chuckled. "Do you have a name?"

"Danielle. Danielle St. Clair. I own a bookstore in Greenville, South Carolina."

Yes, that fit her image to a T. "I'm called Dutch," he returned."But my name is Eric van Meer."

"Are you Dutch?" she asked.

He nodded. "My parents were."

"It must be nice, having parents," she said with unconscious wistfulness. "I was small when I lost both of mine. I don't even have a cousin."

His eyes darkened and he turned his face away. "I hope they serve lunch on this flight," he remarked, changing the subject with brutal abruptness. "I haven't had anything since last night."

"You must be starved!" she exclaimed. She began to dig in her bag as the plane jerked and eased toward the runway. "I have a piece of cake left over from the autograph party. I didn't have time to eat it. Would you like it?" she asked, and offered him a slice of coconut cake.

He smiled slowly. "No. I'll wait. But thank you."

She shrugged. "I don't really need it. I'm trying to lose about twenty pounds."

His eyes went over her. She was a little overweight. Not fat, just nicely rounded. He almost told her so. But then he remembered what treacherous creatures women were, and bit back the hasty words. He had concerns of his own, and no time for little spinsters. He leaned back and closed his eyes, shutting her out.

The flight passed uneventfully, but if he'd hoped to walk off the plane in Veracruz and forget about his seatmate, he was doomed to disappointment. When the plane finally rolled to a stop she stepped out into the aisle, juggling her luggage, and the sack containing her books broke into a thousand pieces.

Dutch tried not to laugh at the horrified expression on

her face as he gathered the books quickly together and threw them into her seat, then herded her out of the aisle.

"Oh, Lord," she moaned, looking as if fate and the Almighty were out to get her.

"Most travelers carry a spare bag inside their suitcases," he said hopefully as the other passengers filed out.

She looked up at him helplessly, all big gray eyes and shy pleading, and for an instant he actually forgot what he was saying. Her complexion was exquisite, he thought. He would have bet that she hardly ever used, or needed to use, beauty creams.

"Spare bag?" she echoed. "Spare bag!" She grinned. "Yes, of course." She shifted restlessly.

"Well?" he prompted gently.

She pointed to the overhead rack.

"We'll wait for everyone else to get off," he said. "Mine's up there, too; it's all right. No big deal."

She brushed back strands of wild hair and looked hunted. "I'm so organized back home," she muttered. "Not a stick of furniture out of place. But let me get outside the city limits of Greenville and I can't stick a fork on a plate without help."

He couldn't help laughing. "We'll get you sorted out," he said. "Where are you booked?"

"Book...oh, the hotel? It's the Mirador," she said.

Fate, he thought with a wistful smile. "That's where my reservation is," he said.

Her face lit up, and the look in her eyes faintly embarrassed him. She was gazing at him with a mixture of blind trust and hopeful expectation.

"Do you know the hotel? I mean, have you been here before?" she faltered, trying not to pry.

"Several times," he confessed. "I come down here once or twice a year when I need to get away." He glanced around. "Let's go."

He got down her suitcase and helped her extricate the spare bag from the case with a wry glance at the neat cotton nightgowns and underwear. She blushed wildly at that careless scrutiny, and he turned his attention to her books, packing them neatly and deftly.

She followed him out of the plane with gratitude shining on her face. She could have kissed him for not making fun of her, for helping her out. Imagine, she thought, a man like that actually doing something for her!

"I'm sorry to have been so much trouble," she blurted out, almost running to keep up with him as they headed toward customs and immigration. She was searching desperately for her passport, and missed the indulgent smile that softened his hard features momentarily.

"No trouble at all," he replied. "Got your passport?"

She sighed, holding it up. "Thank God I did something right," she moaned. "I've never even used it before."

"First time out of the States?" he asked pleasantly as they waited in line.

"First time out, yes," she confessed. "I just turned twenty-six. I thought I'd better do something adventurous fast, before I ran out of time."

He frowned. "My God, twenty-six isn't old," he said.

"No," she agreed. "But it isn't terribly young, either." She didn't look at him. Her eyes were quiet and sad, and she was thinking back of all the long years of loneliness.

"Is there a man?" he asked without quite knowing why.

She laughed with a cynicism that actually surprised him, and the wide eyes that looked up into his seemed ancient. "I have no illusions at all about myself," she said, and moved ahead with her huge purse.

He stared at her straight back with mingled emotions, confusing emotions. Why should it matter to him that she was alone? He shook his head and glanced around him to break the spell. It was none of his business.

Minutes later she was through customs. She almost waited for her tall companion, but she thought that one way or another, she'd caused him enough trouble. The tour company had provided transfers from the airport to the hotel, but a cab seemed much more inviting and less crowded. She managed to hail one, and with her bag of books and suitcase, bustled herself into it.

"Hotel Mirador," she said.

The cab driver smiled broadly and gunned the engine as he pulled out into the crowded street. Dani, full of new experiences and delightful sensations, tried to look everywhere at once. The Bay of Campeche was blue and delightful, and there were glimpses of palms and sand and many hotels. Veracruz was founded in the early 1500s and looked as many old cities of that period did, its architecture alternating between the days of piracy and the space age. Dani would have loved to dive straight into some sightseeing, but she was already uncomfortable in the formidable heat, and she knew it would be foolish to rush out without letting her body acclimate itself to its new environment.

As she gazed at the rows of hotels, the driver pulled into one of them, a two-story white building with graceful arches and a profusion of blooming flowers. It had only been a few minutes' ride from the airport, but the fare was confusing. And a little intimidating. Twenty dollars, just for several miles. But perhaps it was the custom, she thought, and paid him uncomplainingly.

He grinned broadly again, tipped his hat, and left her at the reservation desk.

She gave the clerk her name and waited with bated breath until her reservation was found. Finally, she had a room. Everything would be all right.

The room was nice. It overlooked the city, unfortunately, not the beautiful bay. But she hadn't expected much for the wonderfully low rates that had come with the package tour. She took off her sweater, amazed that it had felt so comfortable back in the States where it was early spring. It was much too heavy here, where the temperature was blazing hot even with the air-conditioning turned up. She stared out the window at the city. Mexico. It was like a dream come true. She'd scrimped and saved for two years to afford this trip. Even so, she'd had to come during the off-season, which was her busiest time back home. She'd left her friend Harriett Gaynor watching the bookstore in her absence. Go, Harriett had coaxed. Live a little.

She looked at herself in the mirror and grimaced. Live a little, ha! What a pity she hadn't looked like that gorgeous stewardess on the plane. Perhaps then the blond giant would have given her a second glance, or something besides the reluctant pity she'd read in his dark eyes.

She turned away from her reflection and began to unpack her suitcase. There was no use kidding herself that he'd helped her for any reason other than expediency. He could hardly walk right over her precious books. With a sigh she drew out her blouses and hung them up.

CHAPTER TWO

BY LATE AFTERNOON DANI felt up to some exploring, and she wandered the ancient streets with the excitement of a child. She'd changed into blue jeans and a loose, light sweatshirt and thongs, looking as much like a tourist as the other strangers in port. Her body was still adjusting to the heat, but the sweatshirt was simply a necessity. She couldn't bear to wear form-fitting T-shirts in public. They called too much attention to her ample bustline.

She found the stalls along the waterfront particularly fascinating, and paused long enough to buy herself a sterling silver cross with inlaid mother-of-pearl. Her pidgin Spanish seemed adequate, because most of the vendors spoke a little English. Everywhere there were colorful things to see—beautiful serapes in vivid rainbow shades, ponchos, hats, straw bags and animals and sea shells. And the architecture of the old buildings near the docks fascinated her. She stared out over the bay and daydreamed about the days of pirate ships and adventure, and suddenly a picture of the big blond man flashed into her mind. Yes, he would have made a good pirate. What was it that Dutch had called pirates—freebooters? She could even picture him with a cutlass. She smiled at her own fantasy and moved on down the pier to watch some men unloading a big freighter. She'd never been around ships very much. Greenville was an inland city, far from the ocean. Mountains and rolling, unspoiled countryside were much more familiar to Dani than ships were. But she liked watching them. Lost in her daydreams, she didn't realize just how long she'd been standing there, staring. Or that her interest might seem more than casual.

One of the men on the dock began watching her, and with a feeling of uneasiness she moved back into the crowd of tourists. She didn't want trouble, and a woman alone could get into a sticky situation.

Dusk was settling over the sleepy city of Veracruz, and the man was still watching her. Out of the corner of her eye she could see him moving toward her. Oh, Lord, she thought miserably, now what do I do? She didn't see a policeman anywhere, and most of the remaining tourists were older people who wouldn't want to be dragged into someone else's problems. Dani groaned inwardly as she clutched her bag and started walking quickly toward the hotel. The crowd dispersed still farther. Now she was alone and still the footsteps sounded behind her. Her heart began to race. What if he meant to rob her? Good heavens, what if he thought she was looking for a man?

She quickened her steps and darted around a corner just as a tall form loomed up in front of her. She jerked to a stop and almost screamed before she noticed the color of his hair in the fiery sunset.

"Oh," she said weakly, one hand clutching her sweatshirt.

Dutch stared at her coolly, a cigarette in one hand, the other in his pocket. He was still wearing the khaki safari suit he'd worn on the plane, but he looked fresh and unruffled. She found herself wondering if anything could rattle him. He had an odd kind of self-confidence, as if he'd tested himself to the very limits and knew himself as few men ever did.

He glanced over her shoulder, seeming to take in the situation in one quick glance. His eyes were very dark when they met hers again. "You'll enjoy your holiday more if you keep out of this part of town after dark," he told her pleasantly enough but with authority in his tone. "You've picked up an admirer."

"Yes, I know, I…" She started to glance over her shoulder, but he shook his head.

"Don't. He'll think you're encouraging him." He laughed shortly. "He's fifty and bald," he added. "But if you purposely went down to the docks looking for a man, you might give him a wink and make his day."

He'd meant it as a joke, but the remark hurt her anyway. Clearly, he didn't think she was likely to attract a man like himself.

"It was more a case of forgetting where I was, if you want the truth. I'll know better next time. Excuse me," she said quietly, and walked past him.

He watched her go, furious with her for letting the taunt cut her, more furious with himself for not realizing that it would. He muttered something unpleasant under his breath and started after her.

But she'd had quite enough. She quickened her pace, darting into the hotel and up the staircase to the second floor instead of waiting for an elevator. She made it into her room and locked the door. Although why she should have bothered was anyone's guess. He wasn't the kind of man who chased bespectacled booksellers, she told herself coldly.

She didn't bother to go downstairs for dinner that evening. Probably he wouldn't have come near her, but she was too embarrassed to chance it. She ordered from room service, and enjoyed a seafood supper in privacy.

The next morning she went down to breakfast, too proud to let him think she was avoiding him. And sure enough, there he was, sitting alone at a window table with a newspaper. He looked good, she thought, even in nothing more unusual than white slacks and a red-and-white half-unbuttoned shirt. Just like a tourist. As if he felt her eyes on him, he lifted his gaze from the paper and caught her staring. She blushed, but he merely smiled and returned his eyes to his reading. She hardly knew what she was eating after that, and she couldn't help watching him out of the corner of one eye.

He was much too sophisticated for a little country mouse, Dani told herself sternly. She'd just have to keep well away from him. He had no interest in her, despite her helpless fascination with him. He was world-weary and cynical, and looked as if she amused him...nothing more.

She made up her mind to enjoy the rest of her four-day holiday, and went to her room, where she got out a one-piece black bathing suit to wear to the beach. She pinned her irritating hair out of the way and stared at her reflection. What ravishing good looks, she thought sarcastically. No wonder he wasn't interested. Looking the way she did, it was unlikely that even a shark would be tempted.

Go to Mexico, have fun, her friend Harriett Gaynor had said. Sparkle! Attract men! Dani sighed miserably. Back home it was spring and things were beginning to bloom, and books were selling well—especially romances. And here Dani was, with nothing changed at all except her surroundings. Alone and unloved and unwanted, as usual. She glared at herself and impulsively she called the beauty salon downstairs and made an appointment to have her hair cut.

They had a cancellation, and could take her immediately. Several minutes later she sat watching the unruly locks of hair being neatly sheared off, leaving her delicate features framed by a simple, wavy short cut that curled toward her wide eyes and gave her an impish look. She grinned at herself, pleased, and after paying the girl at the counter, she danced back upstairs and put on her bathing suit. She even added some of the makeup she never used, and perfume. The result wasn't beauty-queen glamour, but it was a definite improvement.

Then she stared at her bodice ruefully. Well, there wouldn't be any miracle to correct this problem, she told herself, and pulled on a beach wrap. It was colorful, tinted with shades of lavender, and it concealed very well. She got the beach bag she'd bought in the hotel lobby and stuffed suntan lotion and her beach towel into it. Then, with her prescription sunglasses firmly over her eyes, she set off for the beach.

It was glorious. Beach and sun and the lazy rhythm of the water all combined to relax her. She stretched, loving the beauty around her, the history of this ancient port. She wondered what the first explorers would have thought of the tourist attraction their old stomping grounds made.

Feeling as if someone were staring at her, she opened her eyes and twisted her head just a little. She saw Dutch wandering along the beach, cigarette in hand, blond head shining like white gold in the sun. He was darkly tanned, shirtless, and her fascinated eyes clung to him helplessly. He wasn't a hairy man, but there was a wedge of curling dark blond hair over the darkly tanned muscles of his chest and stomach. His legs were feathered with it, too, long, powerful legs in cutoff denim shorts, and he wore thongs, as most of the people on the beach did, to protect against unexpected objects in the sand.

She turned her head away so that she didn't have to see him. He was a sensuous man, devastating to a woman who knew next to nothing about the male sex. He had to be aware of her naiveté, and it probably amused him, she thought bitterly.

He watched her head turn, and irritation flashed in his dark eyes. Why was she always gazing at him with that helpless-child longing? She disturbed him. His eyes narrowed. New haircut, wasn't it? The haircut suited her, but why in hell was she wrapped up like a newly caught fish? He'd yet to see her in anything that didn't cover her from neck to waist. He frowned. Probably she was flat-chested and didn't want to call attention to it. But didn't she realize that her attempts at camouflage were only pointing out her shortcoming?

He glowered at her. Long legs, nice legs, he mused, narrowing his eyes as he studied the relaxed body on the giant beach towel. Nice hips, too. Flat, very smooth lines. Tiny waist. But then there was the coverup. She'd said she needed to lose weight, but he couldn't imagine where. She looked perfect to him.

She was just a woman, he thought, pulling himself up. Just another faithless flirt, out for what she could get. Would he never learn? Hadn't he paid for his one great love affair already? Love affair, he thought bitterly. Never that. An infatuation that had cost him everything he held dear. His home, his future, the savings his parents had sacrificed to give him...

He tore his eyes away and turned them seaward. Sometimes it got the better of him. It had no part of the present. In fact, neither did Miss Frump over there.

He turned, blatantly staring at her, a tiny smile playing around his mouth. She was a different species of woman, unfamiliar to him. He found he was curious about her, about what made her tick.

He moved forward slowly, and she saw him out of the corner of her eye. She felt her pulse exploding as he came closer. No, she pleaded silently, closing her eyes. Please, go away. Don't encourage me. Don't come near me. You make me vulnerable, and that's the one thing I mustn't be.

"You won't get much sun in that," he remarked, indicating the top as he plopped down beside her. He leaned on an elbow, stretched full-length beside her, and she could feel the heat of him, smell the cologne that clung to him.

"I don't want to burn," she said in a strangled tone.

"Still angry about what I said last night?" he asked on a smile.

"A little, yes," she said honestly.

He leaned over and tugged her sunglasses away from her eyes so that they were naked and vulnerable. He was worldly and it showed, and so did her fear of him.

"I didn't mean to ridicule you. I'm not used to women," he said bluntly. "I've lived a long time without them."

"And you don't like them, either," she said perceptively.

He scowled briefly, letting his eyes drop to her mouth. "Occasionally. In bed." He chuckled softly at her telltale color. "Don't tell me I embarrass you? Not considering the type of reading material you carry around with you. Surely every detail is there in black and white."

"Not the way you're thinking," she protested.

"Little southern lady," he murmured, watching her. She had a softness that he wasn't used to, a vulnerability. But there was steel under it. He sensed a spirit as strong as his own beneath shyness. "Do I frighten you?"

"Yes. I…don't have much to do with men," she said quietly. "And I'm not very worldly."

"Are you always that honest?" he asked absently as he studied her nose. There were a few scattered freckles on its bridge.

"I don't like being lied to," she said. "So I try very hard not to lie to other people."

"The golden rule?" He fingered a short strand of her brown hair, noticing the way it shone in the sunlight, as sleek as mink, silky in his hand. "I like your haircut."

"It was hot having it long…" She faltered. She wasn't used to being touched, and there was something magnetic about this man. It was unsettling to have so much vibrant masculinity so close that she could have run her hands over his body. He made her feel things she hadn't experienced since her teens, innocent longings that made her tense with mingled fear and need.

"Why are you wearing this?" he asked, and his hand went to the buttons of her shapeless overblouse. "Do you really need it?"

She could hardly swallow. He had her so rattled, she didn't know her name. "I…no, but…" she began.

"Then take it off," he said quietly. "I want to see what you look like."

There had been a similar passage in the latest book by her favorite author. She'd read it and gotten breathless. But this was real, and the look in his dark eyes made her tremble. She forgot why she was wearing the wrap and watched his hard face as he eased the buttons skillfully out of their holes and finally drew the garment from around her body.

His breath caught audibly. He seemed to stop breathing as he looked down on what he'd uncovered. "My God," he whispered.

She was blushing again, feeling like a nervous adolescent.

"Why?" he asked, meeting her eyes.

She shifted restlessly. "Well, I'm…I feel…men stare," she finished miserably.

"My God, of course they stare! You're exquisite!"

She'd never heard it put that way. She searched his eyes, looking for ridicule, but there was none. He was staring again, and she found that a part of her she didn't recognize liked the way he was looking at her.

"Is that why you wear bulky tops all the time?" he persisted gently.

She sighed. "Men seem to think that women who are…well-endowed have loose morals. It's embarrassing to be stared at."

"I thought you were flat-chested," he mused, laughing.

"Well, no, I'm not," she managed. "I guess I did look rather odd."

He smiled down at her. "Leave it off," he said with a last lingering scrutiny before he stretched out on his back. "I'll fend off unwanted admirers for you."

She was immediately flattered. And nervous. Would he expect any privileges for that protection? She stared at his relaxed body uneasily.

"No strings," he murmured, eyes closed. "I want rest, not a wild, hot affair."

She sighed. "Just as well," she said ruefully. "I wouldn't know how to have one."

"Are you a virgin?" he asked matter-of-factly.

"Yes."

"Unusual these days."

"I believe in happily-ever-after."

"Yes, I could tell by your reading material," he said with a lazy smile. He stretched, and powerful muscles rippled all up and down his tanned body. Her gaze was drawn to it, held by it.

He opened his eyes and watched her, oddly touched by the rapt look on her young face. He'd have bet a year's earnings that she'd never been touched even in the most innocent way. He found himself wondering what she might be like in passion, whether those pale eyes would glow, whether her body would relax and trust his. He frowned slightly. He'd never taken time with a woman, not since that she-wolf. These days it was all quickly over and forgotten. But slow, tender wooing was something he could still remember. And suddenly he felt a need for it. To touch this silky creature next to him and teach her how to love. How to touch. The thought of her long fingers on him caused a sudden and shocking reaction in his body.

He turned over onto his stomach, half-dazed with the unexpected hunger. Was she a witch? He studied her. Did she know what had happened to him? No, he decided, if she did, it would be highly visible in those virginal cheeks. She probably didn't even know what happened to men at all. He smiled slowly at the searching wonder in her eyes.

"Why are you smiling like that?" she asked softly.

"Do you really want to know?" he murmured dryly.

She rolled over onto her stomach as well, and propped herself up on her elbows, looking down at him, at the hard lines of his face, the faint scarring on one cheek. She felt drawn to him physically, and couldn't understand why it seemed so natural to lie beside him and look at him.

His eyes were fixed on a sudden parting of fabric that gave a tantalizing view of her generous breasts, and when she started to move, he reached up and held her still.

"You won't get pregnant if I look at you," he whispered.

"You're a horrible man," she said haughtily.

"Yes, but I'm much safer than any one of these wily Latins," he told her. "The lesser of two evils, you might say. I won't seduce you."

"As if any man would want to." She laughed, and started to move away again. This time he let her, looming over her as she lay back, with his forearms beside her head and his eyes boring into hers at close range.

"If we weren't on a public beach, I'd give you a crash course in arousal, doubting Thomasina," he murmured. "Something just happened to me that shocked me to the back teeth, and it's your fault."

Her eyes widened as her mind tried to convince her that she hadn't heard him make such a blatant statement.

"I see you understand me," he said with a lazy smile. "What's wrong, southern belle, have you led such a sheltered life?"

She swallowed. "Yes." She studied his hard face. "Yours hasn't been sheltered."

"That's right," he told her. "I could turn your hair white with the story of my life. Especially," he added deliberately, unblinkingly, "the part of it that concerns women."

Her eyes dilated as they held his. "You…aren't a romantic."

He shook his head slowly. "No," he said quietly. "Occasionally I need a woman, the oblivion of sex. But that's all it ever is. Sex, with no illusions."

Her eyes searched his, reading embarrassing things in them. "There's a reason," she said softly, knowingly.

He nodded. "I was twenty-four. She was twenty-eight, wildly experienced, and as beautiful as a goddess. She seduced me on the deck of a yacht, and after that I'd have died for her. But she was expensive, and I was besotted, and eventually I sold everything I had to buy her loyalty." His eyes darkened, went cold with memory and rage as Dani watched. "I'd helped buy my parents a small home for their retirement with money I…earned," he added, not mentioning how he'd earned the money. "And I even mortgaged that. The bank foreclosed. My father, who'd put his life savings into his part of the house, died of a heart attack soon afterward. My mother blamed me for it, for taking away the thing he'd worked all his life for. She died six months later."

He'd picked up a handful of sand and was letting it fall slowly onto the beach while she stared at his handsome profile and knew somehow that he'd never told this story to another living soul.

"And the woman?" she asked gently.

The sand made a small sound, and his palm flattened on it, crushing it. "She found another chump…" He glanced at Dani with a cold laugh. "One with more money."

"I'm sorry," she said inadequately. "I can understand that it would have made you bitter. But—"

"But all women aren't cold-hearted cheats?" he finished for her, glaring. "Aren't they?"

"The one boyfriend I ever had was two-timing me with another girl," she said.

"What a blazing affair it must have been," he said with cold sarcasm.

She searched his face, seeing beneath the anger to the pain. "I loved him," she said with a gentle smile. "But he was more interested in physical satisfaction than undying devotion."

"Most men are," he said curtly.

"I suppose so." She sighed. She rolled over onto her back and stretched. "I've decided that I like being alone, anyway. It's a lot safer."

He eased onto his side, watching her. "You disturb me," he said after a minute.

"Why? Because I'm not experienced?" she asked.

He nodded. "My world doesn't cater to inexperience. You're something of a curiosity to me."

"Yes. So are you, to me," she confessed, studying him blatantly.

He brushed the hair away from her face with strong, warm hands, callused hands that felt as if he'd used them in hard work. She liked that roughness against her soft skin. It made her tingle and ache with pleasure. He looked down at the bodice of the bathing suit, watching her reaction. The material was thin and the hard tips of her breasts were as evident as her quickened breathing.

She started to move her arms, to cover herself, but he caught her eyes and shook his head.

"That's as natural as breathing," he said in a voice that barely carried above the sound of the surf. "It's very flattering. Don't be ashamed of it."

"I was raised by a maiden aunt," she told him. "She never married, and I was taught that—"

He pressed his thumb over her mouth, a delicious contact that made her want to bite it gently. "I can imagine what you were taught." He let his dark gaze drop to her mouth and studied it slowly as he touched it, watching it tremble and part. "I like your mouth, Dani. I'd like to take it with mine."

The thought was exciting, wildly exciting. Her gaze went involuntarily to his hard, chiseled mouth. His upper lip was thin, the bottom one wide and sensuous. She would bet he'd forgotten more about kissing than she'd ever learned.

"Have you been kissed very much?" he asked.

"Once or twice," she said lightly, trying to joke.

"French kisses?" he provoked.

Her body was going crazy. She could feel her heart trying to escape her chest, and her breathing was audible. It got even worse when his hard fingers left her mouth to run down the side of her neck, across her collarbone and, incredibly, onto the swell of her breast above the swimsuit.

Her gasp whispered against his lips and he smiled. "Shocking, isn't it?" he murmured, watching her eyes dilate, her face flush as his fingers lazily slid under the strap. His body shielded her from other sunbathers, and there was no one in front of them. "No one can see us," he whispered reassuringly. He laughed softly, wickedly, as his fingers slid under the fabric with a lazy teasing pressure that was more provocative than frightening. Her body reacted wildly to being teased, and she knew that he could see what was happening. He was much too sophisticated not to know exactly what she was feeling.

"Skin like warm silk," he breathed, his mouth poised just above hers while his fingers brushed her like whispers of sensation, and she tensed and trembled as the pleasure began to grow.

She wanted more. She wanted him to touch the hard, aching tips of her breasts; she wanted to watch him do it, to see him possess her with that callused, expert hand. Her face even told him so.

His eyes were getting darker now, and the indulgent smile was vanishing as well. "If you keep looking at me like that," he said under his breath, "I'm going to slide my hand completely over you and to hell with spectators."

Her lips parted. She felt reckless and abandoned and vulnerable. Four days in which to store a lifetime of memories, she thought bitterly. Every one of her friends was married, every one of them had some happiness. But not Dani. Not ever. And now this man, who could have had any woman on the beach, was playing with her, amusing himself, because he saw how vulnerable she was…and she was letting him.

Her eyes clouded, and something deep inside the blond man stirred helplessly when he saw it.

"No," he whispered with aching tenderness. "Don't. I'm not playing."

She bit her lower lip to stop sudden tears. He saw so much, for a stranger. "Yes, you are," she protested. "You—"

His mouth lowered onto hers, just enough to let her lips experience its texture before he withdrew it. His hand, resting warmly under the strap of her bathing suit, began to move.

Her body trembled, and he whispered, "Hush," brushing his mouth tenderly over the bridge of her nose. "No one can see what I'm going to do to you." His lips went to her eyes, brushing them tenderly closed. His long fingers nudged under the fabric, farther and farther.

Her hands were on his shoulders, her fingers clinging, her breath sighing out unsteadily against his tormenting mouth. "Eric," she whispered experimentally.

He hesitated for an instant, lifting his blond head. He looked down into eyes that were full of new sensations, wide and soft and hazy. His free hand eased to the back of her neck, stroking it softly. He held her gaze as his hand moved slowly down, and then up, and she felt the warm roughness of his palm against the hard point of her breast.

"Is this the first time?" he whispered.

"Can't you…tell?" she whispered back brokenly.

Her body moved helplessly, so that she could experience every texture of his hand where it rested, and an odd, tearful smile touched her mouth. "Thank you. Thank..."

He couldn't bear it. The gratitude hurt him. He moved his hand back up to her face and kissed her mouth softly, with a tenderness he hadn't shown any woman since he was little more than a boy.

"You speak as if you think it's a hardship for me just to touch you," he said quietly. "If you knew more about men, you might realize that I'm as aroused by you as you are by me."

"Me?" she repeated, her eyes wide and bright and full of magic.

"You, you voluptuous, exciting little virgin," he said, his voice rough with laughter. "I ache all over."

She began to smile, and his attention was caught by the sunniness of it, by the sudden beauty of her face. And he'd thought her drab and dull. How odd. He sensed a deeply buried sensuality in that voluptuous body, and he wanted it.

He propped himself up on an elbow, his free hand still tugging absently at her short hair.

She gave her eyes the freedom to roam that powerful body, taking in its bronzed sensuousness, the light covering of dark blond hair on his chest, his rippling stomach muscles, his strongly muscled thighs. He even had nice feet. And his legs weren't pale, as most American men's were. They were broad and dark, and looked good.

"I like your legs, too," he murmured.

She glanced back up. "Do you mind?" she asked gently. "I know I'm gawking like a schoolgirl."

"You're very honest, aren't you?" he remarked for the second time that day. "It's vaguely disconcerting. No, I don't mind if you look at me. Except that it—"

"It…?" she persisted.

"Arouses me," he said frankly.

"Just to be looked at?" she asked, fascinated.

He smiled a little. "Maybe it's my age," he said with a shrug. "You have very expressive eyes, did you know? They tell me everything you're thinking."

"Do they really?" She laughed, looking up at him. "What am I thinking now?" she asked, her mind carefully blank.

He pursed his lips and smiled slowly, and she felt a deep, slow ache in her body that was intensified when she looked at the broad sweep of his chest.

"That you'd like to have dinner with me," he hedged. "How about it?"

"Yes. I'd like to. If you won't seduce me for dessert," she added.

He sighed softly. "I'd like to have you," he confessed. "But I couldn't quite take you in my stride, either. A virgin would be something of a rarity for me. Most of my one-night stands have been the exact opposite of virgins."

She tried not to blush, but her cheeks betrayed her.

He searched her eyes. "I wouldn't hurt you," he said suddenly. "And with you, it would have to be lovemaking, not sex."

Her body felt boneless as he searched her eyes, and

there was a flash of something like tenderness in the look he gave her. "I'm sorry," she said.

"Why?"

She dropped her eyes to his chest. "Because I think...I'd have liked you...for a lover."

"Yes, I think I'd have liked you for one," he agreed softly. He tilted her face back to his and searched her eyes. "Wrong time, wrong place. We should have met ten years ago."

She smiled ruefully. "You wouldn't have liked me at sixteen," she said. "I really was twenty pounds overweight."

He drew in a slow breath. "And I was in the early days of some pretty raw living," he agreed. "What a pity." He lifted her hand and kissed the soft palm, watching her face color with pleasure. "How long will you be here?"

"Four days," she said miserably.

His teeth bit into the soft flesh. "Make some memories with me," he whispered.

"That will only make it worse..." she began.

"We'll keep it light," he said. "I won't seduce you."

"By tomorrow I'll probably beg you to," she said unhappily, studying him with helpless longing. "I'm frighteningly vulnerable with you."

His eyes went along her body and he felt himself going rigid with desire. "Yes. I'm pretty vulnerable myself."

She had to force her eyes to stay on his face, and he smiled wickedly, knowing exactly what she was thinking.

He laughed and she rolled over onto her stomach again.

"Don't worry," he murmured as he stretched out beside her. "I'll take care of you. Don't sweat it."

She turned her eyes toward his and searched them, and then she smiled. "You're so handsome," she whispered helplessly.

"You're a knockout yourself," he said. "Flat-chested, hell." He laughed. "You're dynamite!"

"Thank you."

He searched her face appreciatively. "So innocent. J.D. would laugh himself sick at me."

"J.D.?" she asked curiously.

"An old friend." He grinned. "Close your eyes and let's soak up some sun. Later, I'll take you sightseeing." His eyes closed and then opened. "Not to the docks," he added, and closed them again.

She closed her own eyes with a smile. Miracles, she thought wistfully, did occasionally happen to lonely spinsters. These were going to be the four most beautiful days of her entire life. She wouldn't take a second of them for granted, starting now.

CHAPTER THREE

DANI WAS GLAD SHE'D STOPPED by the little boutique in the basement of the hotel on her way up to change for dinner. She'd bought a white Mexican dress with an elastic neckline and lots of ruffles, and when she put it on she looked slightly mysterious, with her brown hair and gray eyes and creamy complexion. Her wire-rimmed glasses weren't so spiffy, she admitted, but they did make her eyes look bigger than they were. And she wasn't really fat, she told herself, smiling at her reflection. It was mostly what was on top, and the dress even minimized that. She got her small evening bag and went downstairs to meet Dutch in the lobby.

He was wearing white slacks with a white shirt and blue blazer, and he rose lazily to his feet from a plush sofa, leaving his evening paper there as he joined her.

"Nice," he said, taking her arm. "What do you fancy? Mexican, Chinese, Italian, or a steak?"

"I like steak," she murmured.

"So do I." He guided her along the hall past the family restaurant and into the very exclusive Captain's Quarters next door. White-coated waiters in white gloves were everywhere, and Dani glanced up at Dutch apprehensively as he gave the hostess his name.

"What is it?" he asked softly, guiding her along behind the well-dressed young woman with the menus.

"It's so expensive," she began, worried.

His face brightened, and he smiled. "Do you mind washing dishes afterward?" he whispered mischievously.

She laughed up at him. "Not if you'll dry," she promised.

He slid an arm around her waist and pulled her close. "You're a nice girl."

"Just the kind your mother warned you about, so look out," she told him.

He glanced down at her. "No. My mother would have liked you. She was spirited, too."

She smiled shyly, aware of envious eyes following them along the way. He was so handsome, she thought, peeking up at him. Muscular, graceful, and with the face of a Greek statue, male perfection in the finest sense. An artist would have been enchanted with him as a subject.

The hostess left them at their table, near the window, and Dutch seated Dani with a curious frown.

"What were you thinking about so solemnly just now?" he asked as he eased his tall form into the chair across from her.

"That you'd delight an artist," she said simply. "You're very elegant."

He took a slow breath. "Lady, you're bad for my ego."

"Surely you look in the mirror from time to time?" she asked. "I don't mean to stare, but I can't help it."

"Yes, I have the same problem," he murmured, and his eyes were fixed on her.

She was glad she hadn't yielded to the temptation to pull the elastic neck of her dress down around her shoulders. It was hard enough to bear that dark stare as it was.

"Shall I order for you, or are you liberated?" he asked after she'd studied the menu.

"I kind of like it the old-fashioned way, if you don't mind," she confessed. "I'm liberated enough to know I look better in a skirt than in a pair of pants."

He chuckled. "Do you?"

"Well, you'd look pretty silly in a dress," she came back.

"What do you want to eat?" he asked.

"Steak and a salad and coffee to drink."

He looked at her with a dry smile, and when the waiter came, he gave a double order.

"Yes," he told her, "I like coffee, too."

"You seem very traveled," she remarked, pleating her napkin.

"I am." He leaned back in his chair to study her. "And you've never been out of the States."

"I've been nowhere—until now." She smiled at the napkin. "Done nothing except work. I thought about changing, but I never had the courage to do it."

"It takes courage, to break out of a mold," he said. He pulled the ashtray toward him and lit a cigarette. "I hope you don't mind, but I'm doing it anyway. This is one habit I don't intend to break."

"'I'll die of something someday,'" she quoted.

"There are lots of other clichés, but I think that one's dandy."

He only laughed. "Smoking is the least dangerous thing I do."

"What *do* you do?" she asked, curious.

He thought about that for a moment, and pursed his lips as he wondered what she'd say if he told her the truth. She'd probably be out of that chair and out of his life so fast... He frowned. He didn't like that idea.

"I'm in the military," he said finally. "In a sense."

"Oh. On active duty?" she continued, feeling her way because he seemed reluctant to elaborate.

"No. Inactive, at the moment." He watched her through a veil of smoke from his cigarette.

"Is it dangerous, what you do?"

"Yes."

"I feel like a panelist on 'What's My Line?'" she said unexpectedly, and grinned when he burst out laughing.

"Maybe you're a double agent," she supposed. "A spy."

"I'm too tall," he returned. "Agents are supposed to be under five feet tall so that they can hide in shrubbery."

She stared at him until she realized he was joking, and she laughed.

"Your eyes laugh when you do," he said absently. "Are you always this sunny?"

"Most of the time," she confessed. She pushed her glasses back as they threatened to slide down her nose. "I have my bad days, too, like everyone else, but I try to leave them at home."

"You could get contact lenses," he remarked as he noticed her efforts to keep her glasses on her nose.

She shook her head. "I'm much too nervous to be putting them in and taking them out and putting them in solution all the time. I'm used to these."

"They must get in the way when you kiss a man," he murmured dryly.

"What way?" She laughed, a little embarrassed by his frankness. "My life isn't overrun with amorous men."

"We can take them off, I suppose," he mused.

Her breath caught as she read the veiled promise in his dark eyes.

"Stark terror," he taunted gently, watching her expression. "I didn't realize I was so frightening."

"Not that kind of frightening," she corrected him. Her eyes lowered.

"Dani."

He made her name sound like a prayer. She looked up.

"Seducing you is not on the agenda," he said quietly. "But if something did happen, I'd marry you. That's a promise, and I don't give my word lightly."

She began to tingle all over. "It would be a high price to pay for one mistake."

He was watching her oddly. "Would it? I haven't thought about marriage in years." He leaned back in his chair to study her, the cigarette burning idly in his fingers. "I wonder what it would be like," he mused, "having someone to come back to."

What an odd way to put it, she thought. Surely he meant someone to come *home* to. She pulled herself up short as she realized that it was just conversation. He was only amusing himself; she had to remember that. Making memories, as he'd put it. They were strangers and they'd remain strangers. She couldn't afford to mess up her whole life because of a holiday romance. That was all this was. A little light entertainment. She'd better remember that, too.

The waiter brought their food, and as they ate they talked about general things. He seemed very knowledgeable about foreign conflicts, and she imagined that he read a lot of military publications. That led to talk of the kind of weapons being used, and he seemed equally knowledgeable about those.

"My best friend's husband likes to read about weapons," Dani volunteered, remembering Harriett's Dave and his fascination with weaponry. "He has volumes on those exotic things like...oh, what is it, the little nine-millimeter carbine—"

"The Uzi," he offered. "It has a thirty-shot magazine and can throw off single shots as well as bursts. A formidable little carbine."

She laughed. "I can shoot a twenty-two rifle. That's about the extent of my knowledge of weapons."

"I know more about knives than guns, as a rule, although I've used both." He reached into his inside blazer pocket, produced a large folded knife and put it on the table.

She stared at it, fascinated. It was made of silvery metal, with a carved bone handle, and when she tugged the blade out, it was oddly shaped and had a sinister look.

"It's not a pocket knife, is it?" she asked, lifting her eyes.

He shook his head. "Although it passes for one, going through customs."

"Where did you find something so unusual?" she asked, fascinated by it.

"I made it." He picked it up and repocketed it.

"Made it?" she exclaimed.

"Sure." He laughed at her expression. "Where do you think knives come from? Someone has to make them."

"Yes, of course, but I didn't recognize... It's very formidable looking," she added.

"I don't carry it for decoration," he said. He leaned forward and sipped his coffee. "Would you like some dessert?"

"No, thank you," she said. "I don't like sweet things very much, thank God."

He smiled. "Neither do I. Let's go walk on the beach for a while."

"Lovely!"

She waited while he paid the check and then followed him out into the darkness.

The night was warm, and she took off her sandals, which she'd worn without hose, and danced in and out of the waves. He watched her, laughing, his hands in his pockets, his blond hair pale and glowing in the light from the hotel.

"How old did you say you were?" he asked when she came running back up the beach, sandals dangling from one hand.

"About ten," she laughed up at him.

"You make me feel old." He lifted a hand and touched her cheek, her lips. There were people farther down the beach, but none close enough to be more than dark shapes.

"How old are you?" she asked.

"Thirty-six," he said. His other hand came out of his pocket. He took her sandals from her nerveless fingers and dropped them down into the sand. The soft thud barely registered above the crashing surf.

"You excite me," he said in a deep, slow tone. He cupped her face in his hands and drew her closer, so that she could feel the pleasant heat of his body against hers. "Do you know how a man's body reacts when he's excited?"

Her face felt blistering hot, and she couldn't seem to move as he released her face only to take her hips in his hands and draw them against him.

Her breath caught and his open mouth touched her forehead. His breathing was audible now, and she was learning fascinating things about him, about the subtle differences in his body that she was apparently causing.

"No protest at all?" he asked quietly.

"I'm...curious," she whispered. "As you've already seen, I know very little about this."

"I don't frighten you?"

"No, not now."

His mouth smiled, she could feel it. His thumbs bit into the soft flesh of her stomach as he urged her closer. "Not even now?" he whispered.

Her legs trembled against his. She felt strange new sensations inside her, dragging sensations that left tingling pleasure in their wake. Her hands clung to his blazer because she wasn't sure her legs were going to support her much longer.

His chest rose and fell roughly against her taut breasts. "I want to be alone with you. And at the moment that's the most dangerous thing we could do."

"You want me," she whispered, realizing it with a strange sense of triumph.

"Yes." His hands moved up her body slowly to her breasts, which were bare under the dress because she hadn't wanted to suffer her hot, longline bra, which was the only strapless thing she had.

She tensed, feeling his hands lift her, cup her, so tender that she accepted them without protest. His thumbs brushed over her, feeling her instant response.

"You want me, too, don't you?" he asked gently.

The sensations his thumbs were producing made her mind go blank. She moved a little, moaning.

His face pressed against her cheek. She could feel his breath at her ear.

"Thank God we don't have an audience," he whispered huskily. "Stand very still, Dani."

His hands rose, moved to her shoulders. He eased the fabric down her arms with a slow, sinuous, achingly tender pressure. Her heart stopped beating as she felt the blood rush through her veins, felt the coolness of the salty night breeze touching her shoulders, her upper arms, and then her breasts as he slid the fabric to her waist.

She moaned again, a catching of breath that acted on him like a narcotic. He felt his own legs go weak at the wholehearted response she was giving him. Giving to him, when he knew instinctively that she'd never have let any other man do this to her.

"I wish that I could see your eyes," he whispered. He lifted his head and looked down at her shadowed face. His hands slid against her face, her throat. "You're so silky-soft," he said under his breath. His hands slid down her arms and back up, his fingers barely touching, experiencing her skin. "Like warm cream. I can feel you trembling, and it brings the blood to my head, did you know? And that little sound you made when I pulled your dress away from your breasts..." His hands moved back to her shoulders. "Sweet, sweet virgin," he whispered. "Make it easy for me. Lift your arms and let me hold you in my palms."

She stood on tiptoe as his hands began to move over her collarbone. Her hands reached up into his thick, straight blond hair as his thumbs moved down ahead of his palms and rubbed sensually at the hard tips of her breasts.

She jerked helplessly at the exquisite contact.

"I want to put my mouth on you," he whispered as his lips brushed hers and his hands slowly, achingly, swallowed her, feeling the involuntary tremors that shook her. "All of this is a natural part of lovemaking, so don't be frightened if you feel my teeth. All right?"

"People," she moaned helplessly.

"There was only an old couple down the beach," he

whispered. "They've gone inside now. Dani, Dani, of all the erotic, unbelievably sexy things I've ever done with a woman, this has to be the sweetest!"

She was arching her body toward him, blind and deaf to everything except sensation. Tomorrow, she told her conscience, tomorrow I'll worry about it.

"You want my mouth, don't you, darling?" he said, and with something like reverence he began to run his lips along her throat, down the side of her neck, over her collarbone, her shoulders. "I'm going to make a meal of you right here," he breathed, and all at once she felt his teeth on her and she stiffened and cried out.

"Eric," she moaned, frightened, her hands catching in his hair.

"It's all right," he murmured against her breast. "I wouldn't hurt you for all the world. Relax, darling, just relax. Yes, like that, Dani. Lie down. Lie down, so that I can get to you...."

He was easing her down onto the sand, and she let him, grateful to have some support under her, because the world was spinning around wildly. She clung to him, glorying in the feel of his lips, his teeth, his tongue, as he showed her how inexperienced she really was. By the time he got back to her mouth she was on fire for him.

With fierce enthusiasm she pulled his body down over hers and kissed him back with a naive but satisfying passion. He laughed delightedly against her open mouth and eased his hips over hers. She was his already.

"Eric," she ventured shakily.

"What do you want?" he asked, tasting her closed eyelids.

Her hands went to the front of his shirt, and he lifted his head. "Do you want to feel me?"

She flushed. "Yes."

"Unbutton it."

He was heavy, but she loved his weight. Overhead there were hundreds of stars. But all she knew was the unexpected completeness of his passion.

She touched his bare, hair-rough skin with hands that tingled with excitement. She'd never touched a man's body before, but she loved the feel of Dutch's. His muscles were padded, warm and strong, and she could imagine that his strength was formidable.

"Move your hands," he said seconds later, and when she did, he dragged his bare chest roughly over hers, shocking her with the force of desire the unexpected action caused in her body.

"Do you like it?" he asked as he moved sinuously above her.

"I never dreamed..." she began huskily. She was trembling, and so was her voice. "Oh, I want you," she confessed on a sob. "I want you, I want you!"

"I want you, too, little one," he whispered, kissing her softly. "But I can't treat you like a one-night stand. I find I have too much conscience."

Tears were rolling down her cheeks. He kissed them all away, and his tongue brushed the tears from her eyelashes, and she realized suddenly that she hadn't had her glasses on for quite a while.

"My…glasses?" she faltered.

"Above your head," he said with a smile. He sat up slowly, catching her wrists to pull her up with him. She was in a patch of light that allowed him a delicious view of creamy, hard-tipped breasts in blatant arousal.

"Oh, you're something else, Miss St. Clair," he said gently. He bent and touched his mouth to the very tip of one breast.

Her breath wouldn't come steadily. She looked down at his blond head. "I…we should…that is…"

He lifted his head. "Suppose in the morning we get married?"

"M-married?"

He nodded. "Married." He pulled up her bodice with obvious reluctance. Then he reached behind her, retrieved her glasses, and put them back on her.

"But…"

His knuckles brushed one perfect breast lazily, feeling it go hard again. "This isn't going to get better," he said. "By tomorrow we'll be in such a fever that nothing is going to keep us away from each other. I haven't experienced anything this powerful since I was about fifteen. And I'm damned sure you're feeling it for the first time."

"Yes, I know that, but we're strangers," she protested, trying to keep her head.

"We aren't going to be strangers for much longer," he said flatly. "My God, I want you," he ground out. "If you won't marry me, I'm getting the hell out of this hotel tonight, and on the next plane out of Veracruz. Because I can't bear to be around you without taking you. And I won't take you without marriage."

"But..."

"Am I so unmarriageable?" he burst out. "My God, I've had women propose to *me*! I'm not ugly, I'm well to do, I like dogs and cats, and I pay my bills on time. I'm in fairly decent health, I have friends...why in hell won't you marry me?"

"But it's only desire," she began.

"Stop trying to be logical," he said gruffly. "I'm not capable of logic when I'm aching like this. I want you. And you want me. For God's sake, put me out of my misery!"

"Would...would we have a divorce if...after we...if you..." she began.

"I'm getting older." He got to his feet and drew her up with him. "I travel a lot, you'd have to get used to that. But until now I've never had anyone of my own. I like you. I like being with you. And I think we'll set fires in bed. It's more than most people start out with. At least we aren't kids who believe in fairy tales like love. I'd rather have a woman who doesn't bore me than an infatuation that wears off."

"And if you fell in love with someone later?" she asked quietly, hearing her dreams die.

"I'll never love again," he said with equal quietness. "But if you do, I'll let you out." He took her hands in his. "Yes or no? I won't ask again."

"Yes," she said without hesitation. Harriett would faint. Nobody would believe it back home, that she'd found a man like this who wanted her. All the questions she'd meant to ask went right out of her mind.

He bent and kissed her—without passion and very tenderly. "My full name is Eric James van Meer. I was born in the Netherlands, although everyone calls it Holland, in a place called Utrecht. I lived there until I was in my teens, when I joined the service. The rest, you know, a little. Someday I'll tell you all of it. When I have to."

"That sounds ominous."

He put an arm around her. "It doesn't have a lot to do with us right now," he said. His arm tightened. "Do you want to be a virgin until tomorrow morning?"

Her lips parted. Her breath came wildly. Of course, she thought, and started to say it. But she couldn't. The words stuck in her throat. She thought of the long night, and her logical mind was booted out of its lofty position by a body that was in unholy torment.

"I want you so much," she said unsteadily.

"No more than I want you," he returned gruffly.

They were in the light of the hotel lobby now. He stopped, turning her toward him. His hands cupped her face and his eyes were dark and hot and full of anguish.

"I was raised a Catholic," he explained. "And in my religion, what I'm going to do to you tonight is a sin. Probably in your religion it is, too. But in the sight of God, for all our lives, I take you for my wife here, now. And tomorrow, in the sight of men, we make it right."

Tears stung her eyes as the words touched her heart. "And I take you for my husband, for better or worse, as long as I draw breath."

He bent and brushed his mouth tenderly over her wet eyes. "In Dutch, we call a married woman *Mevrouw*," he whispered.

"*Mevrouw*," she repeated.

"And darling," he added, smiling, "is *lieveling*."

"*Lieveling*," she repeated, smiling back.

"Upstairs," he said, turning her, "I'll teach you some more words. But you won't be able to repeat them in public." And he laughed at her expression.

CHAPTER FOUR

DUTCH'S ROOM WAS NOTHING like Dani's. It overlooked the bay, and its quiet elegance would have suited royalty. She watched him lock the door, and nervously went to stand on the balcony where she could see a lighted ship in port.

The wind blew her hair and her dress, and she felt like a voyager on the brink of a new discovery.

"One of the passenger ships," he remarked, nodding toward the brilliantly lighted vessel. "Beautiful, isn't she?"

"Yes. I don't know much about ships, but I like looking at them."

He lit a cigarette and smoked it quietly. "I used to sail," he said unexpectedly.

She turned, looking up at the stranger who, in less than twenty-four hours, would be her husband and her lover. "Did you?"

"I moved to Chicago about eight years ago," he said. "I have an apartment on the lake, and I had a sailboat. I got drunk one night and she turned over with me. I let her sink."

Her eyes narrowed uneasily as she stared up at him, and he stared back, unblinkingly.

"I'm not an alcoholic," he said gently. "I probably

sound like one to you, with these veiled references to the past. I don't drink often, but there are times when I get black moods. I won't drink around you. Ever."

It sounded as if he were willing to make any compromise, and something warm and soft blossomed inside her. She went close to him, her eyes trusting, quiet and deep. "I can make compromises, too," she said quietly. "I'll live anywhere you like."

He searched her eyes. "I don't mind readjusting."

"Yes, I know, but your work is in Chicago, I gather, or you wouldn't live there."

"My work is international," he said, and scowled. "I don't work out of Chicago. I live there because I have friends there."

"Women friends?" she blurted out.

He only smiled. He finished the cigarette, tossed it into an ashtray and drew her gently against him. "You're going to be the first woman I've been with this year," he murmured with a mocking smile. "Does that answer the question?"

She felt and looked shocked. "But…but don't you need…?" She couldn't find a delicate way to say it.

"I thought I was beyond all that, until you came along," he confessed. "I can't even remember the last time I felt this way about a woman."

"Are you sure you want to marry me?" she asked.

"Don't worry so," he told her, bending to kiss away the frown. "Yes, I want to marry you. I'll still want to marry you in the morning, too. That was no lie to get you in bed with me."

Part of her had thought that, and she lowered her eyes to his collar.

"Second thoughts?" he asked.

Her fingers toyed with the buttons on his shirt. "I'm afraid."

"Yes, I imagine so," he said matter-of-factly. "The first time was hard for me, too. I was nervous as a cat." He laughed.

"I can't imagine you being nervous," she said.

"It was forever ago. But I haven't forgotten. I'll go slowly." He bent and touched her mouth with his, very gently. "I just want you to remember two things. The first is that there are no set rules in this—it all depends on what pleases the people involved. Will you try to keep that in mind?"

She swallowed. "Yes."

"The second thing is that I'm not superhuman," he said softly. "Inevitably, there will come a moment when I lose control absolutely. Hopefully, I can bring you to that point before I reach it. But if not, I'll make it up to you afterward. Okay?"

"It all seems so mysterious," she whispered, as if even the night had ears.

"It won't by morning." His gaze went slowly over her, from head to toe and back up again, and his breathing began to change. "Rosebud," he muttered softly as he suddenly swung her up into his hard arms.

She relaxed a little and burrowed her face into his warm throat. He smelled of expensive cologne, and she loved the strength that made her seem so light in his embrace.

He laid her down on the bed gently. She expected him to start undressing himself or her immediately, and she lay there uneasily, a little frightened.

But he sat down beside her and laughed gently at the look on her face. "What are you expecting, I wonder. That I'll strip you and take you without preliminaries?"

Her eyes filmed. "I'm sorry...."

He touched her mouth with a hard finger. "Think about how it was on the beach, when I bent you back into the sand and kissed you, here." His fingers traveled down to her soft breasts. "And you threw back your head and moaned and begged me."

Her lips parted as she remembered vividly the sensations he'd aroused.

"That's how it's going to be now," he said, bending to her mouth. "Except that this time I'm not going to let you go."

His mouth opened hers with practiced ease, and his warm, callused hands were on her bare back, caressing it slowly and confidently, while all her inhibitions melted slowly away.

Seconds later the dress began to ease away from her body, and she felt his lips follow its downward movement. But she couldn't protest. The fires were burning again, and she moaned as his mouth covered her breasts, nipping at them with a tender pressure that was more arousing than frightening. His mouth followed as the dress merged with her tiny briefs and then was swept downward along with them. Shockingly, she felt his lips on her thighs, on the soft inner skin of her legs, and her body moved as the edge of his teeth followed the same path. Incredible, she thought through a fog of anguished desire, incredible that people could survive this kind of pleasure!

She wasn't even aware of what he was doing anymore; she was all sensation, all aching hunger. Her eyes were closed, her fists clenched beside her arched neck as his mouth searched her hips and her flat stomach. At the same time he was lazily divesting himself of his own clothing, making it so much a part of his seduction that she didn't even realize he'd done it until finally he slid alongside her and she felt him.

Her eyes flew open and went helplessly down the length of his body before she realized what she was doing. And then it was too late; she couldn't look away. He was glorious. Absolutely the most beautiful sight she'd ever seen, tanned all over without the slightest streak of white, as if he'd sunbathed in the nude all his life.

And meanwhile his hands touched her in a new intimate way. She started to draw away, but his mouth opened hers and his hands began a soft, tender rhythm, and soon she was weeping helplessly against his lips.

In seconds she was trembling and pleading with him. He moved, dragging his aching body into a sitting position against the headboard, his dark eyes glittering with frank desire. He lifted her over him and guided her, his body rigid with self-control, his face hard with it.

She gasped at the contact and her hands clenched on his shoulders as she found herself looking straight into his eyes.

"You do it," he told her huskily. "That way you can control the pain."

She started to argue, but she knew that it was becoming unbearable for him. She swallowed down her fear, closed her eyes, bit her lip and moved. She caught her breath and tried again.

"Help me, Eric," she begged, guiding his hands to her hips. "Please...oh!"

"It's bad, isn't it?" he ground out. "I'm sorry, I'm sorry...." His fingers contracted as his body began to fight his mind. The hunger was exploding in him. He began to tremble, his hands clenched. "Dani...!"

She opened her eyes at the new note in his voice and looked at him. The sight of his face took her mind off the pain. She watched him, fascinated. His eyes opened and found hers. Then his body seemed to take control away from his mind. His face changed, his breathing changed, the movements of his body intensified as she stared into his wild face. He arched and his face contorted, and all at once she realized what she was seeing and blushed wildly.

He was still for an instant, then he shuddered. His eyes opened slowly, looking into hers. His body still throbbed, his breathing unsteady and strained. His hands on her hips became caressing.

"I thought...you were dying," she whispered.

"I felt as if I were," he whispered back. His voice trembled, like his body, in the aftermath. His eyes searched her face. "You were watching me. Were you shocked?"

"Yes," she confessed, but she didn't look away.

"Was it bad?" he asked.

"Yes. Until I started watching you."

He brought her fully against him, still a part of him, and held her gently, with her face against his damp chest. "I think that was what pushed me over the edge," he murmured. "I saw you watching me and my head flew off."

"You looked as though you were being tortured to death."

"And you can't imagine pleasure so intense?" he chided her gently. He laughed, but it wasn't a taunting laugh. His hands caressed her back. "When I've rested for a few minutes I'm going to watch it happen to you."

"Will it?"

"Oh, yes. You just needed a few more seconds than I could give you. The second time," he added, easing her away from him, "always takes longer, for a man."

She looked into his eyes. "You're my lover now," she declared.

He looked down where they were still joined. Her eyes followed his and she blushed furiously.

"I'm still your lover," he told her. His hands pressed against her thighs, dragging her even closer, and all at once something happened that even her inexperienced body understood immediately.

He laughed softly. "Yes, you know what's going to happen now, don't you?" he growled. He shifted, easing her down onto the mattress as he loomed over her.

"Now," he said hotly, blazing with renewed passion. "Now watch what I'm going to do to you. Look!"

Her eyes dilated as she watched him. But the sensations were unexpected, and she cried out helplessly, her body lifting toward him as if it recognized its master.

"Shh," he hissed, smiling as her face began to contort. "Yes, you're going to feel it for me this time. I'm going to make you feel it, just as it happened to me. Yes, Dani, yes, yes...!"

She throbbed with a new rhythm. She moved and twisted and tried to throw him off, and tried to bring him back; she cried and pleaded and bit and whimpered and finally threw back her head and moaned so harshly that she sounded as if every bone in her body had snapped suddenly. And then it was all freefall. Bonelessness. Purple oblivion.

When her eyes opened again she was exhausted. He sat on the bed beside her with a warm, damp cloth in his hands, bathing her gently.

"Is it always like that for men?" she asked, needing to know.

He shook his head. "It's never been like that for me with anyone. The second time was even more intense. I cried out."

Tears touched her eyes as she looked up at him. "Thank you."

"Oh, God, don't," he implored her, bending to kiss her. Once he kissed her he couldn't seem to stop. He put the cloth aside and took her into his arms, holding her, touching her face, brushing his lips over every soft, flushed inch of her face with a touch that was more healing than passionate.

She trembled in his arms, and they tightened, and she gloried in the delicious warmth of his skin against hers, the feel of her soft breasts being gently crushed by his hard-muscled chest.

"You cried out, too," he said at her ear. "Just as you felt it. I had to cover your mouth with mine so that no one would hear."

"Even in my dreams it never happened like that," she confessed.

"I'm glad it happened with me," he told her, lifting his head. "Thank you for waiting for me."

She smiled slowly. "I'm glad I waited."

"I didn't use anything," he said then. "Do you want to see a doctor tomorrow, or do you want me to take care of it until we get back to the States? A wife I can handle, but not a baby. Not yet."

"Then, could you...?" She hesitated. "I'd rather see my own doctor."

"Okay." He bent and brushed his mouth over hers.

"Do you want children eventually?" she asked because it was important.

He brushed the hair away from her eyes. "Perhaps," he said finally. "Someday."

"Too much, too soon?" she murmured dryly.

"Getting used to a wife is enough for now," he said. He let his eyes wander slowly over her. "You have a beautiful body."

"So have you."

He kissed her softly. "We'd better get some sleep. And, sadly enough, I do mean sleep." He sighed as he rose, cloth in hand. "I'm not prepared for anything else until we go into town. Unless…there are other ways if you really want…"

She blushed wildly and changed the subject. "Where are we getting married?"

"In a little chapel down the street." He grinned. "They're open at ten o'clock. We'll be waiting on the doorstep."

"You aren't sorry?" she asked as he started into the bathroom.

He turned, his body open for her inspection, his face faintly smiling. He shook his head. "Are you?"

She shook her head, too. He laughed and went on into the bathroom. Minutes later she was curled up in his arms, both of them without a stitch on, the lights off and the sounds of the city at night purring in through the window.

"You can have one of my undershirts if you like," he said gently.

"I'd rather sleep like this, if it won't bother you," she murmured.

"I prefer it this way, too," he confessed. He drew her closer. "Breathing may be a little difficult, and I may die of a heart attack trying not to indulge myself a third time, but I prefer it like this. Good night, *lieveling*."

"Good night, Eric." She curled up against him with a trusting sigh and was surprised to find herself drifting off to sleep only seconds later.

CHAPTER FIVE

DANI WAS DREAMING. She felt as if she were floating, drifting, her body bare and fulfilled. She stretched, smiling, and a voice brought her awake.

"Don't struggle, darling," a male voice chuckled. "You'll make me drop you."

Her gray eyes flew open along with her mouth, and she realized that Dutch was carrying her into the bathroom, where a huge steaming bathtub waited.

"Don't you want a bath?" he murmured dryly.

"Oh, yes," she said sleepily. "I had planned on waking up before I got in the water." She curled into his chest, snuggled her face against his throat, and closed her eyes with a sigh. "But my pillow started moving."

He laughed, realizing with a start that he'd laughed more in the past two days than in the past ten years. He looked down at her creamy body, her full breasts pressed into the rippling muscle and feathery hair of his chest. She was vulnerable with him. Yet, he sensed that she was much like him in her independence, her wild spirit.

"Wake up or you'll drown," he said.

"I thought I already had, and gone to heaven," she replied, smiling against his throat. She wasn't even surprised to find herself with him. She seemed to have dreamed about him all night long.

"We have to get married," he said.

"Going to make an honest woman of me, hmm?" she teased, peeking up at him.

But he didn't smile. "You're already an honest woman. The first I've ever known. Hold on."

He eased her down into the warm silky water and then climbed in beside her. They soaped each other lazily, enjoying the different textures of their bodies, exploring openly.

"I feel like a child playing doctor," he told her with a wicked glance.

"It's old hat to you, I suppose," she said, watching her hands move on his muscular chest, "but I've never touched a man like this. It's all very new to me just now."

He moved her hands down, watching the flush on her face and the panic in her yes. "All right," he said gently as she resisted. "You're still shy with me. I won't insist."

"Old maids have lots of hang-ups," she said quietly.

"I'll get rid of yours before the week's out," he promised. "Want some more soap?"

She let him lather her back. Something was niggling at the back of her mind, and she glanced at him worriedly as he rinsed her.

"What is it?" he asked gently.

"Something you said last night. About…about precautions."

"There's no problem," he said carelessly. "I'll stop by a drugstore. When we get back to the States, if you'd rather not risk the pill, there's some minor surgery a man can have—"

Her eyes were horrified. The drawn look on her face stopped him in mid-sentence.

"You don't ever want children, do you?" she asked, choking on the words.

He looked hunted. "Hell," he bit off. Why had she brought up the subject! He watched her scramble out of the tub and fumble a towel around herself.

"We aren't even married yet, and you're harping about a family," he burst out, rising to his feet, his handsome face hard with anger. "What the hell do we need kids for? They're a permanent tie. A bond."

"Isn't marriage?" she asked huskily.

"Of course," he grumbled, grabbing up a towel. "But not like kids."

"You never answered me," she said quietly. "You don't ever want them, do you?"

"No," he said flatly, tired of the pretense, hating the memories the discussion was bringing back. "Not ever."

She turned and walked back into the bedroom. She didn't know him at all. And the first thing she was going to do was cut her losses. She'd go back to her room and forget him. How could she expect to live all her life without a child? What kind of man was he?

Tears blinded her. She got as far as the bed and sat down, feeling empty and sick and alone. She'd dreamed of children. Since she was eighteen she'd haunted baby shops, quietly touching the little crocheted things and imagining her own baby in her arms. She had no one of her own, but a baby would be part of her. The tears rippled down her cheeks in silvery streams, and she closed her eyes.

The man at the bathroom door, watching her, saw them, and something painful exploded inside him. She was snaring him, he thought furiously. Swallowing him up whole with her unexpected vulnerabilities. With a muffled curse he threw the towel aside and went to the bed.

He caught her by the waist, lowering her back against the rumpled covers so quickly that she gasped.

"Eric!" she called uncertainly.

His mouth covered hers, but there was none of the violence she'd expected. His lips played with hers, so gentle that she barely felt them, while his hands removed the towel and whispered over her body until she trembled.

"Draw your legs up," he breathed. He helped her, positioning his body so that they were curled together, his knees beside her, his chest on hers, his hips against her hips and thighs.

She looked up, fascinated at the look in his dark eyes.

His big, warm hands cupped her face. "Open your mouth now," he whispered, bending, "and kiss me the way I taught you last night."

She obeyed him, liking the way her tongue tangled softly with his, liking the intimacy of this slow, tender kissing.

His knuckles brushed over her breasts, making their tips hard and sensitive, and when she gasped, his mouth took advantage of it to make the kiss even deeper. His hands searched over her, sliding under her hips to lift her to the slow descent of his body.

She felt his fingers contract on her thighs and caught her breath at their steely strength. And still he kissed her, whispery contacts that drained her of will, that made her weak. Her body trembled as he explored it with even more intimacy than the night before, each new touch intensifying her hunger for him.

He paused, hesitated, his lips touching hers. His eyes opened, holding hers, and his body lowered.

She caught her breath at the intensity of feeling she knew as he let her experience the very texture of his body with the slowness of his movement.

"Now," he said, closing his eyes, "we really make love for the first time."

She didn't understand at first. And then it began to make sense. He was so tender, so exquisitely gentle, that every movement seemed to stroke a nerve of pleasure. She clung to him, matching his tenderness, trying to give him back the beauty he was giving her. Her eyes fluttered closed and her fingers tangled in his cool blond hair, her body trembling under the expert movements of his. As the pleasure built slowly she began to writhe helplessly. And as fulfillment came closer, she wondered if she was going to survive it.

"Eric?" she whimpered against his mouth.

His own body was trembling, too. "*Lieveling,*" he said huskily. "*Mijn lieveling, mijn vrouw!*"

The hands holding her clenched, and he rocked with her, smooth, tender movements that were exquisitely soft. He whispered to her in Dutch, words that she couldn't understand, but they were breathlessly tender.

She kissed his tanned cheek, his mouth, his chin, and he lifted his head for an instant, his dark eyes glazed, his lips parted.

"Yes," he told her. "Yes, like that."

He closed his eyes and let her kiss him, savoring the softness of her mouth on his eyes, his cheeks, his straight nose, his lips.

She moved, trembling with need, letting him feel her body as she drew it with smooth sweetness to either side.

His eyes opened again, reading the intensity of hunger in hers.

"Yes," he said. "Yes, now it happens. Now…"

His voice didn't change, but his breathing did. He looked down at her, lengthening his movements, deepening them, so that although the tenderness remained, the urgency grew.

Something was happening to her that she didn't understand. Terrifying tension, hands buffeting her, a blazing tide of warmth that speared through her like tiny needles. Her mouth opened because she could no longer breathe. Her body began to shudder helplessly, tiny little shudders that matched the tenderness that was devouring her.

"I'm…afraid…" she managed, and her fingers clenched at his back as she felt her body beginning to contract.

"Hush," he said softly. His movements deepened, and still he watched. "Yes, feel it. Feel it now. There's nothing to be…afraid of, *lieveling*. No, don't turn away, let me see you…."

He turned her head back to him, and his face blurred. She thought he smiled, but she was all bursting fireworks, a flare lighting up the night sky. She felt gentle explosions all through her body, and for a moment her heart stopped, her breathing stopped. And then she cried, because it had been so beautiful, and so brief.

Even as the tears came, she felt his own body go rigid, heard the tender, surprised exclamation at her ear, and then her name….

He didn't move for a long time. Neither did she. She felt incapable of movement. What had happened surprised her. He'd said they wouldn't make love again until they got married, so why had he done it? And why that way? So tenderly, so gently, as if he cared about her.

Experimentally, her hands moved on the damp muscles of his shoulders.

He lifted his head and searched her eyes slowly. He touched her face with gentle fingers. "In my life there was never such a tender loving before," he said. "I didn't know that men and women were capable of it." He brushed away the tears. "I hurt you?" he asked.

"No." She swallowed. "It was…so beautiful," she faltered.

"Yes. For me, too." He drew away from her with exquisite slowness, watching her. He sighed heavily, and frowned. After a minute he turned back to the bathroom. "We'd better get dressed."

She got up, too, a little shaky and puzzled by his odd

behavior. He'd meant to comfort her, she was certain of it. But the comfort had gotten out of hand. And the way he'd loved her...

As she dressed she wondered if she was doing the right thing, marrying a total stranger. Then he came out of the bathroom, wearing nothing except his slacks, his blond hair neatly combed, his face slowly curving into a smile. And she knew that she'd die to wear his ring, babies or no babies. She smiled back.

They were married in a small chapel, with people all around them who spoke little English. The minister beamed at them when it was over, inviting the new husband to kiss his bride.

Dutch bent and brushed his mouth softly against hers, smiling at his own folly. Well, it was done now. And it wouldn't be so bad, he told himself as he studied her radiant young face. She could wait for him at home, and they'd see each other whenever he was there. It might even be good that way. No routine to bore him. She could go on with her life, and there would be no ties. He frowned for a minute as he thought of what had happened this morning, then he shook off the instant fear of consequences. Surely to God, he hadn't made her pregnant. He'd just have to be careful from now on. No more lapses. The thought of a child terrified him. That would make a tie he couldn't break.

Dani saw that frown, and worried about it. She wondered why he'd really married her, when he seemed the kind of man who was self-sufficient and didn't need anyone else.

"You aren't sorry?" she asked finally when they were walking back to the hotel.

He stopped, lifted his blond head and smiled, a little puzzled. "What?"

"Sorry that you married me," she continued. She searched his eyes nervously. "You've been so quiet. I know I'm not much to look at, and we don't know each other at all. I…we can always get a divorce," she finished miserably.

"I'm quiet because I have a logistical problem to work out," he said then. "Not because I'm regretting that we got married. When you know me better, you'll learn that I never do things unless I want to. I can't be pushed or coerced." He reached out and curled her fingers into his. "I like being with you," he said, meeting her eyes. "Like this, and in bed. We're both old enough to want someone to be with."

"Yes," she confessed. Tears stung her eyes and she lowered her lids before he could read her thoughts. "I never thought it would happen to me," she added. "I thought I'd be alone all my life."

"So did I." He smoothed his fingers across the back of her hand. She had pretty hands, he mused. "Do you play anything?" he asked unexpectedly.

She laughed. "The piano. Badly."

"I like piano. I play a little, too." He slid his fingers in between hers, feeling oddly possessive as he saw the bright little gold band that encircled her ring finger. "A wedding ring suits you. Feel better now about what we did last night?" he asked with a slow smile, as if he understood her uneasiness about intimacy without marriage.

"I'm old-fashioned." She sighed miserably.

"You don't have to apologize for it, not to me." His eyes gleamed suddenly as he looked at her. Short brown hair, creamy, oval face, wide gray eyes. "I liked being the first."

There was a deep, possessive note in his voice that surprised her. She smiled slowly. Her fingers squeezed his, and she looked into his eyes for so long that she flushed.

"This morning," he said softly, holding her eyes, "was my first time. I didn't realize that I was capable of tenderness. I let go with you in a way I never could before with a woman. I trusted you."

Her face was bright red, but she didn't look away. "I...trusted you." She let her eyes fall to his hard mouth, remembering with a surge of desire how it felt on her body. "One of my friends got married two years ago. She said her husband shocked her speechless on her wedding night, and made fun of her...."

His fingers contracted. "I think it would kill something in you to have a man treat you so," he remarked.

Her eyes came up, stunned at the way he understood.

He nodded. "Yes. It's that way with me, too. I don't like ridicule."

Her expression said more than she wanted it to, and she knew that he could read the worshipful look in her eyes. But she didn't care. He was her whole world.

His breath caught at that look. It bothered him, and he let go of her hand. "Don't ever try to build a wall around me," he said unexpectedly, staring at her. "I'll stay with you only as long as the doors remain open."

"I knew that the first time I saw you," she said quietly. "No ties. No strings. I won't try to possess you."

He started walking again. He wondered what she was going to do when she knew the truth about him. He glanced up, searching her face quietly. She was so damned trusting. She probably thought he was in the army reserves or something. He almost laughed. Well, she'd just have to get used to it, he told himself, because he didn't know how to change.

After they'd changed their status at the hotel desk and switched everything to his room they went downstairs for lunch. Dani picked at her food, wondering at the change in Eric. Something was on his mind, but she didn't know him well enough to ask what it was. She glanced at him with a slow-dawning mischief in her eyes. Well, she couldn't dig it out of him, but she could help him forget it.

"Hey," she called.

He glanced up, cocking an eyebrow.

"I have this great idea for dessert," she murmured, making her first attempt at being a siren.

Both eyebrows went up. "You do?"

She dropped her eyes to his throat. "I could smear whipped cream all over myself…"

"Honey tastes better."

She blushed furiously, and he laughed. He leaned forward, moving his plate aside, and lifted her fingers to his mouth.

"Do you want me?" he asked bluntly, smiling at her averted face.

"Yes," she confessed.

"Then say so. You don't have to play games with me." He got up, helped her up, and paid the check. They were back in the hotel room before he spoke again.

He backed her up against the door and pinned her there with just the threat of his body. "You can have me anytime," he said quietly. "All you have to do is tell me. That's what marriage should be. Not some kind of power game."

Her eyes narrowed. "I don't understand."

He brushed the hair away from her face and curled it behind her ear. "Bargaining, with sex as the prize."

"I'd never do that," she said. She watched him, amazed that this handsome man was actually married to her. "You were worried about something. I wanted to...to give you peace."

He seemed to freeze. His lips parted on a hard breath. "I constantly misread you, don't I?" He touched her throat with the lightest touch of his fingers and lifted his eyes to hers. "Do you want me?"

"I'll want you on my deathbed," she said shakily.

He bent and kissed her softly, tenderly. "I'm more grateful than I can tell you, for such a sweet offer. But I don't think you can take me again today, not without considerable discomfort." He lifted his head. "Can you?"

She bit her lower lip. "Well..."

"Can you?"

She dropped her eyes to his chest. "Oh, shoot!" she mumbled. "No."

He laughed softly and drew her into his arms, rocking her slowly. "That's why I was so gentle this morning," he murmured into her ear, lying a little. He didn't want to admit that she'd been the victor in that tender battle.

"Oh." That was vaguely disappointing, she mused. She slid her arms around him with a sigh, delighting in his strength, the corded power of his warm hard body. "It isn't like this in books," she concluded. She smiled as her eyes closed. "Women always can, and they never have discomfort, and—"

"Life is very different," he said. He smoothed her hair. "We'll wait a day or so, until you recuperate. Then," he added, tilting her face up to his amused eyes, "I'll teach you some more subtle forms of sensual torture."

She laughed shyly. "Will you?"

He took a deep breath. "I've never known anyone like you," he said, the words reluctant. He drew her up on her tiptoes and kissed her very softly. "Feel what's happening already?"

"Yes," she answered him.

"We'd better cool it, if you don't mind. I hate cold showers."

She laughed. "You're terrific." She sighed.

"So are you. Get on a bathing suit and let's go swim."

She started into the bathroom, met his mocking eyes, and stuck out her chin. "You're my husband," she said aloud, to remind both of them.

"Yes, I was wondering if you might remember that."
He chuckled.

She undressed and he watched, his eyes quiet and full
of memories. When she started to pull on the bathing
suit he moved in front of her and stayed her hands.

"Not yet," he said quietly.

She looked up, hungry for him, and watched as he
studied her body and saw for himself just how much she
wanted him.

"How is it, for a woman?" he asked suddenly, and
sounded genuinely curious. "How do you feel when
you want me like this?"

"It's frightening, a little," she told him. "I get shaky
and weak and I can't quite control myself. I ache…"

"Does this…help the ache?" he asked as he bent to
her breasts.

She moaned. It was impossible not to, when she felt
the warm moistness of his lips eating her. She didn't
have a mind left after the first two seconds. She was
hardly aware that he was lifting her onto the bed.

He made a meal of her body, tasting, touching, looking at it, broad daylight streaming in the windows, while
she gloried in the luxury of being married and enjoyed
his pleasure in her.

"I love looking at your body," he said quietly, sitting
beside her. His hands swept up and down, lingering on
her soft curves. "I love touching it. Tasting it. I've never
seen anything half so lovely."

"My husband," she whispered.

He looked up. "My wife."

Her body ached, and she knew he must feel the same longing she did. Her eyes asked a question, but he slowly shook his head.

"I won't do that to you," he said curtly. "Not ever will I take my pleasure and not give a thought to yours."

She ground her teeth together to stop the tears.

"And it isn't pity," he said, glaring at the look in her eyes. "I do nothing out of pity, least of all marry because of it, so you can stop looking at me that way. I want you and I'm getting irritable because I can't have you. So suppose you put on the bathing suit and I'll go have that damned cold shower and we'll swim."

He got up and she lay there, watching him as he discarded his clothing. Her lips parted as the last of the clothing came off, and she saw the urgency of his desire.

His body trembled as he looked at her, and she wanted to cry because of the torment she saw in his face.

"You said once…that there are…other ways," she ventured to ask. "Are there?"

His face hardened; his eyes glittered wildly. "Yes."

She held out her arms, her body throbbing, her blood running like a river in flood as she sensed that violence of his hunger. He hesitated only for a second before he came down beside her.

THE DAYS PASSED WITH miserable speed. They did everything together. They swam and talked, although always about general things rather than personal ones; they danced and sampled new delicacies at the dinner table. And at night he loved her. Sometimes in the early morning. Once on the bathroom floor because the strength of their desire hadn't left them time to get to bed. Sometimes he remembered precautions, but mostly he didn't, because his desire matched her own. She walked around in a sensual haze that blinded her to the future. But eventually, the day came when they had to look past Veracruz. It came suddenly, and too soon.

CHAPTER SIX

THE LAST DAY OF THEIR STAY DAWNED unwelcomed, and Dani packed with a long face. She'd changed her plans so she could be with Dutch for his whole vacation, but at the end of the week he told her that he had a job waiting and couldn't spare any more time. She stared at him across the room as he got his own clothing together, wondering how dangerous his line of work was. A soldier, he'd said. Did that mean he was in the reserves? Probably, she told herself. That was why he wouldn't mind moving to Greenville.

She'd thought about that a lot, about picking up stakes and moving to Chicago. It wouldn't matter, although she'd miss Harriett and her friends from the bookstore. She'd have followed him anywhere. When she realized how little time they'd had together, she could hardly believe that so much had happened so quickly. It seemed like a lifetime ago that the taciturn blond giant had dropped down beside her on the airplane. And now he was her husband. Her husband, about whom she knew so little.

He seemed to feel her puzzled frown, and turned. Then he smiled at her. "Ready?" he asked as he picked up his duffel bag.

"Ready," she agreed. She drew her two bags up to where his were sitting by the door.

He glared at the smaller one and sighed. "You and your books." He chuckled softly down at her. "Well, at least now you know what they're all about, don't you?" he added.

She cleared her throat, reddening as she recalled the long, sweet nights. "Oh, yes, indeed I do, Mr. van Meer," she agreed fervently.

"No regrets, Dani?" he asked softly.

She shook her head. "Not if this were the last day of my life," she said. "And you?"

"I'm only sorry we met so late in life," he replied, searching her face. "I'm glad we found each other." He checked his watch. It was an expensive one, with dials and numbers that meant nothing to Dani. "We'd better rush or we'll miss our flight."

Dutch had made the reservation for the two of them and they had adjoining seats. She sat beside him with her heart in her throat, smiling at him with hopeless hero worship. He was so handsome. And hers. Harriett really wasn't going to believe this.

He glanced down at her, still amazed that he had a wife. J.D. and Gabby would be shocked, he thought. And Apollo and First Shirt, Semson and Drago and Laremos would never let him hear the end of it. Dutch, married. It was incredible, even to him. But it felt nice.

It was Gabby's influence, probably, he admitted to himself. He'd heard so much about her from J.D. even before he'd met her that some of his old prejudices against women had slackened. Not much, but a little. Gabby had trekked through a commando-infested jungle for J.D. and even risked her own life to save him from a bullet. He glanced again at his companion with narrowed dark eyes. Would she do that for him? Did she really possess the fiery spirit he sensed beneath her timid manners? And how was she going to react when she learned the truth about him? That hadn't bothered him for the past few days, but it bothered him now. A lot. His gaze went to the bag of romance novels tucked under her pretty feet. Fluff, he thought contemptuously, and a smile touched his firm mouth as he thought how nearly like fiction some of his exploits might seem to the woman beside him.

Dani saw him starting at her books and shifted uncomfortably in her seat. "Well, we can't all conquer the Amazon," she muttered.

His eyebrows shot up. "What?" He laughed.

"You were giving my books contemptuous glares," she said. "And if you're thinking it's all mushy nonsense, you might be surprised." She fished down and held up a book with a cover that featured a man armed with an automatic weapon. There was a jungle setting behind him and a woman beside him.

Dutch blinked. Automatically, his hand reached for the book and he scowled as he flipped through it and glanced over the blurb on the back of the book jacket. The novel was about two photojournalists, trapped together in a Central American country during a revolution.

"Not what you expected?" she asked.

He lifted his eyes and studied her. "No."

She took the book from his hand and stuffed it back in her sack. "Most of us are armchair adventurers at heart, you know." She sighed. "Woman as well as men. You'd be amazed at how many of my customers fantasize about being caught up in a revolution somewhere."

His face hardened. He gave her a look that sent shivers through her.

"Dani, have you ever watched anyone die?" he asked bluntly.

She faltered, shocked by the icy challenge in his deep voice.

"No, of course not," she said.

"Then don't be too eager to stick your nose in some other country's military coups. It isn't pretty." He touched his pocket, reaching for a cigarette, then glanced up and noticed that the No Smoking sign was still lit as the plane climbed to gain more altitude. Then he also remembered that he'd chosen a seat in the no-smoking section to be near Dani, who didn't smoke. He said something rough under his breath.

"Have you?" she asked unexpectedly. "Stuck your nose in somebody's military coups?" she added when he lifted an eyebrow.

"That would hardly concern you," he said, softening the words with a smile.

He wasn't exactly rude, but she turned quickly back to the window in silence. She felt uneasy, and tried to banish the feeling. He was her husband now. She'd have to learn not to ruffle him. She leaned back, closed her eyes and convinced herself that she was worrying need-lessly. Surely there were no dark secrets in his past.

Someone in the seat ahead of them rang for the stew-ardess, and Dani closed her eyes, thinking what a long flight this was going to be. They'd planned to stop over in Greenville and then decide who would move and who wouldn't. He wanted to see where she lived, he'd said, to meet her friend Harriett and see the little book-shop she owned. She'd been flattered by his interest.

She had just closed her eyes when she heard a loud gasp and then a cry from nearby. Her eyes opened to see the stewardess being held roughly by a man in brown slacks and an open-necked white shirt. He had a foreign look, and his eyes were glazed with violence. At the stewardess's neck he was holding a hypodermic sy-ringe. Another man who had been sitting with him got calmly to his feet, walked around the man with the sy-ringe and went into the cockpit.

There was a loud yell and the copilot appeared, took one look at what was happening and seemed to go white.

"Yes, he's telling the truth, as near as I can tell," the copilot called into the cockpit.

There was a buzz of conversation that was unintelli-gible, then the captain's voice came over the loud-speaker and Dutch stiffened, his dark gaze going slowly over the man with the syringe.

"Ladies and gentlemen, this is Captain Hall." The deep voice was deceptively calm. "The plane is being diverted to Cuba. Please keep calm, remain in your seats and do exactly as you're told. Thank you."

The unarmed man came out of the cockpit, twitching his thick mustache, and fumbled around with the intercom until he figured it out.

"We wish no one to be harmed," he said. "The syringe my friend is holding to the neck of this lovely young lady is filled with hydrochloric acid." Shocked murmurs went through the crowd, especially when the shorter, bald man took the syringe to one side and deliberately let one drop fall on the fabric of the seat. It smoldered and gave a vivid impression of the impact it would have on the stewardess's neck. "So for the young lady's sake, please keep calm," he continued. "We will harm you only if you make it necessary."

He hung up the intercom and went back into the cockpit. The man with the syringe tugged the petite blond stewardess along with him, ignoring the passengers. Apparently, he thought the threat of the syringe was enough to prevent any interference.

And it seemed he was right. The other passengers murmured uneasily among themselves.

"Professionals," Dutch said quietly. "They must want to get out of the country pretty badly."

Dani eyed him uncomfortably. "Who are they, do you think?"

"No idea," he said.

"They wouldn't really use that acid on her?" she asked, her voice soft with astonishment.

He turned and looked down at her, into gray eyes more innocent than any he'd ever seen. He frowned. "My God, of course they'd use it!"

Her oval face paled. She looked past him to where one of the men was barely visible, his arm still around the stewardess.

"Can't the captain do something?" she said then.

"Sure." He leaned back in his seat and closed his eyes, clasping his lean, tough hands over his stomach. "He can do exactly what they tell him until they get off the plane. All they want is a free ride. Once they've had it, they'll leave."

She gnawed on her lower lip. "Aren't you worried?" she asked.

"They aren't holding the syringe to my neck."

His indifference shocked her. She was terrified for the stewardess. Horrified, she forced her eyes back to her lap. For God's sake, what kind of man had she married?

He closed his eyes again, ignoring her contemptuous stare. He regretted the need to shock her, but he needed time to think, and he couldn't do it if she was talking. Now he had sufficient quiet to put together a plan. They wouldn't hurt the girl if their demands were met. But glitches sometimes happened. In case one developed, he had to think of a way out. There were two men, but only one was armed. And obviously, they hadn't been able to get anything metallic through the sensors. That was good. They might have a plastic knife or two between them, or a pocket knife like the one Dutch was carrying—a knife that had special uses. His was balanced and excellent for throwing. And he had few equals with a knife. He smiled.

Dani glanced at Dutch with mingled hurt and curiosity and rage. He was asleep, for heaven's sake! In the middle of a hijacking, he was asleep! She sighed angrily. Well, what did she expect him to do? Leap up from the seat like one of the heroes in the books she read and deliver them all from the terrorists? Fat chance!

A hijacking. She sighed, nervously fingering her purse. She wondered how the poor stewardess felt. The woman was doing her best to stay calm, but it couldn't have been easy. Knowing what was in that syringe, and how quickly it would work if she were injected with it...Dani shuddered at just the thought. In her innocence she'd never believed that there were such fiendish people sharing the world with her.

Dutch opened one eye and closed it again. Dani gave him an exasperated look and clasped her hands to still their trembling. The taller of the hijackers had something in his hand that looked suspiciously like a grenade, and as the plane grew closer to Cuba, he began to pace nervously.

The shorter hijacker, the bald one who was holding the stewardess prisoner, moved into view. He forced the stewardess into the front seat, which was just one ahead of Dutch and Dani, and sat beside her, with the syringe still at her throat.

He was tiring, Dutch mused. And the other one was getting a little panicky. His dark eyes narrowed thoughtfully. He'd bet his life that the grenade was plastic. How else could they have cleared airport security? One of the magazines on covert operations ran advertisements for the fakes—they were dirt cheap and, at a distance, realistic enough to fool a civilian. Which Dutch wasn't.

He'd wait until the plane landed in Cuba. If they were granted asylum, fine. If not, he was going to put a monkey wrench into their act. He owed it to Dani, sitting so quiet and disillusioned beside him. She still believed in heroes, although God alone knew what she thought of him right now.

When the plane landed in Havana the shorter man stayed beside the stewardess while the taller one went into the cockpit. He stayed there only a few minutes, and then burst out the small doorway with wild eyes, cursing violently.

"What is it? What is it!" the smaller man demanded.

"They will not let us disembark! They will not give us asylum!" the taller man cried. He looked around wildly, clasping the forgotten grenade in his hands and ignoring the horrified looks and cries of the passengers. "What shall we do? They will give us fuel but not asylum. What shall we do? We cannot go back to Mexico!"

"*Cuidado!*" the older man cautioned sharply. "We will go to Miami. Then we will seek asylum from our backers overseas," he said. "Tell them to fly to Miami."

Now, that was interesting, Dutch thought as he watched the taller man hesitate and then go back into the cockpit. He had a hunch that the gentlemen with the stage props were Central American natives. But obviously they had no wish to be connected with any of the Central American countries. And that talk of comrades overseas sounded very familiar. As almost everyone knew, there were foreign interests at work all over Central America.

The taller man was back in a minute. "They are turning toward Miami," he told his companion.

"*Bueno!*" The short man sounded relieved. "Come."

He forced the stewardess to her feet and dragged her along with him as he urged the tall man toward the cockpit. "We will explain the demands the pilot is to present to the American authorities," the short one murmured.

Dutch's eyes opened. "How much courage do you have, Mrs. van Meer?" he asked Dani without turning his head. His voice was low enough that only she could hear it.

She tensed. What in the world did he mean? "I'm no coward," she managed.

"What I have in mind could get you killed."

Her heart leaped. "The stewardess!"

He looked down at her. His eyes were dark and quiet and his face was like so much granite. "That will depend on you. When we approach that airport I want you to distract the man with the syringe. Just distract him. Force him to move that syringe for just a fraction of a second."

"Why do anything?" she asked softly. "You said that they'd leave—"

"Because they're desperate now," he said quietly. "And I have no doubt whatsoever that one of their demands is going to be for automatic weapons. Once they have those, we've lost any chance of escape."

"The authorities won't give them weapons," she said.

"Once they've used that acid on a couple of people they will," he said.

She shuddered again. She could taste her own fear,

but Dutch seemed oddly confident. He also seemed to know what he was doing. She looked up into his eyes with returning faith. No, she told herself, she'd been reading him wrong. All that time he'd been quiet, he'd been thinking. And now she trusted him instinctively.

"You could be killed," he repeated, hating the words even as he said them. How could he put her in danger? But how could he not take the chance? "There's a risk; I won't minimize it."

She sighed. "Nobody would miss me, except maybe you and Harriett," she said dryly.

He felt odd. She didn't say it in a self-pitying way. It was just a simple statement of fact. Nobody gave a damn. He knew how that felt himself, because outside the group nobody cared about him, either. Except for Dani. And he cared about her, too. He was suddenly vulnerable because of her, he realized.

She looked up at him with wide gray eyes that had seen too little living to be closed forever.

"There's a chance I could manage it alone," he began slowly.

"I'm not afraid," she said. "Well, that is, I am afraid, but I'll do whatever you tell me to."

So Gabby wasn't a freak after all, he told himself, gratified to find Dani so much like his best friend's wife. This little dove had teeth, just as he'd suspected.

He smiled faintly. "Okay, tiger. Here's what I want you to do…."

She went over it again and again in her mind in the minutes that followed. She chewed her lower lip until it was sore, and then chewed it some more. She had to get it right the first time. The poor stewardess wouldn't have a second chance. If they failed—and she still didn't realize how Dutch was going to get to that man in time—the stewardess would die.

She agonized over it until the captain announced that the plane was on its approach to Miami. He cautioned the passengers to stay calm and not panic, and to stay in their seats once the plane was on the ground. He sounded as strained as Dani felt. That hand grenade was the most terrifying part of all, and she wondered how Dutch was going to prevent the second man from throwing it.

The plane circled the airport and went down, landing roughly this time, bumping around as it went toward the terminal. Dani got her first glimpse of Miami and thought ironically that she sure was getting to see a lot of the world!

As soon as the plane came to a halt, Dutch touched her arm and looked down at her. Dani closed her eyes on a brief prayer.

The man with the syringe had just moved back into the cabin. He looked taut and nervous as well. The stewardess looked as though she'd given up all hope of living and had resigned herself to the horror of the acid. Her eyes were blank.

"Uh, *señor...*?" Dani called, getting halfway out of her seat.

The short man jumped at the sound of her voice and his arm tightened around the stewardess. "What you want?" he growled.

"I…oh, please…" Dani clutched the back of the seat and her gray eyes widened as she fought to make the words come out. "I have to go…to the rest room, please…"

The short man cursed. He called something in another language to the man in the cockpit, who looked out, angrily.

"I have to!" Dani pleaded, looking and sounding convincing.

The tall man muttered something and the short one laughed curtly. "All right," he said after a minute, during which Dani aged five years. "Come on, then."

She slipped over Dutch, and while she was moving, his hand went slowly to his inside jacket pocket.

Dani moved into the aisle and started carefully toward the rest room on the other side of the man with the syringe. Two more steps, she told herself. Her heart pounded, and she kept her eyes cast downward in case the man saw the terror in them and reacted too quickly. One more step. Please don't fail me, she said silently to Dutch. This is insane, I'm only twenty-six, I don't want to die, I've only just gotten married!

One more step. And she stopped and swayed, putting a hand to her temple. "I'm so sick!" And it was almost the truth. She deliberately let herself fall toward him.

It was enough. It was enough. He instinctively moved to catch her, and at that instant Dutch threw the knife. The syringe went to the floor as the hijacker caught his middle. Dutch was out of his seat in a heartbeat. It was 'Nam all over again. Angola. Rhodesia. He ignored

Dani, who was watching with incredulous eyes, tore the stewardess out of the hijacker's helpless grasp, threw her into a seat and kicked the hypodermic out of the way. He was through the cockpit door seconds after he'd thrown the knife, ignoring the groaning bald man on the floor as he went for the taller man.

"I will throw it, señor!" the man threatened, and grasped the firing pin of the grenade.

"Go ahead," Dutch said, and kept going. With two movements of his hands, so quick that the pilot didn't even see them, the hijacker went down with the grenade in his hand.

"He's pulled the pin!" the young copilot yelled, and there was pandemonium in the airplane.

"For God's sake," Dutch growled, retrieving it, "what are you afraid of, flying bits of plastic?" And he tossed the cheap imitation into the pilot's lap.

The copilot started to dive for it, but the pilot, a man in his late forties, just laughed. He turned toward Dutch and grinned.

"I should have realized why he was so nervous."

The copilot was still gaping. "It's a fake!"

"Keep it for a souvenir." The pilot sighed, tossing it to his colleague. "How's Lainie?"

"If you mean the stewardess, she's okay," Dutch said. "But his buddy isn't. You'd better get a doctor out here."

"Right away. Hey. Thanks," the pilot said with a quiet smile.

Dutch shrugged. "Pure self-interest," he said. "He was holding up my coffee."

"I'll buy you a cup when we get out of here," the captain offered.

Dutch grinned. "Take you up on that."

He left the cockpit. "It wasn't a live grenade," he called, the authority in his voice pacifying the nervous passengers. "It's all over, just sit quietly."

Dani was sitting on the floor, staring horrified at the groaning man with the knife in his stomach while she tried to deal with what was happening. She looked up at the stranger she'd married without even recognizing him. Who was he?

Dutch was sorry she'd had to see it, but there was no other way to do it. He bent and caught her by the arms and pulled her up gently.

"He'll be okay," he said. "No sweat. Let's get off this thing." He pulled her toward the door. Two other flight attendants came rushing from the back of the plane, embracing the stewardess, apologizing for not being able to help.

"It's okay," the little blond said shakily. "I'm fine."

She turned to Dutch, all blue eyes and gratitude. "Thank you. Thank you both!"

"All in a day's work," Dutch said carelessly. "How about getting this door open? That man needs a medic."

The groaning man got their attention. One of the flight attendants bent over him, and the copilot was just frog-marching the second terrorist, whose hands were belted together behind him, into the service compartment.

"Wait and I'll show you to the office," the captain

called to Dutch. "We'll need to speak to the police, I'm sure."

"Okay," Dutch told him. He propelled Dani, who was still half shocked, down the stairs with him, out into the darkness. "Oh," he said, turning and addressing the male flight attendant, "would you please get the lady's books and purse out of seat 7B and bring them to the office?"

"Be glad to, sir," came the reply.

Dani was still shocked, but her mind registered what he'd just said. In the middle of all the furor he'd remembered her blessed books. She looked up at him uncomprehendingly, her eyes wide and frightened and uncertain and still bearing traces of sick terror.

"I had to," he said quietly as he recognized the look. "I couldn't have reached him in time."

"Yes, I—I realize that. I've just never seen anybody…like that."

"You were superb," he said. "I can think of only one other woman who would have kept her head so well."

She wondered whom he meant, but there were more immediate questions. "What…what you did," she faltered as they waited for the captain. "You said you were a soldier."

He turned her gently and held her in front of him, holding her wary gaze. "I am. But not the kind you're thinking of. I make my living as a professional soldier. I hire out to the highest bidder," he told her bluntly, without pulling his punches, and watched the horror that filled her face. He hadn't realized how devastated she was going to be, or how he might feel when he saw the horror in her innocent face. Her reaction surprised him. It irritated him. What had she expected, for God's sake, a clerk?

"A mercenary," she said in a choked tone.

"Yes," he replied, his whole stance challenging.

But she didn't say anything more. She couldn't. Her dreams were lying around her feet, and she hurt all the way to her soul. This news was much more devastating than what she'd seen on the plane. She didn't lift her eyes again; she didn't speak. Seconds later the pilot, co-pilot and stewardess who'd been held prisoner joined them, and they went to the airport office. Dani walked apart from Dutch, not touching him. He noticed that, and his face was grim when they got into the building.

Minutes later they were sitting in a small office, going over and over what had happened for the airport security people and three men who looked very much like federal officers. It didn't take long, and they were told that they'd have to appear in court, but Dani hardly heard any of it. She was trying to deal with the realization that she was married to a professional mercenary soldier. And she didn't know what to do.

Her eyes studied him as he spoke to the other men. He didn't look like one. But the air of authority that had puzzled her, his confidence, the way he seemed to take command of things—yes, it made sense now. She even knew when it had happened, back when that woman had made a fool of him. That was the beginning. And now he had a lifestyle he liked, and a biddable little wife who'd be waiting back at home while he went around the world looking for trouble.

She lifted the cup of coffee they'd brought her and sipped it quietly. No, sir, she thought, her eyes narrowing. No, sir, she wasn't going to be his doormat. She cared for him, but there had to be more to a relationship than sex. And if that was all he wanted from her, he could go away.

A cold sickness washed over her as she realized how much a part of her life he'd become. So quickly, he'd absorbed her. All she had to do was look at him and she ached to hold him, to be loved by that warm, powerful body. She knew so much about him, things she blushed even remembering. But none of it was real. She couldn't sit alone at home while he went out and risked his life. My God, she thought, no wonder he didn't want children! How could he have kids in his line of work? They'd never even see their father! As for Dani, how could she live with worry eating at her like an acid? Every time he left she'd be wondering if she'd ever see him again. She'd wonder, and not know, and eventually the not-knowing would kill her soul. No, she thought miserably. Better to have a sweet memory than a living nightmare. He'd have to divorce her. She knew already that he wouldn't give up his way of life. And she couldn't stay married to him under the circumstances. So there was nothing left. A dream, ending too soon.

After the meeting was over they walked quietly outside the terminal. The captain followed them, along with the male flight attendant who brought Dani's purse and her sack of books.

"What now?" she asked helplessly.

"The airline will pay for hotel rooms," the captain said with a kind smile. "Tomorrow we'll fly you to Greenville."

Dutch looked hunted as he glanced over the captain's shoulder. "The press corps has taken up residence," he growled.

"No stomach for stardom?" the captain grinned.

"None whatsoever," came the taut reply. "Dani and I are catching the next flight out of here tonight," he added flatly. "I'm afraid that the international wire services will have a field day."

"Probably so," the captain agreed. "It seems our erstwhile hijackers have some interesting ties to a certain Central American dictator and a few communist strings as well." He sighed. "They'd have wanted weapons once we landed," he said, glancing at Dutch.

"Yes. And they'd have gotten them," the blond man said. He lit a cigarette.

"Used that knife very often?" the captain asked quietly.

Dutch nodded. "Far too often, in years past."

"Would you mind telling me what occupation you're in?" he was asked.

Dutch eyed him quietly. "Care to make an educated guess?"

"Covert operations."

He nodded, noticing Dani's hollow-eyed stare. He looked down at her with unreadable eyes. "I'm a professional mercenary. My specialty is logistics, but I'm handy with small arms as well, and I have something of a reputation with that knife. I made it myself." He glanced at the captain. "When the surgeons get it removed, I'd like to have it back."

The captain nodded. "I'll have it gold-plated, if you like. You saved us one hell of a mess. Any time you need help, just let me know."

"That isn't likely, but thank you."

The captain walked away and Dutch smoked his cigarette quietly while the press converged on the pilot once he was alone.

"Is that why you wanted to avoid the press?" Dani asked hesitantly. He frightened her. Despite the fact that she'd read *The Dogs of War* twice and seen the film three times, she could hardly believe what she was hearing. It was like watching a movie. All of it. The hijacking, the way he'd handled the hijackers, the matter-of-fact way he'd dealt with all of it. Her eyes were glued to his face while she turned it all around in her mind. She was married to a soldier of fortune. Now what was she going to do?

He saw that look in her eyes and could have cursed. Fate was giving him a hard time.

"I don't like publicity," he said. "My private life is sacred."

"And where do I fit into your life?" she asked quietly. It was too soon to ask that, but things needed to be said now.

"You're my wife," he said simply.

"Why did you marry me?" she asked.

He looked hunted. His eyes narrowed, his jaw clenched. He took a deep puff of his cigarette before he replied. "I wanted you."

So that was all, she thought. It didn't hurt, although she was sure it was going to, when the numbness wore off. She was still in a state of shock. She had risked her life, seen a man wounded in front of her eyes, learned that her husband was a mercenary....

He was watching her face, and he felt a violence of emotion that made him dizzy. She was under his skin. In his very soul. How did he get her out?

"Yes, I thought so," she said too casually. She searched the face her hands had touched so lovingly. "And what did you expect that our married life would be like? That I'd sit home and wait while you went away and came home shot to pieces year after year?"

He felt shocked. Taken by surprise. He stared at her intently. "I thought...we'd each have our own lives. That we could enjoy each other. Belong to each other."

She shook her head. "No. I'm sorry. I couldn't live that way. You'd better divorce me."

It was almost comical. His spinster wife of a week was showing him the door. Him! Women had chased him for years. They'd practically hung out windows trying to snare him because of his very elusiveness. And this plain little frumpy bookseller was showing him the door!

"You needn't look so shocked," she told him. "I'm only saving myself a little heartache, that's all. I can't live with the knowledge that your life is constantly in danger. I'd be destroyed."

"I'm not suicidal, for God's sake," he began.

"You're not superhuman, either," she reminded him. "There are scars on you. I didn't realize what they were at the time, but now I know. And one day you'll stop a bullet. I don't want to be sitting alone waiting for the phone to ring. I'm strong. But I'm not that strong. I care too much."

It amazed him that he felt those last four words to the soles of his feet. She cared about him. Of course she did; it was written all over her, in the soft gray eyes that had worshipped him when he loved her, in the hands that had adored him. It was infatuation or hero worship, he knew, but it had been flattering. Now it meant something more to him. Now it mattered that she was turning him away.

"We'll talk when we get to Greenville," he said firmly.

"You can talk all you like," she said, walking away from him. "I've had my say."

"You little frump!" he burst out, infuriated.

"Look who's calling whom a frump!" she threw back, whirling, all big angry gray eyes behind her glasses and flying hair and flushed cheeks. "Who do you think you are, big, bad soldier. God's gift?"

He wanted to strangle her, but he laughed instead.

"And don't laugh at me," she fumed. "It was all a line, wasn't it? You told me I was beautiful to you, but I was just a pickup, something to play with between wars!"

"At first," he agreed. He finished his cigarette and ground it out under his shoe. "But not now."

"That's right, now I'm a liability," she told him. "I'm a holiday interlude that's over."

He shook his blond head. She got prettier by the day, he mused, watching her. He'd called her a frump only because he was so angry. He smiled slowly. "You aren't over, pretty girl."

"I'm a frump!" she yelled at him.

A passing flight attendant grinned at her. "Not quite," he murmured, and winked.

Dani picked up her bag of books and started walking toward the terminal.

"Where are you going?" Dutch asked.

"Back home," she told him. "I've got a bookstore to run."

"Stop."

She did, but she kept her back to him. "Well?"

He hesitated. It was uncharacteristic. He didn't know what to do next. If he pushed her, he could lose her. But he couldn't let go, either. She'd become important to him. He didn't want to think about never seeing her again.

"Think about it for a while," he said finally. "For a few weeks, until I get back."

"Back?" She turned, not caring if he saw her pain. Tears bit at her eyelids and she felt sick all over.

Oh, God, it hurt to see her like this! He glared toward the horizon, jamming his hands into his pockets. He'd never seen that expression on a woman's face in his life. He'd come to the brink of death with cool disdain more times than he cared to remember, and now the look on a woman's face terrified him.

She fought to get herself under control. She took a slow, deep breath. "I won't change my mind," she said, sure now that it would be suicide to stay with him.

"All the same, I'll be in touch."

"Suit yourself."

He met her eyes, searching them. "I'm already committed to this job. I can't back out." It was the first time in years that he'd explained himself, he realized.

"I don't want to know," she said firmly. "You have your life, and I have mine. If you'd told me in the very beginning, I wouldn't have come near you."

"I think I knew that," he said softly. He sketched her with his eyes, memorizing her. "Take care of yourself."

"I always have." She let her eyes love him one last time. She ached already at their parting. It would be like losing a limb. "You take care of yourself, too."

"Yes."

She stared at her wedding ring, and he saw the thought in her eyes.

"Leave it on," he said gently. "I—would like to think that you were wearing my ring."

The tears burst from her eyes. She didn't even look at him again, she turned and broke into a run, suitcases and all, crying so hard that she could hardly see where she was going. Behind her he stood quietly on the apron, alone, watching until she was out of sight.

CHAPTER SEVEN

NOTHING WAS THE SAME. The first day she was home Dani went into the bookstore the same as always, but her life was changed. Harriett Gaynor, her small, plump friend, gave her odd looks, and Dani was almost certain that Harriett didn't believe a word of the story her employer told her about the Mexican holiday. Then the next day the papers hit the stands.

"It's true!" Harriett burst out, small and dark-eyed, her black hair in tight curls around her elfin face. "It's all here in the paper, about the hijacking, look!"

Dani grimaced as she looked down at the newspaper Harriett had spread over the counter. There was a picture of the pilot, and a blurred one of the injured hijacker being carried off the plane. There wasn't a picture of Dutch, but she hadn't expected to see one. He seemed quite good at dodging the press.

"Here's something about the man who overpowered the hijacker…" Harriett frowned and read, catching her breath at the vivid account. She looked up at Dani. "You did that?"

"He said they would have asked for automatic weapons once we were in Miami," Dani said quietly.

Harriett put the paper down. "A professional merce-nary." She stared at her best friend. "I don't believe it. Didn't you ask what he did before you married him?"

"If you saw him, you wouldn't be surprised that I didn't," Dani told her. She turned away. She didn't want to talk about Dutch. She wanted to forget. Even now, he was on his way to another conflict….

"No man is that good-looking," Harriett said. "Not even Dave." Dave, a pleasant man, wasn't half the scrap-per his pint-sized wife was. "By the way, Mrs. Jones called to thank you for her autographed books."

"She's very welcome. It was nice, getting to meet some of the authors at the autographing." She checked the change in the cash register as they started to open the shop.

"Where is he now?" Harriett asked suddenly.

"Getting a good lawyer, I hope," Dani said, laugh-ing even though it hurt to say it. "We're setting a new record for short marriages. One week."

"You might work it out," came the quiet reply.

Dani wouldn't look at her friend. "He makes his liv-ing risking his life, Harrie," she said. "I can't spend mine worrying about him. I'd rather get out while I still can."

"I suppose you know your own mind," Harriett said, shrugging. "But when you decide to go adventuring, you sure go whole hog, don't you? Marrying strangers, overpowering hijackers…"

She went away muttering, and Dani smiled at her re-treating back. Yes, she'd had an adventure all right. But now it was over, and she'd better tuck her bittersweet memories away in a trunk and get on with her life. The first step was to put Dutch out of her mind forever. The second was to stop reading the newspaper. From now on, every time she learned about a small foreign war, she'd see him.

Of course, it wasn't that easy. In the weeks that followed, everything conspired to remind her of him. Especially Harriett, who became heartily suspicious when Dani began losing her breakfast.

"It's the curse of Montezuma," Dani said shortly, glaring at her friend from a pasty face as she came out of the bathroom with a wet paper towel at her mouth.

"It's the curse of the flying Dutchman," came the dry reply.

Dani laughed in spite of herself, but it was brief. "I am not pregnant."

"I had a miscarriage," Harriett said quietly. "But I've never forgotten how it felt, or how I looked. You're white as a sheet, you tire so easily it isn't funny, and your stomach stays upset no matter what you do."

It was the same thing Dani had been dreading, hoping, terrified to admit. But she'd arrived at the same conclusion Harriett had. She sat down on the stool behind the counter with a weary sigh.

"You crazy child, didn't you even think about contraceptives?" Harriett moaned, hugging her.

Harriett, only four years her senior, sometimes seemed twice that. Dani let the tears come. She wept so easily these days. Last night a story on the news about guerrilla action in Africa had set her off when she spotted a blond head among some troops. Now, Harriett's concern was doing it, too.

"I'm pregnant," Dani whispered shakily.

"Yes, I know."

"Oh, Harrie, I'm scared stiff," she said, clutching the older woman. "I don't know anything about babies."

"There, there, Miss Scarlett, I doesn't know anything about birthin' babies my own self, but we'll muddle through somehow." She drew away, smiling with a genuine affection. "I'll take care of you." She searched Dani's eyes. "Do you want to have it?"

Dani shuddered. "I saw a film once, about how babies develop." She put her hand slowly, tenderly, to her flat abdomen. "They showed what happened when a pregnancy is terminated." She looked up. "I cried for hours."

"Sometimes it's for the best," Harriett said gently.

"In some circumstances," she agreed. "But I'll never see it as a casual answer to contraception. And as for me," she said shifting restlessly, "I...want his baby." She clasped her arms around herself with a tiny smile. "I wonder if he'll be blond?" she mused.

"He may be a she," came the dry reply.

"That's all right. I like little girls." She sighed dreamily. "Isn't it amazing? Having a tiny life inside you, feeling it grow?"

"Yes," Harriett said wistfully. "It was the happiest time of my life."

Dani looked up and smiled. "You can share mine."

Harriett, tougher than nails, grew teary-eyed. She turned quickly away before Dani could see that vulnerability. "Of course I can. Right now you need to get to a doctor and see how far along you are."

"I already know," Dani said, remembering the morning in Dutch's room, the exquisite tenderness of that brief loving. "I know."

"You'll need vitamins," Harriett continued. "And a proper diet."

"And baby clothes and a baby bed..." Dani was dreaming again.

"Not until after the seventh month," Harriett said firmly. "You have to be realistic, too. Sometimes it happens, sometimes it doesn't. But it helps not to get too involved too soon."

"Spoilsport!" Dani burst out, half-irritated.

"The doctor will tell you the same thing," Harriett said. "Dani, I bought baby furniture when I was a month along. I miscarried at four months, and had all those bright new things to dispose of. Don't do it."

Dani immediately felt repentant. She hugged Harriett warmly. "Thank you for being my friend. For caring about me."

"Someone has to." She glowered up at Dani. "Are you going to tell him?"

"How?" Dani asked. "I don't even know his address."

"My God, she's married to a man and she doesn't know where he lives."

Dani laughed at the expression on Harriett's face. "Well, we didn't spend much time talking."

Harriett started at the young woman's belly. "So I noticed."

"Stop that!" Dani sighed wearily. "Besides, he said he never wanted children. He'd go right through the roof if he knew. It's just as well that the divorce go through without his finding out."

"How can you divorce a man you can't find?" Harriett asked reasonably.

"He's getting the divorce, not me. He has my address."

"Lovely. Shall we sell some books? Call the doctor first," Harriett said, and went back to her pricing.

Dani was healthy, and after her family doctor put her on prenatal vitamins, she began to bloom. Dr. Henry Carter laughed delightedly every visit she made to his office for checkups, pleased with her progress as well as her attitude toward being pregnant.

"You really love being pregnant, don't you?" he asked when she was having her third checkup, at a little over four and a half months.

"Every second!" She touched the swell of her abdomen. "I think he moved this morning," she added excitedly. "Little flutters, like a bird trying to get free."

"Yes," he said with a warm smile. "That's what it feels like, I'm told. The first sign of a healthy baby. The tests we ran assured us of that."

She'd liked the test. It was done with ultrasound, and they'd given her a polaroid picture of the baby's head, just visible in the X-ray, an n-type sound scan.

"Has there been any word from your husband?" he added quietly.

Dani felt herself go cold. "No." She stared down at her hands. "He might…never come back."

"I'm sorry. The reason I asked is because I'd like you to sign up for natural childbirth classes. Even if you don't want to have a natural delivery, they'll help you cope with labor," he explained. "They involve exercises that prepare you for childbirth. And, sadly, they require a partner."

"Can—can Harriett do it?" she asked.

He knew Harriett, and he grinned. "Best person I know for a coach. All she really has to do is stand beside you and tell you when to breathe."

"She already does that very well," she said dryly.

"Okay. Next month I'll sign you up. You're doing fine. Get out of here. And don't exert yourself too much. The heat's terrible this summer."

"Tell me about it," she murmured, sweating even in her loose sleeveless tent blouse and elastic-fronted skirt. "See you next time."

She made another appointment and dawdled on her way back to work. It was a lovely summer day, the kind that lures dreamers to quiet ponds and butterfly-laden meadows full of flowers. She sang a little as she walked along, feeling the tiny flutters in her stomach and laughing as she went. What a beautiful world. How wonderful to be pregnant and healthy.

Finally, she gave in and went back to the bookstore, because she knew Harriett would worry if she was gone too long. She strolled lazily along the small shopping center in the heart of Greenville, oblivious to shoppers and the sounds of children playing on the sidewalk.

With a slow, dreamy smile, she opened the door of the shop and walked inside. And came face-to-face with Dutch.

He was wearing khakis—a bush shirt with slacks—and there was a new scar on one cheek. He looked as though he'd lost a little weight, although he was as handsome, as physically devastating, as ever. Harriett must have thought so, too, because she was openly staring at him, wide-eyed.

Dutch did some staring of his own. His eyes were on her stomach, and their expression was frankly terrified. He felt as if he'd never breathe again. He'd come back to see if they could work out a compromise, if she might be willing to rethink her position. Only to find—this!

Dani saw the stark terror in his eyes. If she'd hoped for any kind of reconciliation, she knew now that it was all a pipe dream. After all the long nights of remembering, worrying, hoping, praying, for him, of thinking how he'd react if she told him about the baby, now she knew.

It was too much all at once. The sight of him, the hunger for him, the weeks and months of worry. He began to blur, and then to darken. And she fainted at his feet.

She came to in the back of the shop, in a storeroom that Dani and Harriett used for lunch breaks. There was a big armchair there, and Dani was lying across it, her shoes off, a cold cloth on her forehead.

"…had a hard time of it," Harriett was saying grimly. "She's healthy enough, but she won't rest."

"I never should have married her," came the harsh reply.

"You're a prize, aren't you?" Harriett was saying. "That child has never had anything or anyone in her life to make her way easier. Her parents deserted her when she was just a baby; she doesn't even know where they are. She never really had a boyfriend of her own. She's had no one except me. And now you sweep her off her feet, get her pregnant, and walk out on her. Mister, you are a walking blond plague, and if there's one iota of human decency left in you, you'll do her a favor and get out of her life."

"And leave her at your mercy?" Dutch came back idly. "Like hell."

Oh, no, Dani thought sickly. She'd known that would happen. World War III. Dutch and Harriett were just alike....

"What kind of mercy would she get from you, you...!" Harriett retorted.

"No," Dani whispered hoarsely, opening her eyes to see them squared off, glaring at each other scant feet away. They both turned toward her. "No," she repeated more strongly. "If you two want to brawl, go stand in the street. You can't do it here. I can't cope."

"I'm sorry, baby," Harriett said softly. "Are you all right?"

"I'm fine, thanks." She sat up, smoothing the wet cloth over her face while Dutch glared down at her with fierce anger in his dark eyes. His blond hair was slightly mussed, his handsome face harder than she remembered it. "Well, you needn't glare at me," she told him shortly. "I didn't get pregnant all alone, remember!"

Harriett had to hide a smile. "I'll leave you two to talk," she offered.

"We'll talk at home," Dani said firmly, glaring at

Dutch. "Where I can throw things and scream. The store cramps my style."

She got up while Dutch tried not to grin at her fury. Glasses and all, she was something in a temper.

"Don't rush around; it isn't healthy," he said, taking her hand in his. He glanced at Harriett. "Can you manage for an hour or so?"

"Of course. Can you?" she returned.

He couldn't help the faint smile. "Yes, Mama," he said mockingly. "I won't hurt your lamb."

He guided her out the door, letting her show him the way to her nearby apartment. It was up a flight of stairs, and he frowned as they climbed. He didn't like the stairs.

"You have to move," he said when she'd unlocked her apartment and they were inside in the white and yellow homey confines of the living room.

She turned and gaped at him. "What?"

"You have to move," he said shortly. "You can't be walking up and down stairs like…that." He indicated her belly.

"It isn't a that. It's a baby," she said firmly, planting her feet as she challenged him. "It's a boy, in fact, and I am going to call him Joshua Eric."

His face gave nothing away. His eyes went over her quietly, and for the first time in months he felt whole again. Leaving her had been the hardest thing he'd ever done. All the time he was away, he thought of her, longed for her, wanted her. He still wanted her. But she was pregnant. He didn't want a baby, he didn't want her pregnant. It brought back memories that were unbearable.

He hadn't even meant to come back; he hadn't wanted his life to change. And his worst fears had confronted him the instant he saw her.

"Do you have the divorce papers with you?" she asked calmly.

He sighed angrily and lit a cigarette without even asking if she minded. "You've put 'paid' to that, haven't you?" he asked, his voice as cold as his dark eyes. "How can I divorce you in that condition? You'll want child support, I imagine?"

He couldn't possibly have hurt her any more, not if he'd knocked her down. Quick tears welled in her eyes, and she glared at him through them.

"Get out!" she shot at him.

"Is it even mine?" he goaded, feeling trapped and straining at invisible bonds fiercely.

She picked up the nearest object, a small statuette of some Greek figure, and flung it at him. "Damn you!"

He ducked and it hit the door, shattering into a hundred pieces.

"Get out of my apartment! Get out of my life!" she choked. "Oh, God, I hate you, I hate—!" The nausea hit her all at once. She turned, running for the bathroom, where she was horribly sick. She cried helplessly, oblivious to the tall man holding the wet cloth to her head and hating himself so much he wanted to jump off a building to make the guilt stop.

"I hate you," she whispered weakly when it was over and she could talk. Her head was leaning against the cold porcelain sink. She could hardly move.

"Yes." He bathed her face gently, her hands. Then he put the cloth aside and lifted her, carrying her into the bedroom. He laid her down and turned on the oscillating fan, positioning it so that it wouldn't blow directly on her.

"Go to sleep," he said quietly. "Then we'll talk."

"I—don't want to," she murmured drowsily, but she was drained and overwhelmed and so tired. Her eyes closed, and seconds later she drifted off.

Dutch sat down on the bed beside her, frightened and sick at what he'd done to her. His eyes ran lovingly over her body, and without conscious thought he eased up the hem of her maternity blouse and moved the elastic of her skirt down, and looked. Her belly was slightly swollen, round and womanly. So that was what pregnancy looked like. He winced, remembering another time, another pregnant woman. But Dani wasn't like that, he told himself. Never like that. His lean fingers touched the soft flesh gently, hesitantly. Yes, it was firm. His child was in there. His child. A boy, she'd said. Could she be so certain? Of course, there were tests they did now. His big hand smoothed over the swell, pressing, and all at once something fluttered against his fingers. He jerked them back with a gasp.

Dani had woken with the first light touch of his fingers, and she found the expressions that flickered on his face fascinating. But that last reaction amused her, and she laughed softly.

His eyes darted to hers. "What did I do?" he asked softly.

"The baby moved," she said simply.

"Moved?" He looked back down, frowning. Hesitantly, he reached down again. She took his fingers and placed them against the side of her belly. She pressed them close, and it happened again. And he laughed. Slowly. Softly. Delightedly.

"When they get bigger, they kick," she told him. "The doctor says the more active they are, the healthier they are. He moves a lot."

"I never knew...." He looked up from her belly to her rib cage. His hand moved up to the bunched top and he glanced up at her face with the question in his eyes. "I've never seen a pregnant woman this way."

"I don't mind if you look at me," she whispered, fascinated by the way he was reacting to her. There was something in his face, a kind of tenderness. She wondered what had soured him on pregnancy, and why he hated the thought of a child.

He lifted the blouse to under her chin and his body stilled as his eyes sought the subtle changes in her breasts.

"You're bigger," he said quietly. "Darker...here." His fingers brushed an enlarged areole, making her tense with remembered pleasure.

"Little changes," she said, fighting for breath. "All that will increase as I get further along. It prepares me so that I can nurse him."

He felt a wild charge of emotion. It showed when he looked into her eyes. "I didn't think women did that anymore."

She smiled. "I want to do everything. I—" She laughed. "I love it. Being pregnant, I mean. I've never had anyone to fuss over, you see," she tried to explain. "Never had anyone of my own to worry about, to care about, to love. He'll be my whole world. I'll take care of him, and sit with him when he's sick, and play games with him when he's older. I'll take him everywhere with me, I'll—" She lowered her eyes at the expression on his face. "What you said, about child support. It's not necessary," she added proudly. "I make a comfortable living from the bookstore. I can take care of him. He'll be my responsibility."

He'd never felt so empty and alone in all his life. He stared at her belly, hearing the words and wanting all that tender caring for himself. But it wasn't possible. She didn't want him. She was telling him so.

He tugged the blouse back down. "You'll be a good mother," he said numbly.

"I'm sorry that you had to find it out this way," she murmured. "I would have written you, but I didn't even have your address."

He drew in a slow breath and got to his feet. He went to the window, smoking another cigarette. He looked so alone. So lost.

"You…weren't hurt?" she asked, averting her face so that he couldn't see her eyes.

"A few scratches." He stared at the glowing tip of the cigarette for a minute before his dark eyes went back out the window to the city traffic. He'd done nothing right since he got off the damned plane. He'd wanted to talk about reconciliation, but when he'd found her pregnant, he'd gone off the deep end. It was because of the memories, of course; they'd haunted him for so long. Perhaps he'd blown the whole incident out of proportion over the years.

He turned back to her, uneasy at the way she looked. That woman, Harriett, had mentioned how tired Dani was. Yes, she was tired. Run down. There had been a radiance in her when she'd come into the bookstore, but it was gone now. He'd taken it away with his cold attitude and stupid accusations. He'd hurt her. Again. And he hadn't meant to.

"What I said, before," he said hesitantly, glancing at her. His hand, holding the cigarette, moved aimlessly. "I know the baby's mine."

"Do you?" she asked with an empty smile as she sat up. "I might have had a legion of lovers since you left."

"I came back to see if we might salvage the marriage," he said after a minute, hoping for some reaction in her face, but there was nothing.

She looked up at him, schooling her features to remain calm. "And now?"

He shifted restlessly, pacing near the window, his blond head bowed, one hand in his pocket. "Now I don't know."

She swung her feet to the floor. "I haven't changed my mind, even if you've started to change yours," she said before he could speak. She looked at him with quiet gray eyes. "It's all I can do to manage carrying the baby and running my business so that I can support him. I can't have any additional pressure right now. I hope you understand."

"You keep referring to it as a 'he,'" he said curtly.

"He is a he," she told him. "They ran some tests."

He felt odd. A son. A little boy who might look like him. He stared at her as if he'd never seen a woman before, studying every line and curve of her body.

"Don't look so worried, Eric, I don't expect anything from you," she mused, getting slowly to her feet. "Now, if you've said all you came to say, I've got to work to do. I'll give you the name of my attorney...."

"No!" The word came out without conscious volition. They couldn't divorce. Hell, he didn't even want to think about it! She had his child, and he...wanted it!

She clenched her fingers together and glared at him. "I won't live with you," she said stubbornly.

His face hardened. "You will."

"Make me."

He stared at her. Mutinous bow mouth, stormy gray eyes, flushed face. Pregnant. He started to laugh helplessly, a deep, rich sound like velvet.

"I like you," he said absently. "I honestly like you. No deceit, no tricks, no lines, no backing away from trouble. You're a hell of a woman."

She shifted from one foot to the other. No, he wasn't going to get around her that way. "Remember me?" she asked coldly. "Miss Frump?"

He put out the cigarette, still smiling faintly, and moved toward her with a gleam in his eyes that made her back away.

"Sexy frump," he murmured dryly. "Very pregnant, very desirable. And I don't want a divorce. I want you."

"I'm not for sale," she told him, moving backward until the wall stopped her. "Go away. Go blow up something."

"I don't blow up things, actually," he murmured, pinning her to the wall with a strong arm on either side of her. "I'm more into logistics and strategy."

"You'll get killed, anyway," she said.

He shrugged. "I could get hit by a car downstairs."

"Not quite as easily," she argued.

"I want you," he said quietly.

"Yes, I know," she replied softly. "But wanting isn't enough. You've already said you'd never fall in love again, so all you're offering me is your body, between wars. It's a gorgeous body, and in bed you're all any woman could ever want. But you're asking me to live with death, day in and day out, and I can't."

He drew in a breath and started to speak, but before he could she took one of his hands and pressed it slowly against her belly.

"I have your son under my heart," she whispered, pressing his palm flat against her. "I can't live with the fear of losing both of you."

He frowned. "I don't understand."

"Eric, I could miscarry," she said, her voice soft with a fear he was just beginning to sense.

"Is it likely?" he asked.

"I'm healthy. So is the baby. But there are no guarantees," she said, lowering her eyes to his chest.

"It…frightens you, to think of losing him?" he asked hesitantly.

She looked up wide-eyed. "Of course it does!"

He was remembering another woman, another time, and he cursed himself for that lapse. Dani wanted the baby. It was written all over her.

"I can't worry about him and you as well," she said curtly. "And he deserves a chance. You're old enough to make your own mistakes, but I'm responsible for him now."

He stared down at her for a long time. Then he turned away with a sigh and lit still another cigarette.

"I've done it for so many years," he said after a minute, staring at the floor. "It's all I know."

"I'm not asking you to change," she reminded him.

He looked up. "We're married."

"We can get divorced."

"I don't want a damned divorce!" he burst out, his eyes black with anger.

She stood there staring at him helplessly, searching for the right words.

He sighed angrily. "I knew you'd be trouble the minute I saw you," he growled. "A frumpy little bookseller with the body and soul of an angel. And you're in my blood like poison. I'd have to die to get you out of my system!"

She lifted her shoulders and smiled ruefully. "Well, look at it this way, you'll never have to fight off other men."

He laughed softly, shaking his head. "Would you care to bet? The way you look right now…"

"I look pregnant," she said. "In two or three more months I'll look like a blimp."

"Not to me you won't."

He averted his eyes to his shoes. "Well, I'll go home and pack. And there are some people I want to see."

"Pack?"

He looked up. "I'm going to live with you," he said. "If you don't like it, that's tough. I am not," he continued, gathering steam, "going to have you working yourself to death and running up and down these damned stairs. Harriett's right. You need looking after. So I'm going to look after you. Until the baby comes, at least," he added. "After that we'll make whatever decisions have to be made."

She wanted to argue. But he looked very formidable. "But, your...your work...."

"To hell with my work," he bit off. He looked frankly dangerous. "I've got enough in foreign banks to buy this damned building you live in. I work because I like it, not because I need money."

"But..."

"Shh. Talking is bad for the baby." He crushed out his cigarette. "I'll get back Saturday."

Things were happening too fast. She was shell-shocked. She watched him walk toward her.

"Little gray-eyed witch," he whispered. He pulled her gently against him and bent to tease her mouth with his. "Open it," he murmured. "I haven't kissed you in months."

"I'll bet you've kissed other women," she said mutinously.

He lifted his head. "Nope." He drew his knuckles over her flushed cheek. "I haven't even looked at one. And yes, there are always women in the circles I move in. Beautiful women, with no principles and eyes like dollar signs. And all I could think of was how it felt with you, that morning when we made such exquisite love on my bed and created this little boy."

Tears burst into her eyes, startling him. "You know?" she breathed.

"Of course. Didn't you?" he asked, smiling at her.

"You're more experienced than I am," she hedged.

"Not in that kind of lovemaking," he murmured ruefully. "I wasn't lying when I said I'd never experienced it before."

"Do you mind very much, about the baby?" she asked, because she had to know.

He smoothed away her frown with a lean forefinger. "I have to get used to the idea, that's all. I've been a free spirit for a very long time. I've had no one."

"Yes, I know." She studied his shirt buttons. "Eric, you don't have to do this. You don't have to come here…."

He stopped the sacrificing little speech with his mouth, opening hers to a delicate, gently probing kiss that had her going stiff with desire all too soon.

His fingers tangled in the short hair at the nape of her neck and eased her head back against the hard muscle of his upper arm. His other hand made slow, torturous forays against her collarbone, her shoulder, the side of her breast.

"Sadist," she whispered shakily as the magic worked on her.

He bit her lower lip gently. "Do you want to make love?"

Her eyes opened, looking straight into his face. "No."

He smiled, and his fingers brushed knowingly over her nipples. She flinched with sudden pleasure, and he laughed gently.

"Yes, you do," he murmured dryly.

"My mind doesn't want to," she amended, trying to save herself from the sensual prison he was trying to trap her in.

He kissed her eyes closed, and his hands slid to her stomach, cupping its firm warmth. "It won't make you miscarry," he whispered. "Not if I'm gentle enough. And I will be."

She trembled at the soft tone, and he smiled and pulled her into his arms, holding her.

"It isn't that," she whispered into his shoulder, eyes open and worried as they stared at the fabric of his shirt. "Don't make me care for you. It will make it all that much harder to let go. Just…just let me pretend that it's Mexico, and we're having a holiday. All right?"

He stood very still, smoothing her hair. "Dani…"

"Please!"

He sighed heavily and let her go. "All right. A holiday." His eyes dropped to her belly and he chuckled. "For the three of us."

"And—and no sex," she added, her eyes dark and frightened.

He searched them, seeing her fear of losing him. It bothered him, but he didn't quite know how to handle it. "Are you sure?" he asked. "We could enjoy each other."

"Yes, I know. But I don't want to."

She was imposing impossible limits on his self-control, but he couldn't turn his back on his responsibility to her. He shrugged, as if it didn't matter. "Okay," he said carelessly. "No sex."

She breathed more easily. She had expected him to argue. He brushed a kiss against her nose.

"Of course," he added, "you can always seduce me if you like."

"Thank you," she replied with a reluctant smile. "I'll keep that in mind."

He winked at her. "See you Saturday. Rest for another hour. I'll stop by your store and tell the mother hen where you are. And watch those damned stairs," he added firmly.

"Yes, your worship." She curtsied.

He laughed shortly as he went out the door, closing it quietly behind him. Dani stared at it for a long time before she went back to lie down. She wondered what she was letting herself in for. He wasn't going to be able to settle down, she was sure of it. It would mean only more heartache. But apparently he felt responsible and he wasn't going to let her out of his sight for five months. She grimaced at the thought of having to cope with Dutch and Harriett together. It was going to be a rough pregnancy.

CHAPTER EIGHT

DUTCH THOUGHT THAT getting married might have been worth it all when he saw the shock on J.D.'s and Gabby's faces.

J.D. Brettman was big and dark. He was an ex-mercenary who now practiced law in Chicago. And Gabby Darwin Brettman had been his secretary before she married him. Dutch had heard a little about her from First Shirt, another member of the team, who'd told him how rough the courtship had been, and he'd met her once himself. Now he needed advice, and he couldn't think of anyone better than J.D. to ask.

"Married." J.D. caught his breath. "You?"

Dutch shrugged. He looked up from his lit cigarette to catch the amused look in Gabby's green eyes, and he laughed in spite of himself. "It's your fault," he told her. "I never would have noticed her, but for you. Until J.D. married you, I thought all women were incapable of honesty."

J.D. touched Gabby's cheek gently. "She changed my own outlook," he said, and a look passed between them that embarrassed Dutch.

Dutch got up and went to the window, staring blankly

out at Chicago. "I don't know what to do," he confessed. "I thought I would keep working and we'd each have our own lives. But she won't agree to that. She says she can't handle knowing what I'm doing when I'm away."

J.D. got up. "I'll make a pot of coffee. Gabby, keep Dutch company, will you?"

"Sure." She got up and went to the window, standing quietly beside the tall blond man, her arms folded over her chest. She looked at him. "I was going to get out of J.D.'s life when I thought he might go back to it," she said honestly. "I couldn't handle it, either." Her shoulders rose and fell. "I'm not a coward, but the worry would have made one of me. If he'd been a policeman or worked in law enforcement, I suppose I'd have had to make the best of it. But the kind of work he did, and you do, isn't easy for a woman to cope with. It's extraordinarily dangerous."

"Gabby," he said, staring out the window, "how would you have felt if J.D. hadn't been able to give it up—and you were pregnant?"

Tears burst from her eyes. He looked down and saw them, and his face contorted. "Oh, God," he breathed roughly.

She turned away. "I'm sorry," she said. "I want a baby so much. But J.D. and I haven't been able to have one. If I were pregnant, and he went off to a war, I think I'd die in my sleep."

He started to speak and couldn't. He lifted the cigarette to his lips, anguish in his eyes.

"I meant to tell you," J.D. said minutes later, after

he'd brought the coffee, "that Apollo's been cleared of any criminal charges."

"You got him off?" Dutch asked with a smile, feeling happy for their old friend and comrade.

J.D. nodded. "It took a little work. But he was innocent; that helped." He pursed his lips and glanced at Dutch. "He's opened his own business."

"Oh? Doing what?" Dutch asked.

"A consulting firm. He specializes in teaching anti-terrorism tactics to international corporations. And already he's got more work than he can handle." He leaned back against the sofa. "It's exciting work. Even a little risky. He asked if you might be interested. He needs someone experienced in tactics and strategy."

"A desk job," Dutch scoffed.

"Not at all. Go see him."

Dutch met J.D.'s level gaze. "I don't know if I can settle down."

"I didn't know, either." He glanced at Gabby, who was writing letters at the small desk, her long hair around her shoulders. "But it wasn't hard to decide which meant more, a few wild thrills, or her. She's my world," he added in a tone that made Dutch look away.

He leaned forward, staring at the carpet. "Dani's pregnant."

J.D. hesitated. "Is it yours?"

He nodded and smiled. "No doubt about it."

LATER, HE WENT TO SEE Apollo Blain, the tall black man who'd been part of their small unit since J.D. and First

Shirt had formed it years ago. Apollo grinned at him from behind his big desk, looking urbane and capable and prosperous.

"Tired of planning battles?" Apollo chuckled as he shook Dutch's outstretched hand. "Help me save paunchy executives from terrorists. It's a hell of a lot safer, and the pay's good."

"J.D. said I might like it," Dutch sighed, settling back in an armchair. "I got married."

"You?" Apollo gaped at him. He felt his own forehead. "My God, I must have an awful fever. I thought you just said you were married."

"I am. And I've got a son on the way," came the amused reply.

"I'd better lie down."

"Not until we discuss this job," Dutch returned.

"Are you really interested?" Apollo asked seriously.

Dutch nodded. "I don't know if I can stick it out. That's up front. But I think I need to try, for her sake."

Apollo whistled. "I'd like to meet this lady. Anything like Gabby?"

Dutch smiled. "Quite a lot."

"I hope there aren't any more of them running around loose." Apollo shuddered. "Even First Shirt's on the verge, with Gabby's mother. Anyway, enough about that. Here's what I had in mind, if you'd like to give it a shot...."

Dutch lit a cigarette and listened quietly. He nodded. Yes, it sounded like an interesting job. Outwitting terrorists. He smiled. Perhaps he might even enjoy it.

He leaned back and crossed his legs as Apollo's deep voice outlined the project.

WHEN DANI TOLD HER BEST FRIEND what was happening, Harriett had little to say about it, except to mutter something about a strong cage and a thin whip.

"He's not at all difficult when you know him." Dani grinned impishly. "And you have to admit, he's rather extraordinarily handsome."

"Handsome doesn't have anything to do with it," Harriett said curtly. And then she smiled. And growled wolfishly. And went off grinning.

Dani stared after Harriett, her own smile being slowly replaced by a frown. Her hand went absently to the swell of her stomach and she walked back behind the counter slowly.

It all seemed like a dream, somehow. The only reality left in her life was the baby. How in the world was she going to cope with a husband who felt trapped? She couldn't forget the look on his face when he'd seen that she was pregnant, couldn't forget what he'd said to her. He'd apologized, but still she couldn't forget. He didn't want this baby for some reason, and although he desired Dani, he didn't love her. His feelings were superficial at best, nothing that a marriage could be built on.

Her eyes went to the order sheet on the counter and she stared at it blankly, oblivious to the sound of Harriett helping a new customer find the books she wanted. Harriett had been right; she should have kept her head in Mexico. How incredible that level-headed Dani had gone off the deep end and married a stranger. It wasn't like her.

And now he felt responsible for what he'd done, and he was going to take care of her. She almost cried. Not because he loved her, but because the baby was his fault. She stared at her neat, short nails. How could she bear seeing him day after day, knowing that only the baby held him to her, that when it was all over, he'd be gone again. Perhaps he'd be killed. Her eyes closed in agony.

"Stop it," Harriett whispered sharply, pausing by the counter. "Stop tormenting yourself. At least he cares enough to look after you, doesn't he?"

Her eyelids lifted, and her anguished gray eyes were fogged from tears. "Does he?"

"He was snarling like a mountain lion," Harriett said, "when he stopped by here on this way to the airport. But it wasn't all guilt, you know. He's really worried about you."

Dani sighed thoughtfully. "He was terrified when he saw I was pregnant, Harrie," she murmured. "And when we got back to my apartment…he said some harsh things."

"None of which he meant, I imagine." Harriett patted her hand. "But you've got to stop worrying. It isn't healthy."

"He said he had to see some people," Dani said tightly.

"So that's it." Harriett glanced toward the browsing customer. "If he said he'd be back, he will. You can't put a rope around a man like that."

"I'd die if I lost him," she whispered, closing her eyes. "I offered him a divorce, and he wouldn't take it. I can't bear being nothing more than a responsibility."

"Once he gets to know you, that might change. Have you thought of it that way?" Harriett asked with a quiet smile. "Now, get busy. That's the best therapy I know for worry. Okay?"

"Okay." But as the days went by, the worries grew. What if he didn't come back at all? What if the people he was seeing told him of another mission, and he couldn't resist taking it?

Friday afternoon, when she left, she asked Harriett to open up the next morning so that she could sleep late. She was tired, and the worry wasn't helping. Harriett started to say something, but apparently thought better of it.

SOMETHING WOKE DANI. A movement beside her, a heavy weight on the bed. She came awake slowly, her face pale and drawn from lack of rest, her eyes heavily shadowed.

Dutch stared at her with unconcealed anxiety. She looked even worse than when he'd left. His eyes went slowly down her body to the swell of her stomach and they darkened. He didn't touch her this time. She didn't want that, he recalled bitterly, she didn't want him in any physical way anymore.

Dani blinked and almost reached out to touch him. Was he real? Her eyes wandered over his broad shoulders in the tan raincoat he was wearing. His blond hair was damp, too, curling a little around the sides of his face, and she wondered if their child would inherit that slight waviness.

"I didn't expect you so early," she said drowsily. "Is it raining?"

"Cats and dogs." He stood up, moving away from the bed. "Harriett's watching the store, I gather?"

"Yes. Would you like some breakfast?" she asked, although the thought of food was giving her problems already.

"I had it on the plane," he said. He lit a cigarette and glanced at her. "Can you eat anything?"

She shook her head. "Not now, I can't. I have toast when I get up."

"I'll go make some."

She gaped at him, and he laughed reluctantly.

"Well, I can toast bread, you know," he said. "We used to take turns with chow when the group and I were on a mission."

Her eyes lowered quickly to the bedspread. She touched the design in the white chenille. "The...people you had to see?" Her glance skipped to his hard face and down again. "I'm sorry. That's none of my business." She got up, standing slowly because any movement could trigger the nausea.

He felt as if he'd taken a hard blow in the stomach. Not her business! For God's sake, didn't she even care?

He turned, striding angrily into the kitchen while she sighed miserably, wondering what she'd done, and made her way into the bathroom.

The toast was on the table when she joined him. She'd thrown on a sleeveless flowered dress and came barefoot into the room, her hair gently brushed, her face white and drawn. He was wearing jeans and a brown knit shirt that made him look even more vital, tanned and powerful than usual.

"Thank you," she said as she sat down.

"You don't look well," he said bluntly.

"I'm pregnant."

"Yes, I noticed that."

She looked up and caught an amused gleam in his dark eyes.

"I don't ever feel well in the morning," she returned. "It's normal. And as for looking well," she added with a glare, "as you like to remind me, I never have looked well. I'm frumpy."

"Talk about bad moods," he murmured, leaning back to smoke his cigarette with an amused smile on his firm mouth. "Eat your toast, little shrew."

She glared at him. "You don't have to feel responsible for me," she said coldly. "I've already told you, it isn't necessary for you to stay here. I can have the baby all by myself."

"Sure you can," he scoffed, his eyes narrowing. "That's why you look so healthy."

"I'd be healthier if you'd go away!" she shot back. She left the toast, started to get up and suddenly sat down again, swallowing rapidly.

Dutch went to fetch a damp cloth and held it to her face, her throat, her mouth, kneeling beside her.

"All right now?" he asked in a tone so tender, it brought quick tears to her eyes.

"Yes," she whispered miserably.

His hand sought her belly and pressed there protectively. "This is mine," he said softly, holding her gaze. "I put it there. And until it's born, and the danger is all over, I'm going to stay with you."

The tears overwhelmed her. "Oh, please go away," she whispered brokenly. "Please..."

He pulled her gently against him, her face against his, his arms warm and strong at her back. He smelled of spicy cologne and cigarette smoke, and her body reacted to him with a crazy surge of pleasure that she tried to fight down. It wasn't permanent, she had to keep reminding herself, it was only temporary, until the baby was born. She'd better not get too attached to the feel of his arms.

"I was going to wait until later to discuss this with you," he said after a minute, "but I think we'd better talk now. Come here."

He lifted her in his arms and stood up in one smooth motion, carrying her back into the bedroom.

He laid her down against the pillows and leaned over her, searching her wide gray eyes behind the glasses.

"You're killing me," she whispered achingly.

"I can see that," he said quietly. "It isn't making my life any easier. I can't love you," he said tersely, and his face was hard. "I'm sorry. I'm...very fond of you," he added, brushing the tears from her cheeks. He took off her glasses and laid them aside, wiping the tear tracks away with a corner of the sheet. "But what there was in me of love died long ago. I can't afford the luxury of caring, not in my line of work."

Her eyes closed and her voice was hoarse with pain. "I love you," she said helplessly, her voice strained.

"I know," he replied. Her eyes opened, and he searched them. What the hell! She needed to know. Perhaps it would help her to understand. He took a sharp breath. "The woman, the one I loved so desperately...she became pregnant with my child," he said coldly. "The day she left me she told me she'd had an abortion. She laughed about it. How absurd, she said, to think that she'd want a child of mine!" His hands gripped her arms fiercely, but she didn't notice it at all. Her shocked eyes were fixed on his tortured face. "She got rid of it," he said harshly, "like so much garbage!"

Now she understood. Now it all made sense. She reached up hesitantly and touched his face.

"I'm raw from thinking about it," he whispered roughly, "from the memories. When I saw you pregnant with my child it all came back like a fever." His eyes blazed. "You don't know me. What I am now, she made me..."

Her fingers touched his hard mouth, feeling its warmth. Everything soft and womanly inside her reached out. Poor, storm-battered man, she thought achingly. Poor, tortured man.

"My parents hated me," he ground out. "They died hating me!"

"Come here." She reached up, drawing him down with her, holding him. He shuddered, and her eyes closed. Perhaps he didn't love her, but he needed her. She knew that even if he didn't. Her arms enfolded him—loving, comforting arms. Her hands smoothed his cool blond hair, and she nuzzled her cheek against it.

"Parents never hate children," she said quietly. "Not really."

"How would you know?" he growled harshly. "Didn't yours desert you?"

She took a slow breath, clinging to him. "Yes." She shifted under his formidable weight. "They were very young. Just children themselves. The responsibility must have been terrible." She held him closer. "They tried to contact me once. My aunt…told them I was dead." He stiffened and she swallowed hard. "I found out only when she was dying herself. It was too late then."

"Dani…"

"We can't go back, either of us," she continued quietly. Her hand brushed the nape of his neck. "We have to do the best we can with what we have."

"Are you sorry that I made you pregnant?" he asked in a tone so quiet she barely heard it.

"I've already told you that I'm happy," she said, and smiled against his cool skin. "I've never had anyone of my own."

It was a long minute before he lifted his head. He drew in a slow, calming breath and met her eyes. His own were stormy, turbulent; his face was terrible with remembered pain.

"I would never hurt you," she said. "Never, in any

way, even if I had the ability. She was a horrible woman, and you were young and vulnerable. But I'm sure your parents understood, even if they were hurt. And I will never believe that they didn't love you," she said, her face soft and caring.

His jaw tautened. He got to his feet and turned away. A long moment later he fumbled to light a cigarette.

Dani, blind without her glasses, didn't see the betraying movement of his hands. She tugged her glasses back on and sat up, straightening her dress, which had ridden up her legs.

"I have to get to the store," she said after the long silence began to grate on her nerves. "Harriett has an appointment to get her hair cut at noon."

He turned, scowling. "You're in no condition to go to work," he said curtly.

She looked up, eyebrows raised. "Fudge! I'm a little shaky on my legs, that's all." She got up, daring him to stop her. "I've got a business to take care of."

"You've got a baby to take care of," he corrected. "Call Harriett and tell her to close up when she leaves."

She glared at him. "No."

He shrugged and watched her pull out a slip and hose, and she thought the matter was settled.

He waited until she started to pull the dress over her head. Then he put down his cigarette and moved forward. Before she had time to react he stripped her, quickly and deftly, and put her under the covers. Then he took her clothes, tossed them into the closet, locked the closet, and pocketed the key.

She lay there with the covers around her neck, staring at him with eyes like saucers. It had happened so quickly, she'd had not time to retaliate.

He picked up the phone and asked for the number of her bookstore. Blankly, she told him. He finished dialing.

"Harriett? This is Dutch. Dani said to close up the shop when you leave. She's staying in bed today. Yes, that's right. Yes, I will." He hung up and retrieved his cigarette. "Now," he told Dani, "you'll stay right there until I say you can get up."

"I won't!" she returned.

"All right," he said easily, sliding one hand into his pocket. "Get up."

She started to, remembered her unclothed condition, and sank back against the pillows. "I want my clothes."

"You can have them tomorrow."

"I want them now."

"Go back to sleep. It's only nine," he said. "I'll clean up the kitchen.

He started out of the room and she stared at him uncomprehendingly, her eyes wide and uncertain. He turned and looked at her, the cigarette in his hand sending up curls of gray smoke.

"You're very much like Gabby," he said quietly.

He was gone before she could reply. Was Gabby the woman in his past? she wondered miserably. She took off her glasses and turned her face into her pillow as fresh tears came. She was sure that he hated her. Why else would he have said such a thing to her?

Eventually, she slept. It was late afternoon when she awoke, to find her clothes at the foot of the bed and a note under the pillow. Drowsily, she unfolded the paper and read it.

You can have your clothes, but don't leave the apartment, it said in a bold black scrawl. *I have gone to do some shopping. Back by five. Dutch.*

She glanced at the clock beside the bed. It was almost five now. She scrambled out of bed quickly to dress before he got back.

When he came in, with a bag of groceries in one powerful arm, she was curled up on the sofa with her ledgers spread around her. He glared and she glared back.

"Well, somebody has to do the paperwork," she said stubbornly. "And you won't let me do my job."

"Tit for tat," he said carelessly. "You won't let me do mine."

"I won't get killed selling books," she returned.

"I like the idea of being a father now that I'm getting used to it," he said as he put down the bag on the kitchen table. "I'm not going to let you risk losing him."

"You make me sound as if I didn't care about him at all," she snapped.

He started putting food into the refrigerator. "Stop trying to pick fights with me," he said pleasantly. "I won't argue with you."

"I'm not picking a fight," she said tautly. She just found it hard to believe that he was really concerned about her. She put her paperwork aside and padded into the kitchen to get something cold to drink. The heat was stifling, and the little air conditioner in the window was barely adequate.

He turned, frowning at her damp skin. "Are you hot?" he asked gently. "I'll get a bigger air conditioner delivered."

"No, you won't," she said stubbornly. "I like the one I've got."

He took her by the arms and held her in front of him. "You won't win," he said quietly. "So stop trying. I have to go to Chicago on Monday."

She wouldn't look up. "Work?" she asked, trying to sound as if she didn't care.

"Work," he agreed. His hands smoothed up and down her soft arms. "I'm not making any promises."

"Have I asked for any?" she murmured, lifting her eyes.

"You wouldn't," he said, as if he knew. "You're too proud to ask for anything that isn't freely given." He bent and started to kiss her, but she turned her face away.

He felt a tremor of hurt and anger go through him. His hands clenched, and he moved away from her with a new and unexpected pain eating at him.

He sighed angrily. How the hell had she gotten so far under his skin? He wanted to throw things.

"I'm not leaving the country," he said curtly. "An old friend of mine has opened a consulting firm. He teaches counterterrorism tactics to corporate executives. He needed someone experienced in tactics, and asked if I'd be interested." He shrugged. "So I told him yes."

It shocked her that he'd even consider changing his profession. Did the baby mean so much? Yes, she thought, probably it did. There were deep scars on his heart. Perhaps he'd never truly get over them. She didn't have the beauty or the sophistication to capture his heart. It wasn't enough that he desired her. Desire was something a man could feel for almost anybody, frumpy or not.

"It's a long way to commute," she said quietly.

"Yes." He moved toward her, but this time he didn't come too close. He studied her, and she looked back, noticing how very tall he was, how powerfully built. He had a face a movie star would have envied—even features, dark velvet eyes, chiseled lips.

"We discussed this a long time ago," he said. "I don't mind commuting. I think it's best, for now, that you stay here. You'd be alone a good bit of the time in Chicago, although I'm sure Gabby wouldn't mind looking in on you."

"Gabby?" She stared at him.

"Gabby Brettman," he said. "She's married to one of my best friends, a trial lawyer." His firm mouth relaxed into a smile. "Gabby followed J.D. through a Central American jungle with an AK-47 under one arm. She actually shot a terrorist with it and saved his life. A hell of a woman, Gabby."

So Gabby hadn't been the woman from his past! And he admired her—he'd said that Dani was much like Gabby. She blushed.

"Now you make the connection, is that it?" he asked softly. "For God's sake, what did you think I meant when I compared you to her?"

Her eyes fell to his chest. "I thought...she was the

woman who betrayed you," she said miserably, and went back to the sofa.

"You don't read me any better than I read you," he said after a minute. "Suppose you come to Chicago with me for a few days? Meet my friends. Learn a little about me."

The invitation excited her, but she hesitated. "I don't know."

"My apartment has two bedrooms," he said icily. "You won't have to sleep with me."

"I can't imagine why you'd want to," she laughed bitterly, curling up on the sofa with her ledgers. "There are a lot of pretty women in the. Eric!"

He was beside her, over her, the ledgers scattered onto the floor as he pinned her down. His eyes glittered, his chest rose and fell harshly. He held her wrists over her head and looked as if he could do her violence.

"I'd never do that to you," he said harshly. "Never! What kind of man do you think I am?"

Tears stung her eyes. "You're hurting me," she whispered unsteadily.

He loosened her wrists, but he didn't let go of them. "I'm sorry," he muttered, still glaring into her white face. "I've hardly done anything else, have I? I picked you up, got you pregnant, forced you into marriage without telling you the truth about myself…and lately all I've done is blame you for it."

Her eyes closed. The tears ran from beneath her lids, and he caught his breath.

"Don't cry," he said with reluctant concern. "Dani,

don't cry. I'm sorry. *Lieveling,* I'm sorry, I'm sorry…" he told her over and over again, his mouth searching across her wet cheek to her mouth. He took it gently, opening it to the moist possession of his own, while his hands freed her wrists and moved to cup her face. *"Lieveling,"* he breathed against her mouth. His body stretched full length over hers, his forearms catching the bulk of his weight. His heart pounded, his breath came unevenly. He wanted her. He wanted her!

She felt him begin to tremble, and against her hips she felt the helpless reaction of his body to her soft yielding. She hadn't wanted this to happen; she hadn't wanted to give in to something purely physical. But it had been months since she'd known the possession of that hard, expert body, and his mouth was driving her mad with its taunting hunger. She reached up hesitantly and slid her arms around his neck.

"Let me have you, Dani," he murmured into her open mouth. He shifted so that his hands could ease up her dress. "Let me have you."

She wanted to stop. But his hands were touching her soft body now, teasing it into reckless abandon, his mouth probing hers in a kiss so deep it became an act of intimacy in itself. Her body moved against his, her hands trembled and clenched on his shoulders and she moaned.

"Yes," he said, his voice urgent now, shaking. "Yes."

"Here…?" she managed in a last attempt at sanity.

"Here," he groaned, pressing her into the cushions with the gentle, carefully controlled weight of his body. "Here…!"

It was as it had been that morning in Mexico. He was breathlessly tender with her, each motion slow and sweet and reverent. His hands trembled as they touched her, guided her. His voice was passionate as he reverted to Dutch, whispering in her ear.

His mouth moved to hers, open and tender and trembling on her own as he began with aching tenderness to possess her.

Her mouth opened, her eyes widened. "Eric…!"

"Shh," he whispered huskily. He watched her as he moved, tender motions that wouldn't harm his child, arousing motions that made her gray eyes dilate, that made her heart beat wildly against his hair-matted chest.

"Oh!" she cried out, a whisper of sound that he took into his mouth.

"Gentle violence," he said into her parted lips. "Rock with me. Take my body, and give me yours. Be my lover now."

"I…love you!" she whimpered helplessly. "I love you!"

It shattered what little was left of his control, to hear her cry it out so huskily, to see it in her eyes as she looked at him with all the barriers down. His mouth crushed softly into hers and his hands held her. He heard her fluttering little cries, felt the wildness in her body, the heat of it burning his hands. He wanted to look, but it was happening for him, too, the tender explosions that were so much more terrible than the fierce passion he'd known before with women. He thought he might die….

He was aware of her in every cell as they lay trembling together in the aftermath. His hands stroked along her relaxed body, feeling its softness in a kind of dazed reality.

"Dani?" he whispered as his eyes opened and he saw the back of the sofa.

"Yes." Her voice sounded like velvet.

"I…didn't meant to do it," he said hesitantly. "I didn't plan it."

"I know." She kissed him. Her lips touched his eyes, his eyebrows, his straight nose, his cheeks, his mouth, his chin.

He loved the softness of her mouth on his face. His eyes closed, so that she could kiss his eyelids, too. He smiled, feeling sated, loved. Profound, he thought dizzily. This, with her, was so much more than a brief merging of bodies. His hands touched her belly and felt his child move.

He laughed softly, delightedly. "He kicks," he whispered. "No more bird flutters."

"He's very strong, the doctor says," she whispered back.

He lifted his head and looked at her, at the tiny line of freckles over her nose. Sometime in the last feverish few minutes her glasses had been removed. He glanced around and saw them on the coffee table and smiled.

"I'd forgotten where we were." He sighed, kissing her again. His hands slid up her sides, and his thumbs moved over her breasts, feeling their swollen softness. "Will you let me watch you nurse him?" he asked lazily, and laughed when she blushed. "Will you?"

"Yes," she said, and buried her red face against his throat.

He kissed her forehead, her closed eyes. "Dani, is it gentle explosions for you, the way it is for me?" he asked hesitantly. "Do you feel what the French call the little death when the moment comes?"

Her breath caught. "Yes," she whispered. She clung to him. "I didn't know…"

"It was never like that for me," he told her softly, and his arms slid further around her. "Never, with anyone, the way it is with you." He shuddered.

Yes, but it was only physical, she thought miserably, and closed her eyes. Still, it was better than nothing. She smoothed the hair at his nape. It was a start.

THEY WENT TO CHICAGO on Monday, after Dutch had taken time to call Dr. Carter to make sure it was safe for Dani to make the trip. He watched her closely, with narrowed dark eyes, every step she took. It was almost amusing, the care he was taking of her. Amusing…and very flattering. Perhaps he was growing fond of her, at least.

He hadn't loved her again. Afterward, he'd been protective and gentle, but he hadn't touched her as a lover. She wondered why, but she didn't provoke him by asking. She'd long since decided to take one day at a time, to accept what he could give without asking for more. Somehow she'd learn to live with him. Because she couldn't leave him now.

CHAPTER NINE

DANI WASN'T SURE WHAT she'd expected Dutch's friends to look like. But when she was introduced to J.D. and Gabby Brettman and Apollo Blain, her face must have given her away.

"Yep—" Apollo nodded as he shook her shyly outstretched hand "—I told you, J.D., she expected us to look like the cover of *Soldier of Fortune* magazine."

Dani blushed and burst out laughing. "Well, I've never seen professional mercenaries before," she explained. "Anyway, at least I didn't come in looking for camouflage netting, did I?" she asked reasonably.

Apollo chuckled. "Nope, little mama, I guess not."

She lowered her eyes with a self-conscious smile, feeling Dutch's arm come around her shoulders.

"Animals." Gabby glared at the men. "Shame on you."

"Well, we're curious," J.D. said defensively. He studied Dani through eyes as dark as Dutch's. All three men were wearing lightweight suits, and Gabby was in a green-patterned dress. Dani felt as though she stood out like a sort thumb in her maternity garb.

"Of course we are," Apollo seconded. "After all, it took some kind of woman to catch Dutch, didn't it?"

"I won't argue with that." Gabby grinned. "Come on, Dani, you can help me in the kitchen while these three talk shop."

"I think I'd better," Dani confided, throwing an impish smile at Dutch. "At least I know a potato from a head of lettuce, even if I don't know an AK-47 from an Uzi."

Dutch smiled at her, possession in his whole look.

She followed Gabby into the kitchen. "What can I do?" Dani asked helpfully.

"You can tell me how you did it!" Gabby burst out delightedly, smiling from a radiant face. "Dutch, married! Honestly, J.D. and I almost fainted!"

"It's a long story," Dani murmured dryly, sensing a comrade in Gabby. She sat down at the kitchen table. "It isn't love, though, you know," she added quietly.

Gabby studied her. "For you it is. Yes, it shows. Are you happy with him?"

"As happy as I can expect to be," Dani said. "I can't hope to hold him, of course. He's very protective, and he wants the baby. But it isn't in him to love."

Gabby poured two cups of coffee, checked the timer on her microwave and sat back down. She pushed a mug of black coffee toward Dani and offered the cream and sugar.

"You know about Melissa?" she asked after a minute.

Dani knew instinctively whom she meant. "The woman from his past?"

Gabby nodded. "I wouldn't know, but Dutch was badly wounded once, and he blurted out the whole story to J.D. Dutch doesn't know," she added, lifting her eyes to Dani's. "J.D. didn't let on. But that woman...!"

"He told me all of it," Dani said quietly, sipping her coffee. "He was devastated when he found out I was pregnant."

"Did you know what he did for a living when you married him?" Gabby asked.

Dani smiled ruefully and shook her head. "I found out when the airplane we were coming home on was hijacked."

Gabby forced air through her lips. "What an interesting way to find out."

"Yes." She lowered her eyes to her cup. "He thought we could make a go of it, each leading our own lives. I didn't. I walked off and left him." She sighed. "Several weeks later I learned that I was pregnant. He came back…." She laughed. "We've been going around and around ever since."

"I remember the first time I ever heard of Dutch," Gabby recalled. "J.D.'s sister Martina had been captured by terrorists and we went to Italy to see about the ransom. Dutch was J.D.'s go-between." She looked up. "J.D. wouldn't even introduce me to him. He said Dutch hated women."

"He told me so," Dani said, smiling. "When did you get to meet him?"

"At the wedding, when I married J.D. He wasn't at all what I expected. At first I was a little nervous around him," Gabby said. "Then I got to know him— as well as he lets outsiders know him." She held Dani's curious eyes. "He talked to me about you when he was here before. He wanted to know how I'd feel if I were pregnant and J.D. couldn't give up the old life. I cried."

Dani drew in a shaky breath. "I've done my share of crying. I don't know what to do. I don't feel that I have the right to ask him to change his life for me. But I can't live with what he does." Her eyes were wide with fear and love. "I'm crazy about him. I'd die if anything happened to him."

"That's how I feel about J.D.," Gabby said quietly. "I envy you that baby," she added with a sad smile. "J.D. and I have tried…" Her thin shoulders rose and fell. "I can't seem to get pregnant."

"I had a girlfriend who couldn't get pregnant at first," Dani said, recalling an old friend from years past. She grinned. "Five years after she got married she had triplets, followed by twins the next year."

Gabby burst out laughing. "What a delightful prospect!"

"What's all the noise in here?" J.D. asked, opening the kitchen door. "Are we eating tonight?" he asked Gabby.

She got up and kissed him tauntingly on his hard mouth. "Yes, we're eating tonight, bottomless pit. And we're laughing about triplets."

His eyes widened. "What?"

"Tell you later. Let's eat!"

It was late when Dani and Dutch got back to his elegant lakeside apartment. She hadn't expected such luxury, and it emphasized once again the difference between her lifestyle and his. During dinner the conversation had inevitably gone back to old times and comrades whose names Dani didn't recognize. And then mention was made of the new job Apollo had offered Dutch, and Dani listened with wide eyes as it was outlined. It wasn't as dangerous as what he was doing now, of course, she reminded herself. There wasn't half the risk. She'd have to get used to it. She could, too, if she tried.

"I don't think I can manage a desk job," he told her as if he sensed her deep, frightening thoughts.

She turned from the window, where she was watching the lights of cars far below, and the city lights near the river. "Yes, I know that."

He looked at her for a long time, hands in his pockets, eyes narrow and dark and searching. "But I'm going to try."

She nodded. "I won't ask you for anything more than that," she said then. "I'll settle for whatever you can give me. I...have very little pride left." She sighed and she seemed to age. "I'd like to go to bed now, Eric. I'm so tired."

"It's been a long day. You can have whichever bedroom you like."

She looked at him across the room, started to speak, and then smiled faintly and walked down the hall.

"Dani..."

She didn't turn. "Yes?"

There was a long, trembling silence. "My room is the first door to the left," he said thickly. "The bed...is large enough for all three of us."

Tears stung her eyes. "If you don't mind," she whispered.

"Mind!" He was behind her, beside her; he had her in his arms, close and warm and protected. His mouth found hers in a single graceful motion. She clung. He lifted her, devoured her. His dark eyes sought hers as he kissed her.

"Now?" he whispered, trembling.

"Now," she moaned huskily.

He bent to her mouth again and she trembled with delicious anticipation as he carried her slowly into his bedroom and closed the door behind them.

TWO WEEKS LATER SHE HAD to go back home for her checkup, and to hire someone else to help Harriett at the bookstore. Dutch flew back with her since the weekend was coming up. But he had to be in Chicago for a conference on Monday.

"I don't like leaving you here," he said curtly, glaring around at her small apartment. She'd become so much a part of his life that it felt odd to leave her behind.

She didn't want the parting, either, but she hadn't switched to a Chicago doctor yet, and she needed to be sure about the baby.

"Don't worry about me," she told him, holding his big hand in hers as she walked him to the door. "I'll be fine. The nights will last forever, but I'll manage," she teased.

He didn't smile. He touched her cheek, feeling tremors all the way to his soul. It was because of the baby that he felt this uneasy, he told himself. Only because of the baby. "I'll be back day after tomorrow," he said.

"We'll spend the week here, getting things in order. Tell Harriett I said to look after you."

"Harrie will." She smiled. "Do I get a goodbye kiss?"

He pulled her against his tall frame. "I wonder if I'll make it out the door if I kiss you?" he murmured with a dry smile. "Come here."

He drew her up on her tiptoes and covered her smiling mouth with his. It was like flying, he mused, eyes closing as he savored the taste of her. Flying, floating. She made his head light. He lifted his lips finally and searched her loving eyes. It didn't bother him so much these days, that adoration. Perhaps he'd gotten used to it.

He brushed a last kiss against her lips. "Behave. And watch these steps, okay?"

"Okay. 'Bye."

He touched her hair. "'Bye." He walked away without looking back. She closed the door, and realized she hadn't felt so alone since her parents had walked away from her years and years ago.

CHAPTER TEN

HARRIETT WAS ALL EARS, fascinated by the news that Dani's unlikely husband was actually going to try to settle down.

"He must feel something for you," she said, smiling at Dani. "I don't care what you say, no man is going to go to those lengths just because of a purely physical involvement."

Dani had been afraid to think that, much less say it. But she stared at Harriett for a long time, wondering.

"In some ways you're still very naive, my friend," Harriett said with a wicked grin. "He's hooked. He just hasn't realized it yet."

If only it were true, Dani thought, praying for a miracle. If only he liked the job Apollo offered him. Even moving to Chicago wouldn't be any hardship. Harriett and Dave would visit. And she could come back to Greenville from time to time. Harriett could be godmother. She smiled.

With her mind on Dutch, not on what she was doing, she went to step up on the long ladder against the wall to get a book from a high shelf. She was halfway up when she slipped. Terrified, screaming as she hit the floor, she looked up at Harriett, her face white.

"Oh, God, the baby!" she sobbed, clutching her stomach.

"It's all right," Harriett said quickly, soothing her. "It's all right, I'll get an ambulance. Lie still! Are you hurt anywhere?"

"I don't know!"

Harriett ran for the phone. Dani lay there, panic-stricken, clutching her stomach. No, please don't let me lose my baby, she prayed. Her eyes closed and tears bled from them as the first pain began to make itself felt in her leg, in her back. Please, please, please!

The next few minutes were a nightmare of waiting, worrying. The ambulance came, the attendants got her on the stretcher, took her to the hospital, and into the emergency room, with Harriett right behind. She hardly knew Harriett was there, she was so afraid of losing the baby.

She was examined by the emergency room doctor, who would tell her nothing. Then the tests began and went on and on until finally they took her to a room and left her shaking with worry. Her doctor would talk to her when they got the test results, she was informed.

She cried and cried. Harriett tried to soothe her, but it was useless. She was feeling a dragging pain in her lower stomach, and she knew she was going to lose the baby. She was going to lose her baby! Harriett asked her for something, a name in Chicago to call, to tell Dutch. Numbly, she gave her J.D. Brettman's name and closed her eyes. It was no use, she wanted to say. Dutch would come, but only out of responsibility…and then she remembered the other time, the other pregnant woman, and she was terrified of what he might do.

Dr. Carter came walking in a few hours later, took one look at her and went back out to call for a sedative. He came in again, took her hand and nodded Harriett toward the door. He didn't speak until she was gone.

"The baby's going to be fine," he said. "So are you. Now, calm down."

The tears stopped, although her eyes remained wet and red. "What?"

"The baby's all right." He smiled, his blue eyes twinkling. "Babies are tough. They've got all that fluid around them, wonderful protection. Of course, you're bruised a little here and there, but bruises heal. You'll be fine."

She leaned back with a sigh. "Thank God," she said. "Oh, thank God. But—but these dragging pains," she added, pressing her stomach.

"False labor. A few twinges are normal," he said, grinning. "Now, stop worrying, will you?"

The nurse came in with a syringe, but before she could go any farther, the door flew open and a blond man burst into the room with eyes so wild that both doctor and nurse actually backed up a step.

"Eric!" Dani whispered, astonished at the look on his face.

He went to her, a wet, disheveled raincoat over his gray suit. He was wild-eyed, flushed as if he'd been running, and half out of breath.

"You're all right?" he asked unsteadily, touching her

as if he expected to find broken limbs. "The baby's all right?"

"Yes," she whispered. "Eric, it's all right!" she repeated softly, and the look on his face was the answer to a prayer. "It's all right, I just fell off the ladder, but I'm—"

"Oh, God." He sat down beside her. The hands that touched her trembled, and there was a look in his eyes that struck her dumb. He caressed her face and suddenly bent, burying his face in her throat. "Oh, God." He was shaking!

Her arms went up and around him, hesitantly, her hands smoothing his hair, comforting him. She felt something wet against her throat and felt her own eyes begin to sting.

"Oh, darling," she whispered, holding him closer. Her eyes closed as the enormity of what he felt for her was laid bare, without a word being spoken. She laughed through her tears. She could conquer the world now. She could do anything! He loved her!

"Reaction," the doctor said, nodding. He took the syringe from the nurse. "Pregnancy is hard on fathers, too," he murmured dryly. "Off with that coat, young man." He removed the raincoat, and the suitcoat, then rolled up the sleeve of the shirt without any help from Dutch, who wouldn't let go of Dani, and jabbed the needle into the muscular arm. "I'll have a daybed rolled in here, because you aren't driving anywhere. Dani, I think you'd do without a sedative now, am I right?" he added with a grin.

"Yes, sir," she whispered, smiling dreamily as she rocked her husband in her arms.

He nodded and went out with the nurse, closing the door behind him.

"I love you," Dani whispered adoringly. "I love you, I love you, I love you…."

His mouth stopped the words, tenderly seeking, probing, and his lips trembled against hers.

He lifted his head to look at her, unashamedly letting her see the traces of wetness on his cheeks. "J.D. came himself to tell me after Harriett called." He touched her face hesitantly. "I went crazy," he confessed absently. "J.D. got me a seat on the next plane. I ran out of the terminal and took a cab away from some people…. I don't even remember how I got here." He bent and brushed his mouth softly against hers as he let the relief wash over him. His wife. His heart. "I was…I was going to call you tonight. I wanted to tell you how much I like what I'll be doing. I found us a house," he added slowly. "On the beach, with a fenced yard. It will be nice, for the baby."

"Yes, darling," she whispered softly.

He brushed the hair back from her face. "I was so afraid of what I'd find in here," he said unsteadily. "All I could think was that I'd only just realized what I felt for you, and so quickly it could have ended. I would have been alone again."

"As long as I'm alive, you'll never be alone," she whispered.

He touched her mouth, her throat, her swollen stomach. "Danielle, I love you," he whispered breathlessly, admitting it at last, awe in his whole look.

"Yes, I know," she answered on a jubilant little laugh.

He laughed, too. "I've never said that before. It isn't hard." He looked into her eyes. "I love you."

She smiled, stretching. "I love you, too. Ooh," she groaned, touching her back. "I'm bruised all over. That stupid ladder!"

"No more stupid ladders," he said firmly. "We're moving to Chicago, where I can watch you. Harriett can visit."

Her eyes searched his. "This is what you really want?"

"How can I take care of you from across the world?" he asked reasonably. His voice was slowing, and he looked drowsy. "Anyway, I was getting too old for it. And I like the challenge of teaching techniques I've learned." He kissed her softly again. "J.D. told me I could do it. When he and Gabby got married, he decided that marriage was more exciting than dodging bullets. I think he has something there."

He looked down at her stomach and the last of the barriers came down. "He's going to be all right, they're sure?" he asked touching the swell.

Her lips parted, smiling. She sat up and touched his face with soft, loving hands. "I'm giving you a baby," she whispered, smiling. "A healthy, strong boy. The doctor said so."

He started to speak, and couldn't. And tried again. "I'll take care of you both," he whispered.

She reached forward and caught his full lower lip gently between her teeth. "I'll take care of you, just as soon as they let me out of here," she teased.

He chuckled softly, putting a hand to his temple. "I may need taking care of. My God, what was in that syringe?"

"A sedative. They brought it for me, but I guess they decided you needed it more."

He smiled ruefully. "I'd like to talk some more, but I think I'd feel better lying down."

Dr. Carter came in with a nurse and a spare bed even as the words were echoing in the room. He glanced at his watch and grinned at Dutch. "I thought you'd be about ready for this. Lie down, father-to-be, and you can both have a nice nap until supper. Feeling okay now, Dani?" he asked.

"Just wonderful." She sighed, trading soft looks with her drowsy husband. The nurse was eyeing him wistfully, and Dani only smiled with the confidence of a woman who is deeply loved. As Dutch lay down her eyes closed on the smile he gave her. Minutes later she was asleep, with the future lying open and bright ahead.

CHAPTER ELEVEN

THE CHRISTENING TOOK place six months later, with little two-month-old Joshua van Meer cradled in his mother's arms. At Dani's side Dutch burned with pride in his young son, and amused looks passed among an odd group on the front pew of the Presbyterian church in the outskirts of Chicago.

Harriett felt uneasy, sitting next to them all, and Dave had actually started to get up except that she'd caught him in time. What a collection of unusual men, she thought, gaping. There was an older, wiry little man sitting beside a wiry, tough-looking woman and they were holding hands. There were two black men, a tall, dignified one and a shorter, grinning one. There was a huge dark-eyed, dark-headed man sitting beside a green-eyed brunette who was obviously pregnant. On the other side was a swarthy Latin, arms folded, looking elegant. Harriett turned her attention back to the minister, who had taken the child in his arms and was walking it up and down the rows of pews. Harriett smiled. Her godchild. Dani had wanted her to stand with them during the ceremony, but she'd twisted her ankle getting on the airplane, and could hardly manage to stand. Just as well, she thought with a smile at the big blond Dutchman. She and that handsome giant were too much alike to ever get along. But even she had to admit that he was a terrific husband and father. A surprisingly domestic man, all around. A really normal man. Except for his friends here.

After the ceremony was over, the group beside Harriett sat still. She wondered for a wild minute if they were escaped fugitives, because they seemed to be looking around them all the time.

Dani rushed forward and hugged her. "Wasn't Joshua good?" she asked enthusiastically, kissing the white-clad baby in her arms. He cooed up at her. "I was so proud of him! Harrie, you haven't met our friends. Gabby!"

Gabby Darwin Brettman drew her tall husband along with her, beaming as she made faces at the baby.

"Isn't he gorgeous! I want a girl myself," Gabby said, her bright green eyes gleaming, "but J.D.'s holding out for a boy."

"I don't care what it is, as long as it's ours," J.D. grinned. "Hi, Dani. Nice ceremony. Dutch didn't even pass out; I was proud of him."

"Imagine Dutch married." The wiry old man shook his head. "And with a child!"

"Could have knocked me over with a feather when I found out," the tall black man joined in.

"Hush, First Shirt," Gabby growled at the older man. "And shame on you, Apollo," she told the tall black man. "Dutch just had to find the right girl, that's all."

Apollo shrugged. "Well, I'm glad he did," he told

Dani with twinkling eyes, "because he's sure made the best vice-president any consulting firm could ask for. Shirt, when are you going to give in and join up? Semson and Drago already did. And I need someone to teach defensive driving."

"You corporate tycoons give me a pain," First Shirt scoffed. "Besides, Mrs. Darwin and I are contemplating a merger." He grinned at the blushing widow beside him, who was Gabby's mother, from Lytle, Texas. "We're going to raise cattle and sand."

"I owe it all to J.D.," Apollo said, smiling warmly at the big, dark man beside Gabby. "He got me off. Years of hiding, over. I'm glad you decided to go into law, J.D."

"So am I," J.D. replied. He looked up as Dutch joined them. "I was just coming to find you. Gabby and I are starting natural childbirth classes. Any advice?"

Dutch grinned as he put an affectionate arm around Dani. "Sure. Go buy a can of tennis balls."

Gabby stared at him. "Tennis...balls?"

"Tennis balls." He leaned forward conspiratorially. "They're for your backache. J.D. is supposed to roll them up and down your spine."

"It really does help," Dani said. She bent and kissed her son. "The best part is when you get to hold him for the first time."

"Yes," Dutch agreed. "Let's go grill some steaks," he said. "Everybody know how to get to our place?"

"Sure," Apollo said. "I'll lead the ones who don't. You got enough steaks?"

"Shirt and Mrs. Darwin brought a boxful. If we make

you stand last in line, there should be enough to go around," he said with a grin.

Apollo glared at him. "I don't eat that much!"

"Only half a ham at a time," Dutch shot back. "Remember Angola, when you ate the rabbit I'd just snared?"

"Oh, yeah, remember 'Nam, when you ate the snake I caught?"

"It's a christening," J.D. said, separating them. "We're supposed to forget old grudges at a time like this."

They both turned at him. "Yeah?" Apollo asked. "Well, you're the turkey that ate the box of cookies my mother sent me...."

"And the plum pudding I scrounged from the camp cook," Dutch added in the same breath.

J.D. drew Gabby beside him. "You can't pick on a man with a pregnant wife."

"I had one of my own until two months ago," Dutch returned.

"Well, I'm not standing too close to you guys," Apollo said gruffly, eyeing them. "It might be contagious."

"You won't get pregnant, Apollo, honest," Dutch said with a wicked grin.

Apollo glared at him and moved away. "Funny man. You know I meant this marriage virus."

"Some virus." J.D. grinned, hugging Gabby close. "What a way to go!"

Dani was laughing wildly, along with Gabby and the others. She moved close to Dutch and nuzzled her dark head against his shoulder. "I'm starved. Let's go home. We've got all kinds of stuff to eat."

"Yes, well, let's just make sure Apollo doesn't get there before us," J.D. teased.

Apollo glared at him. "I'm returning the Christmas present I bought you."

"It's almost March," J.D. reminded him.

"That gives you ten months to look forward to not getting one," Apollo said smugly.

"Come on," Dutch chuckled. "Let's go celebrate."

"Yes," Dani said, so that only Dutch could hear. "I have a different kind of celebration in mind for later," she murmured. "My doctor said I could."

Dutch's eyes lit up as he studied her bright eyes. "Did he? Hmm," he murmured, drawing her close to his side and smiling down at the baby sleeping in her arms. "Well, we'll have to think up some new things to try, won't we?" he asked, watching her with smug delight. He whispered into her ear, and despite months of marriage and a baby, she colored delightfully.

She felt more alive than she ever had in her life. She looked up at him with such love that the roomful of people seemed to disappear. His fingers touched her mouth.

"Tonight," he whispered, holding her gaze, "I'll love you the way I loved you that morning in Veracruz."

"You'll get me pregnant again," she whispered, her heart throbbing wildly.

His own breath caught. "We'll talk about it tonight."

"Yes." She searched his eyes slowly. "No regrets?"

He shook his head. "Not one. Watching that baby

being born was the most exciting thing I've ever done; next to loving you," he added softly.

She reached up and touched his hard cheek gently. He smiled, and for a moment, they were alone in the world.